PRETTY BAD THINGS

PRETTY BAD THINGS

C.J. SKUSE

Chicken House

SCHOLASTIC INC. / NEW YORK

Text copyright © 2011 by C. J. Skuse

First published in the United Kingdom in 2010 by Chicken House,
2 Palmer Street, Frome, Somerset BA11 1DS.
www.doublecluck.com

"Everlong" lyrics by Dave Grohl (© 1997). Produced by Foo Fighters and Gil Norton, and released by Foo Fighters in August 1997 as the second single from their album *The Colour and the Shape* (© Roswell/Capitol Records, 1997).

Library of Congress Cataloging-in-Publication Data

Skuse, C. J.
Pretty bad things / by C. J. Skuse. — 1st American ed.
p. cm.
Summary: When they were six years old, twins Beau and Paisley were famous for surviving on their own after their mother died of a drug overdose, and now, at sixteen, they escape from their abusive grandmother to look for their father, who is out of prison and, unbeknownst to them, has been writing them letters since he was put away.

ISBN 978-0-545-28973-3

[1. Twins—Fiction. 2. Brothers and sisters—Fiction. 3. Family problems—Fiction. 4. Missing persons—Fiction. 5. Fathers—Fiction. 6. Criminals—Fiction.] I. Title.

PZ7.S43748Pr 2011
[Fic]—dc22

2010015640

10 9 8 7 6 5 4 3 2 1   11 12 13 14 15
Printed in the U.S.A.   23
First American edition, July 2011

The text type was set in Zurich and Meridien.
The display type was set in Hand of Sean.
Book design by Whitney Lyle

FOR MY DAD

PRETTY BAD THINGS

PAISLEY

ONE

Simpson fumbled getting the tape into the VCR. She was all, *Which button is it?*

And I was like, *How old are you and you can't even work a friggin' VCR?*

"I'd like you to watch this and tell me how you feel about it," she said, finally getting her fat ass out of the way so I could see the screen. The music started up over CNN's flashy intro. The words came up: CNN BREAKING NEWS: SIX-YEAR-OLD NEW JERSEY TWINS MISSING. MOTHER FOUND DEAD. CNN's Kim Slaughter appeared—devil-red lipstick, concrete bouffant, gray suit, serious face—shuffling her papers.

"Good morning, I'm Kim Slaughter, and this is the news you're waking up to on Monday, March twentieth. It's seven A.M. We take you live now to New Jersey, where Jake Williamson is outside the house where this tragic story is unfolding. Jake, what's going on down there?"

Yeah, do tell, Jake, I thought. *What is going on down there?*

"Thanks, Kim. And tragic is definitely the operative word in this story. I'm here standing outside the Argent family's house on Forest Way, Clifton, a quite unassuming residence where an extraordinary story began to unfold earlier today."

Cue montage of worried faces, woman in a red coat biting her lip, sniffer dogs in bushes. Then back to Jake.

"This is what we know: At three fifty this afternoon, Fae Wong, who lives next door to the Argents, dropped off the twins Beau and Paisley at home after school, as she normally does, and went home with her own children. And then, approximately five minutes later, a 911 operator received this call:"

Cue the blue screen and scratchy tape recording.

OPERATOR: 911 emergency.

GIRL: Hi, um . . . I think my mom needs an ambulance.

OPERATOR: Is your mom sick?

GIRL: Uh-huh. She's on the couch.

OPERATOR: Is she awake or asleep?

GIRL: Asleep. (Background crying.) I said, "Mom, wake up," and she didn't say anything.

OPERATOR: Okay. Are there any grown-ups around?

GIRL: No.

OPERATOR: What's your name, honey?

GIRL: Paisley Jane Argent.

OPERATOR: That's a pretty name. Can you tell me where you live?

GIRL: 1175 Forest Way, Clifton, New Jersey. (Background crying.)

OPERATOR: Is someone else there with you, Paisley?

GIRL: Beau's here.

OPERATOR: Who's Beau?

GIRL: He's my twin brother.

OPERATOR: How old are you, Paisley?

GIRL: We're six and ten days old.

OPERATOR: You're very smart to call 911. Did you learn that at school?

GIRL: Mmm-hmm.

OPERATOR: Okay, there'll be someone to help you real soon. You just keep talking with me and we'll wait for them. They're coming.

Jake appeared again. I was kinda glad. I started lip-synching along with him.

"We now know that the little girl on the tape there, Paisley Argent, didn't stay on the line. An ambulance showed up at the house approximately seven minutes later, and the body of her mother, Sylvia Argent, was found in the living room. But Paisley and twin brother Beau were nowhere to be found . . ."

Maggie Simpson stopped the tape. The picture went to black. She set the remote down on the table and put her hands in her lap. Maggie Simpson wasn't her real name. That was just what I called her 'cause she had spiky blonde hair and would sit there in our sessions pouting and puckering her lips as she listened to me, like a baby sucking a pacifier.

"You okay?" she said, eyebrows peaked in fake sympathy.

I looked at her. "What did you expect?"

"I thought maybe that might have brought back some bad memories for you, hearing yourself as a little girl."

All these counselors had one mission: to get me to cry. And there was no way—even if they pricked my eyeballs with pins or splashed lemon juice into every cut—no way was I gonna cry.

"Would you prefer that I start bawling?"

"No. I just want to know how it made you feel, seeing that news story again."

I shrugged. "Hunky-fucking-dory."

Simpson smiled, and there was a definite roll of the eyes. "Can you relate to that little six-year-old girl anymore?"

I sat back in my leather chair and played with my hair. I was running out of boredom indicators. She didn't have a clue how to deal with me. None of them did. It wasn't my choice to go to counseling. I was forced to have it. I was one of the school's "special cases." Like the piano genius in my music class who only ate orange food. Or the autistic girl in science who liked banging her head against the fire door.

"Tell me about what happened. You and your brother came home from school, found your mom . . . and you went to find your dad to tell him she was sick."

"She wasn't sick. She was dead. I *do* know the difference."

"Okay, so you both headed out to go tell your dad. But you got lost, didn't you? In the woods. Were you scared?"

"No, we had the time of our lives. No parents, no peer pressure . . ."

"Why did you go into the woods?"

"We didn't mean to go into the woods. The woods were behind the country club."

"Your father worked there?"

"I thought you read my file? No, he sometimes went there for dinner after work," I sighed, in the same singsongy way little kids read out poetry.

"Was your brother scared when you were in the woods? Did you look after him?"

I didn't answer.

"Your brother's name is Beau, isn't it? Are you close?"

Still nothing. We were having a staring competition now.

"You're twins, aren't you?"

I was rock solid. Not even blinking.

"Is he the younger one or the older one?"

I wasn't going to talk about Beau. Beau was off-limits. I didn't want him going through this torture, too.

"The sooner you speak up, the sooner you can leave."

"Yeah, we're twins."

"Some twins don't get along. Do you?"

"Yes."

"Do you ever experience that strange telepathy with Beau that some twins get? You know, do you feel pain at the same time as him? Have the same dreams? The same feelings?"

"I sometimes get the urge to touch my dick."

"I am trying to help, you know."

"No shit."

"Would you at least try to open up? Just go with it. No one else can hear."

She had a pockmark on her face that kept catching the light. We're talking crater-sized. The last counselor was better than her. I called her The Jawbreaker 'cause she had this really large lower face and big donkey teeth that could crush rocks. Then there was Pretty Shitty Blah Blah at Sacred Heart. I called her Pretty for short. Except she wasn't. She was the kind of person who looks pretty to start with but gets uglier the more you learn about them. I could call most people Pretty.

This one, Simpson, was so nervous I only had to sneeze and her coffee cup would rocket up to the ceiling. Such was my reputation, I guess.

"Your father's imprisonment . . . ," she began, then stopped for me to fill in the blank. I wasn't going to. But then I did, 'cause she was looking at me and going all puckery again like she was gonna explode.

"He didn't kill her, if that's what you're thinking. Our mom."

I could see her balk, checking her notes again. *Father robbed hotel staff at gunpoint. Been in prison for the last ten years. Mother overdosed. No wonder. No fucking wonder.*

"What do you think about your recent behavior? Do you know why you felt compelled to do that to the piano?"

I shrugged. "I was bored. I'm a fuckup. That's what fuckups do."

I had to meet with the school counselor—whoever it happened to be that semester—every Tuesday and Thursday after school to talk through my "issues," while sitting on a beanbag with my shoes off. I'd done this as long as I could remember. In every school it was the same—different days and different color·beanbags, but the same setup. The rooms always stank of coffee, and the walls were always plastered with posters of kids with their heads in their hands, saying things like, "We get the blues, too" and "Amy didn't like being laughed at." I'd feed them all the usual crap of finding life so tough 'cause I was away from my brother and Mommy never showed me any affection, and they'd look at me sympathetically and give me meditation exercises and all that kinda fuckery. It was bullshit.

"Do you ever think about your mom? How do you feel about her?"

"She hated me. It's no biggie."

What was I supposed to say? My mom did hate me. She hated Beau, too. She hated us so much she used to drink to forget we were there. She'd hit us. She'd lock us in the basement for hours on end. She hated us so much she took her own life. I don't know what that is if it isn't hate.

Simpson looked at me, eyes all smoky with compassion. Luckily my bullshit shield kept out oncoming attacks of kindness. What's that stuff they freeze Han Solo in at the end of *The Empire Strikes Back*? Anyway, it was like I had that all around me. No one could get through my shield of "that."

Immaculate Conception Academy (ICA) was the best boarding school in New Jersey—highly academic—turning out America's finest girls since 1908. It was also the most expensive. I knew that 'cause I'd been kicked out of all the crappy ones. Our Lady of the Oranges, Rambuteau, Satan's School for Girls (Bayonne High), and Sacred Heart Academy—been there, done that, broke the windows. My grandmother realized that to keep me out of her way permanently she had to spend some real dough. I supposedly had this "volatility" problem. My dad got the blame.

Simpson checked her notes. "Your father's in prison, isn't he?" she started again. She was getting confident. "How do you feel about that? Do you miss him?"

I picked my nails. I wasn't gonna answer that. I didn't want to tell her anything about my dad. I only ever talked about him to Beau.

"Your grandmother tells me that when you went home for the summer you didn't argue as much."

"That's probably because we're not talking as much."

"Oh. You had a fight?"

"We always fight. So we don't talk to each other."

"Why don't you get along?"

"Uh, because she hates me?"

"She must think a lot of you."

"And why the hell would you think that?"

"Well, she's spending a lot of money to give you a good education."

"No, she's spending a lot of money to keep me as far away as possible."

I remembered the day she'd dropped me off at Our Lady of the Oranges when I was seven. There was little me, drowning in my huge uniform, standing on the huge mosaic steps with the principal's hands on my shoulders. My grandmother, Virginia, stood there, too, with Beau beside her. Nowadays I call her the Skankmother. She's too Botoxed to be called Granny. As we stood there, she kept straightening my tie. I hated that.

"You'll make lots of friends. We'll see you at spring break."

I looked up at her. "I'll be good, I promise. I won't say any more bad words and I'll help clean my room and I won't be mean to Beau . . ." I would've said anything to go back to Los Angeles and go to school with my brother.

"We have to catch our plane. You take Mrs. Lloyd's hand."

Beau held out his toy owl, Two Wit, to kiss my owl, Two Woo. "Bye, Pais."

"Why can't I go with Beau?" I kept asking, but she didn't seem to hear it. "Why can't Beau stay with me?!"

She finally looked down at me. "Stop whining and go with Mrs. Lloyd, please."

"We'll keep you informed, Mrs. Creed," said the principal. "And we'll take good care of Jane."

Five schools later and they still always called me by my middle name. I hated that.

"Do you want to talk about those marks yet?" said Simpson, scoping my legs.

8

I sighed. When were they gonna learn? I decided to throw her a bone. "No. It . . . it's too painful," I lied, pulling down my skirt hem to hide my cuts. Counselors were born to be lied to. I liked to watch them lean forward and get all excited 'cause they thought they were on the brink of something.

"You know, some young people do it because it's the only outlet they allow themselves. Opening their skin becomes a way of leaking out what's troubling them. Do you have any friends that you talk to about it?"

I shook my head. "No. I'm saving up for some of those Harajuku girls. You know, those Japanese chicks you can pay to be your friends and they don't say anything, they just carry your bags and stuff. Gwen Stefani used to take hers everywhere. You can tell *them* to get out of your face, and they'll fucking listen."

She did the lean-forward thing. "You can talk to me. You can always talk to me. You can think of me as a friend, if you want."

That was a big fat hairy lie. The older I got, the bigger and fatter and hairier the lies got. She was no friend. Just like the counselor at the hospital when we were six. *It's okay, you're gonna be all right. Your dad'll be here soon, okay?* she'd said. Yeah, in about ten years, maybe. Eight with good behavior.

I reached into my pocket for my peanut M&M's.

Simpson took a deep breath, then blew it right out. "You remember in our last session together we spoke about the possibility of you moving to another facility, one that might be able to help you. . . ."

"Yeah, a nuthouse," I said. I popped a blue M&M in my mouth and began flicking it around on my tongue. I liked to suck them until just the peanut was left.

"No, a behavior-modification facility—it's a positive place. And there's one in California, so you'd be closer to your grand-mother. . . ."

I scoffed.

"Well, closer to your brother, then."

The M&M almost shot right out of my mouth. Closer to Beau? *Yeah, sure, where do I sign?* I thought. But of course there would be a catch, and I knew what it was.

"That's right. Get me all cozy in this nice little nuthouse, regular visits from my brother, trips to the zoo, all nicey nicey, and then zap the fuck out of my brains. I can see it now. I'm just staring into the abyss with drool dripping down my chin. Shuffling around in my slippers. *Buh buh buh buh buh buh buh buh.* I've heard electric shock treatment is killer."

"It wouldn't be like that."

"Oh, please. I know how this works. You just want me outta Jersey. If you can't turn me into a *High School Musical* wannabe, you ship me off to La La Land, where they'll put those little wires on my temples and turn me into a vegetable."

"I can assure you that's not what happens. But it's true that your problems may be a little beyond my expertise. . . . Have you tried reading that book I lent you?" She looked down at my legs again.

I looked down at my legs again. "No," I said, bowing my head. *Chicken Soup for the Teenage Soul.* I was using it to balance my nightstand. Simpson breathed a little sigh. Her breath reeked of stale coffee.

I wasn't *really* cutting myself, duh. I only liked them to think that. I just sucked at shaving. I have no patience, no interest in doing it right at all. I scrape and scratch away and I'm done in, like, five minutes. I don't see the point.

My M&M was ready, just the peanut left. I took it out of my mouth and split it in two. The little bunny was there. The bunny that was always there whenever I opened a peanut. It had been something I'd noticed when I was about eight. I don't think I was the first to discover it, though. That was probably Columbus or somebody. It's the middle part where the two halves join.

"So, I be crazy. Is that what I put in my next letter home to the folks?"

Simpson sighed. "No, I wouldn't put it like that. But you do seem to be incredibly . . . tense. You have a lot of frustration, and I can completely understand that, after what you've been through. And if we could identify what's causing . . ."

I crunched down on the nut and tuned out. I was so frickin' fed up of hearing the same old same old. Yeah, I was tense. Yeah, I needed help. Yeah, I was all outta love. I'd read somewhere that the best tension reliever was sex, and that would have been great if I could get it. Only problem was, Immaculate Conception Academy for Girls was pretty dry of tension relievers. No men, just three hundred and sixty-five mechanically engineered lesbians who'd do it with a broom handle if it looked at them the right way.

But a week after that crunch meeting with Maggie Simpson and the threat of being sent to the cabbage patch, a miracle happened. A blinding light shot down from the August sky and this angel appeared before me in paint-splattered jeans. His name was Jason, and he was helping the school gardener. He was seventeen, had a perfect V-shaped torso and spiky brown hair. I was convinced we were soul mates. I even took more interest in the classics—you know, Jason and the Argonauts? I imagined that was him, sailing forth to retrieve the Golden Fleece and doing all this heroic shit, when really he was downstairs filling wheelbarrows with weeds. As a rule, I don't like dropping the L-bomb, but I guess, maybe, it was sorta love. In a way.

I was sneaking a smoke before class when he said his first words to me.

"Who are you?"

"Paisley. Who are you?"

"Jason." He grabbed both handles of his wheelbarrow and checked out my skirt, or more accurately my belt. "You always dress like that, or is it just for me?"

"What, too long?" I said, hitching it up a little higher.

Pretty soon we were sharing cigarettes behind the toolshed, talking about movies. And then it got physical. I've always seen couples pawing each other and going all cupcakey and sending text messages every five seconds and stuff, but me and Jason weren't like that. We were more your frantic smash-and-grab sessions. Kissing but missing, like magnets. Grappling like wrestlers. Not Elizabeth and Darcy, but romantic all the same. And then I kinda understood the point of shaving.

I remember everything about our nights inside the toolshed after all the other immaculate girls had gone to bed. The sweet smell of deodorant and the stinking rubber of new tennis balls. The candlelight flickering, making our shadows bigger on the wall. His hot breath in my ear. His skin on mine, his hands on my back. Feeling down my glossy, smooth legs. All that kind of crap.

We'd talk, too, all night long about nothing in particular, and he'd listen to me. Just like Beau did. Not interrupting. Not going off on some boring tangent. Just listening. Laughing. Passing cigarettes and laughing. It was like having Beau there, in a weird way. Although with me and Beau it had been candy, not cigarettes.

It felt like it was the start of something. The start of me feeling something other than anger.

"Tell me you love me," I'd say to him.

"I totally do. I love you so much," he'd say. And I'd believe him.

"I love you, too," I'd whisper into his shoulder and hold him tight.

How sweet. How heartbreakingly sweet.

We talked. We kissed. He tasted of green apples. He smelled of grass cuttings and lawn-mower gasoline. He held my head and stroked my earlobes. And for a short while at school, I was happy. I lived for our nights in the toolshed. A softer, kinder Paisley was born. Desk lids were scored with *P.A. Luvs J.T.* instead of *When I Die Bury Me Upside Down So The Whole World Can Kiss My Ass*. My grades rose. I noticed birds and clouds. Tension drained through me like a sieve.

So you can kinda guess what came next.

BEAU

TWO

9976 CAHUENGA BLVD EAST,
HOLLYWOOD, CALIFORNIA

I shouldn't have been there, ergo I should never have known about it. What happened was, I had to come home from school early to change my clothes. O'Donnell and his merry men had found a new way to humiliate me—they'd dunked me headfirst into the trash cans by the cafeteria. Despite the walk back in the California sunshine, my Eels T-shirt clung to my skin like Saran Wrap.

I walked in through the back door and our maid, Concepción (Connie to us), was in the kitchen reading a letter.

"Hey," I said, making her jump about a mile in the air, and she fumbled the letter back into its envelope.

"Ooh, what's that, Connie?" I asked, thinking it might be from her son, Nando, who'd been sent back to Mexico a few months earlier. I knew she was desperate to hear from him.

"It's nothing. No, don't worry," she said, flapping her arms like she had ants down both sleeves. She noticed my soggy T-shirt. "Oh, you are wet. I will wash—"

"No, I just had an accident at school," I said, trying to sound nonchalant.

She attempted to tuck the letter into her apron, and I saw the front.

"That's addressed to me and Paisley." That's when my heart started to thump real hard. I asked her who it was from, but she wouldn't tell me, just kept going on about taking my clothes off so she could wash them. She practically had my shirt up over my head before I wriggled away.

"Connie, if that letter's for me, I wanna see it, 'kay?" I tried my best to be polite, for real; I still felt bad about catching her off guard.

She sighed, took the letter out of her pocket, and placed it quietly on the counter. Then she walked out of the room, and I heard her go upstairs.

I looked at the envelope. *Mr. Beau and Miss Paisley Argent.* It was postmarked Paradise, Nevada. I picked it up and slowly pulled out what was inside. Words scrawled in blue pen covered one side of a small piece of white paper. And this is what it said:

> To my Wonder Twins,
>
> Well, here I am in Paradise, like I said. It's not Las Vegas but it's close, so maybe when you come visit we can go see the lights. Eddie's putting me up for now in his suburban ranch. It's kinda on the small side, but it has four walls and a shower, so it's good enough for me. As I've explained in all my other letters, it's just a stopgap. I'll get a good job in time and my own place and maybe then you guys could come see me. You're both probably doing so well, you don't need your old man back in your lives, sticking his nose in your business. But whatever you think, I'll be here waiting,
>
> Dad xx

There was a rush through my whole body and this water-clear release in my head. Dad. He wanted us. He'd always wanted us. He'd gone to jail when we were six, charged with armed robbery. Now he was out of jail. A free man. A free Dad! We hadn't seen him, hadn't even heard from him the whole time he'd been inside. I held in my hands the first shred of contact we'd had with him in ten years.

But "other letters"—what did that mean? When did he say he'd be staying in Paradise—wherever that was? Who was Eddie? How did he know we were doing "so well"? I didn't think we were doing so well. Who'd told him that?

"Connie?"

I couldn't hear her upstairs and found the lack of floorboard creaks troubling. I heard a distant clatter coming from the far end, near my room. I two-stepped it up the stairs, finding her in the spare bedroom, sitting on the floor in front of the bureau, a shoe box full of letters on her lap. She was crying into the hem of her apron.

"This is all," she said to me. "Miss Virginia made me throw away the presents. This is all yours now. I want no more of this. It is too sad."

I looked down at the letters. There must have been fifty of them. "How long has he been writing to us?"

She smiled, her wide eyes melting into moons. "You and Paisley were seven. Your seventh birthday, a card came. He loves you so much, Beau. So much . . ."

I started bawling, as is my wont. My sister, Paisley, says I cry way too easily. She never cries if she can help it. Once when we were kids we were freewheeling on our bikes down the street, and Paisley fell off and slid along the concrete until she'd scraped off all the skin down the side of her leg. When I got to her, she was pretending like she hadn't shed a single tear, blinking her eyes and saying she was fine. She could barely walk. "I'm gonna have a cool scar," she said, and got right back on the bike like nothing had happened, the blood still trickling down. She's always been like that. I think it's because she knows if she starts crying, it'll be hard to stop. She says tears are a sign of weakness. At least that's what our grandmother always told her.

"You kept them from us?" I said.

Connie got up and handed the box to me, closing the bureau drawer behind her. I hated to see her cry. She'd always snuggle me if I cried as a child. It had always been her job to feed us, tuck us in, take us shopping, and give us hugs.

I still stank of the rotten kitchen waste I'd been dunked in at school but offered her a hug anyway. I tentatively put my arms around her, feeling her tense up, and then go limp and hug me back.

"You kept them all this time?" I said, feeling her nod against my head.

"I might lose my job."

"It's all right."

We released each other and she tapped the top of the box. "These are yours now. Please, I don't want them. You read them." She pinched my T-shirt on my shoulder. "Please change your clothes; I will wash them before I go."

And then she left the room and me and the box, and disappeared down the stairs. Moments later I heard the vacuum cleaner humming in the den.

I stripped off my rancid T-shirt and sat there, all afternoon, reading through every single letter Dad had sent us from prison. Letter after letter that my sister and I had never seen. I held each one like it was some ancient document that would disintegrate beneath my finger grease. Each one took me back ten years in time, back to New Jersey. Back to Paisley and me as children. Back to Dad and how it used to be when he took us out. To the park, to the country club, to eat pancakes on low-lying tables where he had to bend over to eat. To hotel lobbies where he'd show us coin tricks and we'd play baby blackjack for candy.

Then I knew who Eddie was. I wandered back in my mind to the times when Dad used to take us with him on his trips into the city (he was a sales rep for New Jersey Gardenia, which sold toiletries to hotel chains). He'd give us Junior Mints and Mike and Ikes if we behaved. We got to go inside these swank hotels and play on the massive winding staircases, go in and out of the elevators, slide around on the pristine marble floors in the bathrooms while he did his work. Just like in that children's book, *Eloise*. Sometimes, if the hotel was really busy, Dad would get someone to watch us—usually a real old geezer who'd keep reminding us how lucky we were and tell us about the crap Christmas presents he used to get as a kid, like oranges and, whatever, a bar of soap or something. But sometimes we'd get a concierge like Eddie.

Eddie, at The Roosevelt, was awesome. Like Will Smith only shorter. He always wore this pristine black uniform with a burgundy collar, and he'd show us coin tricks like Dad's and make us laugh with stories about the guests, telling us who was superrich and which ones were just superweird. "Suits" he called them. Suits with golden wives. Certain companies would hold conferences in the hotel and there'd be a horde of suits with matching designer luggage. The men would always do the checking-in and the wives would stand around, sighing and clicking their heels against the marble. Me and Paisley would take our candy up to the mezzanine and find ourselves a quiet nook where we could look down on the marble lobby, staring at the twinkling chandelier, watching the tourists check in and out, and waiting for Dad to emerge.

I remember the last time he took us into the city. It was our birthday the following day, and as a pre-birthday treat he took us to this restaurant in Grand Central Station, where we had burgers and cheese fries and Dad had a BLT. After lunch we looked down from the marble balcony at all the intense New York commuters running for their trains. I was dying to ask him about the fight he and Mom had had the night before. Our neighbor, Mr. Wong, had even called to complain because it was thumping through his walls. Mom going all high and screechy, Dad being all deep and defensive. And then him all high and defensive and her all deep and judgmental. Paisley and I shared a room above the kitchen, which was where most of their arguments took place. That night Mom had called us "little shits" and complained that Dad was never home to help, and always gave us candy to curry favor. That part is sort of true. Dad did buy us a lot of candy. You want me or my sister to do anything, you give us candy. It's kind of a key to get in with us.

In the diner, Paisley had ketchup all around her mouth. She asked Dad about the wives at The Roosevelt.

"Are they made of gold, Dad?"

"No, honey. Why d'you say that?"

"'Cause they look gold."

"No, they're not gold. They sure got a lot of it, though. I wouldn't mind a piece of it myself."

"Do they have jobs?"

"No, I don't think so."

"What do they do all day?"

"I don't know, honey."

I couldn't wait any longer. "Are you and Mom going to get a divorce?" I said.

I remember him chewing really hard on his sandwich and frowning. "Why d'you ask, B?"

"'Cause we heard you shouting again last night."

He took another bite of his sandwich and scrunched up his napkin to wipe his chin. Then he said, "I'm sorry, guys. We thought you were asleep."

"We were," said Paisley. "It woke us up."

Dad shook his head. "We just had a little argument, like you two do sometimes. We're not getting divorced."

"Where does it hurt you, Dad?" Paisley asked him.

"What do you mean, baby?"

"You told Mom you were broke. Where are you broke?"

Dad bowed his head and wiped his chin again with his napkin. When he came back up, he was smiling. He grabbed a menu from the stand. "Who wants cheesecake? Let's see what they got . . . ooh, strawberry, I think. Or chocolate swirl. Who wants chocolate swirl?"

We both nodded and dunked our fries in our joint pot of ketchup.

I remembered it so clearly. On the way home, Dad throwing Peppermint Patties over his shoulder to us in the backseat, them raining down on us like stars. Me and Paisley snuggling into the old wool blanket we always kept in the car.

"Try and get some sleep, okay, guys? Traffic's gonna be pretty bad on the way back to Jersey. We got a long drive."

About a week later, Dad went to work like usual but didn't come home. We just assumed that Mom had kicked him out, and we were too afraid to ask her. We didn't know about him going to prison until later. Mom spoke to us less and less and started talking to bottle necks more and more. And then, pretty soon, she wasn't saying anything at all. Paisley and I were the ones who found her.

Paisley misses Dad like crazy, even now. She's always talking about him. His on-the-spot bedtime stories in which we had starring roles. His BLT subs—the best in Jersey, he always said. The way he always called us his Wonder Twins. I kinda resigned myself years ago to the fact that he didn't want us anymore. Finding the letters threw me all out of whack. I didn't know how I felt now. I didn't know what to do.

All afternoon spent worrying about it and reading and rereading the letters brought me to one conclusion: I needed to tell Paisley. That was the next step I had to take. But I didn't know how to do it. She was banned from all the computers at her school, so I couldn't e-mail her. I tried calling, but I kept hanging up the second I heard a voice on the other end. I couldn't figure out what I would say. I knew I'd get all tongue-tied and say the wrong things, and she'd go on a rampage and get all Paisley about it. For the sake of her school, I needed time to work out the best way of telling her. I decided to write a letter. I spent all evening on it. My numerous attempts lay beneath me on the carpet in slowly uncurling balls.

Pais, I have to speak to you urgently . . .
Sis, you are seriously not going to believe . . .
Dearest Paisley, this is such a hard letter to write,
    I don't know how you're going to take it. . . .
Pais, I don't know how to tell you this . . .
Paisley, this is really difficult to say, so I'll just come right
    out and say it. . . .
PJ: Well, look what just turned up on our doorstep! . . .
Dear sis, you will NOT believe what happened today.
    I came home from school and Connie was in the
    kitchen . . .
Paisley, I have some really big news, so call me. . . .
P, it's about Dad. . . .

*Pais, remember our dad? Well, he didn't just abandon us
from his prison cell after all; he's actually been writing
to us for ten years and our grandmother didn't bother to
tell us. . . .*

However I ended up phrasing it, I knew one thing for sure: She
was gonna go ballistic.

PAISLEY

THREE

IMMACULATE CONCEPTION ACADEMY FOR GIRLS,
LODI, NEW JERSEY

I caught Jason screwing a cheerleader. What a friggin' cliché. And not a significant cheerleader, either; not Emily-Jane Bulow or Jessica Walsh, the two most popular bitches in school, but Mandy Fugazi, aka Paris Hilton in a broken mirror. Diseased little alley cat, too. She'd once done two St. Anthony's boys behind the tennis courts, using an empty potato chip bag for protection. All right, I'll admit, I'm no Jonas Brother when it comes to chastity, but Mandy had those kinda eyes. A slut's eyes.

Seeing those two skanks together became another one of my instant replays. Like the time we found Mom's body. In those moments between being awake and asleep, my brain has a habit of puking up bad memories. Finding Mom dead, for example. Being lost in the woods. The time Dad was pushing me on the swing and it swung back and caught his head and made him bleed. And from that day on, this scenario: getting to the toolshed twenty minutes early. Taking three tokes of my cigarette. Hearing the floorboards creak, a giggle. Rubbing a space on the dusty window. My cigarette dropping to the ground. Seeing them naked. Her lying beneath him like a doll. Him looking up at the window and smiling. Him thrusting on. Harder.

I ran back to the dorms. Ran and ran and ran, like some stupid hamster on its wheel, running off its night energy. When I got to the building, I stopped, knowing that my heavy breathing and wheezing would wake up the others. I couldn't go in. But I couldn't go back. And because I'd stopped running, I started to feel it. The punch to my stomach. The big black boot stamp to my rib cage. I needed to keep running so it wouldn't get me. So I ran deeper into the woods behind the school and spent the night there, nestled in the nook of a large tree trunk. I think I was born to live in a fucking tree trunk.

And when my breathing got less and the pain came back, I started thinking about my brother, Beau. The last time I went all Girl Scout under the stars, he was with me. But now I was on my own. No frightened twin brother to hold my hand. No more angel of salvation in paint-splattered jeans. Just me. Fucked-up, fucked-off me. I let it take me over. This was why I didn't cry. Because it hurt so damn much.

I acted like I'd forgotten about it when I saw Jason pushing his lawn mower up the lacrosse field a few days later. I had this stinging sensation behind my eyes like I wanted to cry, but there was no way I was gonna. There was no way I was gonna punch him, either. Why would I waste my calories on that son of a bitch? No, I would not be conquered, not by a guy. I took *my* big black boot sole and stamped down hard on any feelings I might have had for him. I wrote myself some angry poetry and this little story about a woman who cut the dicks off her former lovers to make necklaces and then sold them on QVC and made a fortune. It helped. I concluded Jason was merely a "get-me-through." Like when you're forced to watch a really boring movie and it's numbing your brain, so you develop a little crush on one of the stars, just to get you through it. A get-me-through. That's all Jason had ever been. That's all any guy would ever be.

Apart from Beau. And Dad.

But even though I'm a vegetarian, I still have a meat-eater's incisors, so naturally I wanted revenge. And it was while I was thinking up how to wreak my revenge on this little douche bag that I got a letter from Beau. And this letter, this little one-line letter, put the whole stupid Jason incident into perspective.

Beau usually e-mailed me, but since I'd been banned from all computers for making fake IDs, he had to go old school and write. When I first saw the letter, I immediately thought it was bad news. A long ramble about a beating he'd gotten from the O'Donnell gang at his school, written by his nurse. A wordy speech about how he was finally at the end of his "infinite tether" with the Skankmother and was planning to run away for sure. But it wasn't. It said just six words.

Paisley, Dad's been in touch. — Beau x

I read it again and again. And it came screaming at me like one of those magic eye posters that your brain has to unscramble before the hidden picture comes into focus. I stopped reading and held it to my chest. Dad. What? Dad's been in touch. Our dad? My dad? I had to say it a couple of times before I wrapped my brain around it.

Over the years, Dad had become this god to me. I constantly thought about him, wore old rock T-shirts that reminded me of the ones he used to wear, watched his favorite movies until they became my favorite movies. *Dog Day Afternoon*, *Serpico*, *Bonnie and Clyde*, *One Flew Over the Cuckoo's Nest*, *Assault on Precinct 13*, *Psycho*. I never stopped wondering why he didn't contact us. Wondering if his brown eyes still twinkled like Beau's did when he smiled. If it would still feel the same to hug him. If he was still as big. At school I'd fantasize about him in class. Him breaking out of jail and stalking across the country to look for us. Putting a bullet through the head of the first guy who stood between him and his kids. Bursting through the door of fourth-period Latin, sunlight flooding in from behind, and saying in his gravelly Dad voice, "Come on, Paisley, I'm gettin' you outta this dump." The fantasies were always killed when the bell rang. I hadn't been stupid enough to think any of them could come true. Until now.

I went from lying in a pit of stinking, slashed-heart despair to being thrust up into the sunlight, like a beach ball held under the water and then bursting up into the sky. I paced up and down our dorm like some crazy-assed bear in the zoo. I had an open-ended plane ticket back to LA, so I could easily get a cab to Newark and be on my way back west within twenty-four hours. But the principal—or Super Turbo Bitch, as I knew her—would never let me leave without the Skankmother's permission. And there was no way Skank was gonna give permission. It meant all the stops would have to be pulled out.

I needed to get myself expelled. ASAFP.

And a week after the traumatic event with Jason, four days after receiving Beau's letter, an occasion presented itself to me.

The whole school lined up for lunch in the long corridor outside the cafeteria. Jutting off at various intervals were our classrooms and the fiction and reference libraries. Right at the end was the school chapel. This was where we'd meet every morning, give praise for stuff, get freaked out by the tall plastic Jesus figure on the altar, and kneel on uncomfortable cushions till the woven imprints of crosses were tattooed on our knees. On the occasion in question, my favorite cheerleader, Mandy Fugazi, aka Sluttina Fug Face, had the misfortune of standing right outside the chapel, and therefore at the end of the lunch line, just as I joined it. The corridor reeked of meat and onions.

"Hey, Mandy," I said.

"Oh, hi," said Fug Face, curling her upper lip at me, then turning away.

I knew exactly what I was gonna say. I'd played it over and over in my mind to get it right. I took a few breaths before delivering it. I didn't want to stutter or mispronounce anything. I wanted it to be just right.

"Mandy," I said, "I've got this great book if you ever wanna borrow it. I know you're into that kinda stuff."

She looked blank, predictably. Fug Face didn't read—she could barely spell out the monosyllabic words in her moronic rah-rah chants. A fluorescent light flickered above our heads among the wooden caves and cobwebs. She had so many zits under her makeup, I could have played connect-the-dots.

"*Kama Sutra*, it's called. Yeah, it shows you all these different sexual positions you can get into with your boyfriend." I leaned in closer. I could smell him. Grass cuttings and gasoline. "You looked kinda stiff on the floor of the toolshed the other day."

Fug's face turned scarlet. The low mumbles of conversation stopped as the others listened in. I could see some of the girls giggling behind their hands. But I wasn't finished. Yet.

"It's okay if that's what the guy likes. But one day you might want to be a bit more adventurous. You know, try opening your legs a little?"

She stared daggers at me. No, not daggers. Swords. Swords with flaming blades and poisoned tips. She lunged at me, pushed me back against the bulletin boards, and grabbed my hair, pulling it any way she could.

"You bitch!" she screamed at the top of her lungs. "You were spying on me! You perv, you complete psycho perv!" Her voice echoed, ricocheting off every wall as we grappled. That's all she could do: grapple and pull hair. She was such a girl. That's how girls fight: They go for the hair. I had never fought like that. Hair-pulling was foreplay to me. I pushed her back and swung, clocking her across the left side of her face. *Thwack!*

Whoomph, down she went. I can still see her eyes close as my fist caught her cheek, the slow-motion jet of blood shooting from her mouth like a little red fish.

My arms were pinned back.

Cries of, "Oh my God" — "Is she dead?" — "What happened?" — "How awful," echoed in my ears as I floated along the corridor, propped up by two teachers, Miss Randle and Mr. Patrick. Every pair of eyes was on me, from the usually jaded seniors all the way down to the freshman in their burgundy and gold jumpers, gawking at me as I passed them. Some had their hands over their mouths, others tried to pretend they were suddenly very interested in their regulation penny loafers. Soon there were no more giggles, no more murmurs of disapproval. Just big eyes. And me, desperately trying to kick and wriggle out of my restraints, screaming at the top of my lungs: "Go ahead, make my day! Do it, you assholes. Put me out of my fucking misery!"

And then *bam*, I was in the principal's office, standing tight-lipped before the massive wooden desk with its row of paperweights and picture frames. Super Turbo Bitch, that day in a gray pantsuit and sad new bob haircut, glared at me all the way through her lecture.

"I'm not tolerating it anymore, Jane Argent," she said finally in her fake English accent, her nose all pointy and high in the air. "Over the past few semesters, your behavior has become progressively worse. Our school motto encourages us to give everyone a fair chance to fit in. But you are an example of everything that is wrong with girls today and everything I want Immaculate Conception to be rid of. I think you'll agree I've given you more than enough chances, spent more than enough of our limited resources to provide you with counseling, and you have done nothing, absolutely *nothing,* to improve."

Here we go again, I thought. *So come on already, do it. You know you want to. Rub this dirty little stain out of your clean little school.*

She stood up and faced me, leaning over the desk. "Punching a student?" The *p* of *punching* was packed with enough spit to spray my entire face. I motioned to wipe it from my eye.

She huffed on. "How am I going to explain to Mandy's parents that she's been punched? By another student? That she may have a broken jaw? Hmm?"

I started laughing. I couldn't help it. "What can I say? Made the bitch famous. They'll be talking about it for years to come." My heart was thumping in my ears. This was my chance. Four schools down, one to go. She was giving me all the right buttons, and I was pressing them all like a little kid on a keyboard.

STB snarled. "Disobedient, arrogant, rude, insolent . . ."

I sucked the tips of my numb fingers in an attempt to give them the warm kiss of life. Every word was a shout. A criticism. An order. As though saying it at maximum volume and spitting it at me like a cobra was gonna make me bow down to her. It wasn't. Nobody could make me do anything.

". . . ruthless, obstinate, rude . . ."

"You already said rude." I picked at my teeth with the tip of my long purple nail. I'd had enough by that point. I couldn't look at the woman anymore, so I concentrated on the greige wallpaper and tall, dark wood bookcases all around me. I don't know if it was my near-hypothermic state in that freezing office or the putrid waft of stale coffee I was getting off her breath, but it all seemed to be closing in on me. Like the garbage crusher in *Star Wars*. Or was it *Empire Strikes Back*? The one where they rescued Princess Leia, anyway. It used to be Beau's favorite movie, up until he saw that French one with the chick on the bike. Now he likes that one better. Thinks it makes him look more intelligent.

"Look, I get the point," I said finally. "I'm crap. Can I go now?"

"That's what you want, isn't it?" she roared, sitting down on her swivel chair and folding her arms, her too-tight jacket straining at the shoulders. "And that's what you got from all your other schools. They couldn't handle you, so they just let you go. I know you too well."

"You don't know me at all!" I shouted. "Most of the time you people ignore me. And when you're not ignoring me, you're whining about me not joining in or not being good enough for this or that . . . and it's 'waaah, waaah, waaah' in this ear, 'waaah, waaah, waaah' in that ear. Is it any wonder I'm so goddamn ANGRY?"

I'd used this same speech when they'd kicked me out of Rambuteau. There were two of them then. I'd managed to bring one to tears and pull off the other one's toupee. STB wasn't a crier. She didn't wear a rug, either.

"With a family history like yours, I'd say your behavior was written in the stars."

Mee-ow. *Okay*, I thought, *let's try this. . . .*

"You can't honestly tell me I'm single-handedly . . . bastardizing the entire private school system. I'm a drop in the ocean compared to some of the things that go on here."

"Such as?" she said, hands searching for things to do on the desk—papers to shuffle, pens to put back in their cup, a stapler to realign so it was perpendicular with the edge of the desk. Everything had to be perfect.

I counted them off on my fingers. "Your highly decorated student council president has her own strip show on YouTube; half the tenth graders are bulimic; I'm pretty sure our drama teacher smokes crack; and your lawn boy has been screwing most of my class."

She looked like she was waiting for a golf ball to drop into her mouth. Her whole body rose and fell with her breath. She picked up the phone.

"I suppose the piano incident wasn't your fault, either?" she said, dialing.

I thought about it for a second. "No, that was me."

She spoke into the phone. "Morrie, send Jason to my office, please. . . . I don't care, it's urgent." She put down the phone.

I leaned in for the kill.

"And since I'm spilling all these unfortunate beans, I don't suppose you've sat in on any of your husband's German classes recently, have you?"

"Don't you—"

"The man can suggest things with a long ruler that would make your eyes bleed."

"—DARE! You HORROR of a girl!" she bellowed, squinting the words out as if the force was hurting her eyes. "I could charge you with slander!" Drawn up to her full height now, she rounded the desk and marched over to the office door. She opened it, turning to deliver her parting shot.

"Get out of my school."

Mission: Accomplished.

"You are a bad seed, Jane Argent. Your future looks *very* bleak to me."

I stepped into the hallway and turned to deliver *my* final blow. "My name is Paisley. And at least I *have* a future. I wouldn't give a bucket of piss for *yours*."

I'd heard that line in a movie once, and I'd been dying to use it. Luckily my great brain managed to bring it to my attention at the perfect moment. The door slammed in my face, the bang echoing around the stony hallway.

"Yeah, thought that'd do it," I said.

I stood there for a moment, blinking myself firmly into reality. Done. I was outta there. My heart still thumped in my ears. I couldn't think about it anymore. I couldn't dwell on it. Five schools. Five schools and not one of them could deal with me. I didn't even know if *I* could deal with me. All I knew was I had to get to Beau and we had to get to Dad. Life would be better then. *I* would be better then, I was sure of it.

There was a school brochure on the table outside the principal's office. All the pictures inside were of happy, fresh-faced girls: a shiny blonde in a pristine tunic lighting a candle in the chapel; a girl sprayed in achievement badges playing the flute in the music room; a circle of cross-legged Girl Scouts sitting around a playground toadstool, listening intently to a fat woman reading a book. I was never the girl in the brochure. I was always the back-of-a-head in the science lab or the out-of-focus blob in the bleachers. I took the brochure in my hands and tore it straight down the middle.

As I started walking up the staircase to the dorms, the front door opened and Jason lumbered in, scraping the dirt from his boots on the doormat. For the splittest of split seconds, I felt that disgusting pang in my chest again, like I still loved him. It was a relief when the anger came back and I remembered what he had done to me. What I had seen.

He looked up and saw me.

"What have you told them?" He glared.

"Everything, darling." I kept on walking.

He came up behind me and grabbed my hand.

"If you told them about us sleeping together . . ."

"Sleeping together, screwing together. Eating Chunky Chips Ahoy together . . ."

"I'll tell 'em it's all bullshit. You're a kid. And you're a kid with a bad rep. They'll never believe you."

At that moment, Super Turbo Bitch appeared in the doorway to her office, behind Jason. She must have heard us. He didn't see her.

"But it did happen, Jason," I said, raising my voice so STB could hear every word and fake crying, lip quiver and all. "You said you loved me."

His hand felt rough and sweaty on mine. "Give it up, Paisley. It won't work. I got a good gig here. You're not gonna blow this for me."

"That's not what you said before!"

"Stop it, all right?" he whispered, leaning closer. "I'm just gonna tell them you're lying, then you'll be out of here and that will be that."

I stopped fake crying and looked at him. "But that *isn't* that, is it? I got proof. I kept our first condom. A souvenir to remind me how much I meant to you."

"Shut up! You know we never even used a condom!" he couldn't help shouting at me, and it wasn't until he turned that he saw Super Turbo Bitch glaring at him with nostrils like caves.

He turned back to me, as gray as a cliff face.

I smiled and whispered, "Don't that just stick it in and break it off?"

In the dorm, I packed up my stuff and found my plane ticket and passport. I threw off my school shirt and tie, replacing it with my AC/DC *For Those About to Rock* T-shirt, an exact copy of the one Dad wore when we were little. I kept my school skirt on and hitched it up another inch. It actually went really well with my chunky socks and boots. I kept my stripy tie, too; it made a cool cuff. Everything else—the blazer, the yellow sweats, the white button-ups—could burn for all I cared.

I could hear them all in the cafeteria as I walked to the school entrance. The echo of, "For what we are about to receive, may the Lord make us TRULY thankful, amen." The eager scraping of chair legs and clank of metal kitchen utensils.

I strode on. "Assholes," I said. "All of them, assholes."

BEAU

FOUR

I was sitting at my desk, awaiting Paisley's call to pick her up from the airport. I couldn't wait to see her. I didn't want to wait to see her. I had been waiting too long. I opened the lid of my hibernating laptop and clicked on the "TVArchivia" link in my favorites, then logged into my account. All my most-watched videos came up as thumbnails. I clicked on Oprah's face.

"They're doing marvelously, yes," said my grandmother in an odd Madonna-esque English accent. Ever the actress, she was rehearsing for a play in London at the time. *"Beau's very good at baseball, and he's taken quite a keen interest in art."* She sat beside us on this huge, squashy lemon couch. Paisley had her hands folded in her lap and her feet crossed at the ankles; I was wearing some kind of lederhosen. Our grandmother retrieved a piece of paper from a nook in the couch and showed the cameras. It was a painting I had done of myself and Paisley playing in the backyard. I remembered doing it at school.

The audience "aaahed" in chorus and Oprah asked, *"And what about Paisley? How are you doing, little miss?"*

The camera zoomed in on my sister, dressed in her little white smock and tights, hair in silky blonde pigtails. She smiled at Oprah and nodded.

"I'm fine, thank you."

And the whole audience just melted. Then Pais started squinting. She developed it not long after we moved to California. Ten years later, I still have my own nervous tic where I can't look anyone in the eye for longer than two seconds when they're talking to me, but Paisley's only lasted a couple of months. It was pretty bad, though, and the camera wasn't on her for long.

"She's just wonderful," said Virginia, smiling widely. *"Yes, she's a very happy little girl. They're both very much loved. I just feel so . . . so blessed that we've been able to make the most of what was a terribly tragic situation."*

I then looked up at Virginia and said, *"What's tragic?"* Oprah clapped and laughed, and there was another round of applause from the studio audience and a pastel-colored cutaway to commercials and a whinnying saxophone. After the break, Team Oprah had wheeled in our new bikes, but that segment of the show wasn't available for download. Virginia didn't let us keep those, anyway. We'd already won bikes on *All-Star Kids Fun House*.

Virginia made sure she got to tell everyone our story. We had interviews on ABC, CNN, *60 Minutes*. Appearances on *Ricki*, *Montel*, *Regis and Kathie Lee*, *Rosie O'Donnell*. We did endorsements for Chunky Chips Ahoy, Lucky Charms, and Wonder Gummies. She even got us invites to the Nickelodeon Kids' Choice Awards as guests of 'N Sync.

Wonder Gummies was this healthy kids' candy that was supposed to contain all these vitamins. When we were lost in the woods, all we ate for three days was a packet of them that Paisley had in her pocket. So there was all this hoopla about this miracle candy, and the company wanted us to be the "spokeschildren" for their new campaign.

I clicked on the Wonder Gummies thumbnail.

I remember being taken down to the TV studio with Paisley, both of us dressed in nasty white overalls with these pink and blue bubbles on the pockets. The ad was pretty corny, even then. We had to pretend we were walking through this plastic forest, rubbing our tummies like we were really hungry. And then we'd come upon this house made of candy and start gnawing on it, like Hansel and Gretel and the gingerbread house.

Then Paisley had to say, "Gee, Beau, this Wonder Gummy house is delicious."

And then I had to lick a wall and say, "Sure is, Paisley. And did you know Wonder Gummies are fat free *and* give us essential vitamins and minerals, too?"

Except I couldn't say "essential." I kept saying "senshal," and Virginia would shoot daggers at me from off-set every time I messed up. It took about twenty takes, and even then the director wasn't happy and changed it to "vital."

"Enunciate, Beau, there's a good boy," Virginia would say. "Big smiles, Paisley Jane. Come on, you can do better than that." And she'd do this quick clap after every order, like we were performing seals or something.

And then this voice-over would announce, "Wonder Gummies are helping keep America fit and healthy. Did you know that a child's daily portion of Wonder Gummies contains as much calcium as a glass of milk? It also provides essential daily nutrients including Vitamins D and E, folic acid, and zinc."

And then Paisley would be licking a gummy window and she'd say, "Hey, try the window, Beau. It's made of Wonder's New Honey Gummy. It tastes good."

Virginia would be screaming at her from the sidelines, "Rich in potassium!"

By that time I'd be sitting on the roof of the house, chewing on the chimney and saying, "I'm not done up here yet. Mmm, raspberry flavor. You gotta try this."

And then the voice would come on again and say, "Give the kids what they love and what they need—" (cue kids shouting) "Wonder Gummies!"

I laughed. I remembered Virginia storming onto the set, pulling my sister's overalls down, and smacking her across her bare legs. I stopped laughing.

"You WILL get it right. You will stay here ALL NIGHT if you have to."

It was good to think of us as kids again, me and Paisley, remember the good times. But the remembrance of every good time was tainted with bad.

I'd always been afraid of Virginia, more fool I. But she didn't scare Paisley at all, even when she hit her. Paisley would always just stare up at her. Whenever she sent Paisley to her room without food, I'd go up afterward and sneak her some Apple Jacks or something, and we'd sit in a little blanket cave on her bed and eat straight out of the box. I knew when she'd been crying. I always knew when Virginia had gotten to her. And there'd sometimes be a new hole she'd kicked in her closet door or a tear in the wallpaper behind her headboard. But only I would ever notice these kinds of things. Nowadays she and Virginia didn't speak to each other at all if they could help it. She was allowed home for the holidays if she was lucky, but that was it.

Paisley always used to say our grandmother was a vampire 'cause she hated garlic, *always* wore dark shades in sunlight, and didn't believe in God. Virginia did have a reflection in our mirrored hallway, though, which I called Paisley out on, but Paisley told me it was because our grandmother was the queen vampire so she could have a reflection. Once, a bird or something crashed into my bedroom window at night, and when we looked outside it was gone. Paisley convinced me it had been Virginia, flying up to check on us, and I didn't sleep right for days after. I hated all that kind of stuff: vampires, werewolves. Paisley's not afraid of things like that. Ghosts and gargoyles. "It's the living you wanna be scared of, Beau, not the dead," she'd say. And I knew she was right. But that's just the way I am. I think when we were babies she won the good genes lottery: She's cute, quirky, blonde. And badass. I'm short, dark, scared. And superfluous.

I clicked on the *Regis and Kathie Lee At Home With* special and scrolled through it. I'd watched it a bunch of times, but I wanted to see the last shot again, of us jumping in the pool. The rest of the clip was just our grandmother standing in our mirrored hallway with a backdrop of her shiny gold-plated Daytime Emmys for Outstanding Supporting Actress, 1984 and 1986.

"We're looking forward to Christmas and, as you can see, the twins are doing great," she said. And then she looked deep into the camera and said, *"And may I just take this opportunity to thank every single person who has sent cards and donations to the twins. We still receive gifts from all over the country, and it is heartening to know that America thinks so highly of them. We are investing in their future and have set up a trust fund for them, which will pay for their education and care. We try to respond to every single letter we receive, but are sometimes a little overwhelmed. We thank you all from the bottom of our hearts."*

I laughed. *We're looking forward to Christmas.* Which Christmas was that? The Christmas she left us with Connie's family to go skiing with the raisin millionaire? Or the Christmas she left us with Connie's family so she could get wasted on Scotch at home because she'd been dumped by the raisin millionaire? I could see through her like she was one of those hallway mirrors. *We are investing in their future.* New pool. State-of-the-art fire pit and sauna. New furniture. Bathroom fixtures. Carpets.

On one particularly brave Saturday afternoon a couple of years ago, I searched Virginia's desk and found the details. Me and Paisley had over ten million dollars coming to us when we were eighteen.

Ten million dollars!

I couldn't believe it. People had been so kind, sending us money when we'd been found, knowing full well that we had nothing else to look forward to. No Mom, no Dad. No home. I checked the desk often when I knew Virginia would be out. The latest correspondence from the bank said they were "looking into the misuse of finances issue" and putting a lockdown on all withdrawals from now on. Since we'd lived with her, she'd creamed off three million dollars of what had been sent for us.

The total then stood at just under seven million.

The day we were sent to live with Virginia was scary for us. You have to remember that we were only six and we were fresh out of a group home, where we'd been placed after leaving the hospital. We thought it was gonna be like *Annie*, when the little curly orphan goes and stays with that bald gazillionaire. We thought we'd walk into the mansion and there'd be footmen twirling around on mops, maids folding silk sheets, and a happy dog padding around all covered in soap suds. What *we* got was a ramshackle bungalow in West Hollywood, a part-time Mexican housekeeper, a gardener named Popeye who had two fingers missing from his right hand, and a grandmother whose sole preoccupation was to get us in the papers. It was better than the children's home and Connie was always good to us, but she had her own family. It never felt like home.

And while the cameras were there, we could never be ourselves. We had to be the children our grandmother wanted us to be. Clean, cute angels with rictus grins and well-rehearsed waves, always happy or studying. Not the kids we were. Me, who sucked on wet washcloths until they were gray and stank like wet dogs. And Paisley, who talked back and stole food for us when Virginia wasn't looking so we could have midnight feasts in our blanket cave on my bed.

When the cameras were gone, we were just messy kids, naughty kids, disgusting kids. We'd chew up cookies, then spread out the chewed mix on top of other cookies and eat them. We'd spit on the back of our grandmother's padded velvet coat when walking behind her in a store and draw patterns in the trails. Once we drew all over ourselves in black marker and pretended we'd gotten tattoos. We broke the lock on the booze cabinet and took sips from all the bottles. We cut each other's hair with gardening shears. We'd wash stray cats in talcum powder. We'd pee in the pool. We'd pee in the fire pit, too. Our knees were always bloody and scraped, and we always had the best time when we were doing something we shouldn't.

In the end, Virginia realized that spanking our butts or locking us in our rooms was no deterrent. She found the hole in the wall between our rooms, the hole Paisley had bored with one of Virginia's own stilettos so we could talk to each other. That was when she lost it and decided to send Paisley away.

It was always new and fun and exciting being a kid. I liked being disobedient. I can't bring myself to do the fun, naughty stuff anymore. I hate being a teenager.

I'm supposed to be shoplifting beer and notching up my STD count. Hanging out behind the bleachers after dark, smoking weed and snorting eight balls. Getting bong flu or getting shit-faced in strip clubs on Hollywood Boulevard or at frat parties in the Valley. I'm supposed to pack a knife and rob old ladies or be planning a shooting on my blog. But that's not me.

I like simple things. Reading. Observing. Watching the green parakeets up on the pylon wires outside the house. I like the cool breeze on my face through my bedroom window when I'm writing at my desk. I like French movies, pop music, pomegranates. I'm reading Sartre and Simone de Beauvoir and trying to teach myself French using a four-CD kit I got at a thrift store. I want to live in Paris someday.

That's why I get called "nerd" or "pussy" and dunked in trash cans. I try not to look them in the eye anymore. I hide behind my hair. But I can't change. I won't change.

I closed my laptop and stared out the window. I had a bag of peanut M&M's on the desk, and I reached over and plucked one out, a blue one. I carefully crunched away the blue shell and licked away the chocolate until just the peanut remained. Then I split open the two halves.

And there inside was the little bunny that lives inside every whole peanut.

Paisley taught me that.

And then the phone rang.

PAISLEY

FIVE

"Hey," he said, with a thin smile and a lift of his eyebrows.

"Hey," I said, dropping my bag. He picked it up and we headed for the exit. I hate airports. "There's too many fucking people in this world."

"It's good to see you, Pais," he said, all puppy dog eyes.

"You, too." We hugged. I'd seen him, like, a month before during summer vacation, so it wasn't one of our usual squeezes, full of unsaid *God I missed you*s. He was definitely fatter since the summer. The Skankmother had been feeding him up. But I didn't mention it. It was too soon to go into that old brother-sister repartee, and I knew he'd get all worried and start going on and on about diets he should try, so instead I cut straight to the chase.

"Did you bring the letters?"

"No, they're at home. I hid them under my bed."

"Good job."

We walked through the automatic doors, and I took my first breath of California air. It felt good. Then we played cab dodge to cross the road to the parking lot where Beau had left the Skank's red Pontiac Fiero.

"D'you wanna grab something to eat? I didn't have breakfast yet, so . . ."

"No. First things last. I wanna get back and see the letters. How many are there?"

"I don't know." Beau started the car.

"She hasn't treated you to your own wheels yet, then?"

He shrugged. "I don't mind. The Fiero's a sweet ride."

"Not yours, though. I thought you were looking at Subarus."

"She said they were too expensive."

"Can't bear the thought of you having a little bit of freedom, can she?"

"It's not like that."

"It so is."

He clearly wanted to change the subject. "So, good flight?"

"Not really," I said, looking out the window at the palm trees. "Didn't sleep."

"You're officially expelled?"

"Yeah. So what else did Dad say? Where is he?"

"Paradise."

"Where the hell's Paradise?"

"Just south of Vegas."

"Why there?"

Beau shrugged. "Remember Eddie from The Roosevelt Hotel? He's staying with him. He's got a place there."

"Oh. So why not come see us first?"

"Maybe he wants to get his soap business up and running again. He talks a little about heading for the Las Vegas Strip. You know, for the hotels . . ."

"But why can't he do all that in LA? We have hotels here. God, we're so close to him, Beau."

He changed the subject. "So what was it this time, why'd they expel you? Demolished another Steinway? God knows you tried everything else to get outta there."

"I punched a girl. And I liked it."

Beau laughed. "Why? What did she do to you?"

I shrugged. "Stuff." That was our code for *Don't ask me about this under any circumstances.*

"Something pretty bad, then," he said. "So I guess *Chicken Soup for the Teenage Soul* fell on deaf ears?"

"Just get me back home."

"As you wish."

Beau eased the Fiero onto Cahuenga and up the slope until we came to the paved driveway of the house. She'd had the outside painted again, white this time, and there were more palm trees out front. It was something different every time I came back; it never looked like the same place. New pool, new downstairs, new dining furniture. Same old Skankmother, though, if you didn't count the injections.

She wasn't home, thank God. Out at the salon having her landing strip do fuzzed, apparently. Connie wasn't there, either. She had finished for the day. The place was spotless and I could smell chocolate as soon as I walked in. She'd baked one of her special chocolate pizzas for us and left it on the kitchen counter. It said *Welcome Home Paisley* in marshmallows. We both tore off a piece and went upstairs to Beau's room. He slid out the shoe box from under his bed and emptied it onto the carpet.

"I can't believe they're from him," I said, yanking one of the letters from its envelope. "But why'd Skank hang on to them? If she never wanted us to have contact . . ."

"Virginia didn't keep them. Connie did," said Beau, munching on his pizza, watching me riffle through the envelopes like a monkey ripping open bananas. "Hey, be careful." He had read through all the letters before, at least twice. I picked up one of the earlier ones.

"This the first?" I asked. Beau nodded. The postmark was EJSP. East Jersey State Prison. Where he was sent after the robbery. I knew the history of the place from the Internet. Beau gulped down the last of his pizza and took the letter from me. He read it aloud.

> I never stop thinking about your mom. She was beautiful. I have this necklace of hers that I carry with me all the time. It was almost taken away from me in jail, but I still got it. I know she put you through some stuff, but she was sick. I should have gotten her treatment. But I kept following this big dream I had of getting some money together so we could all get out of Jersey. Make a better life somewhere else. Do you know she taught you both how to swim? I'll tell you all that and more when we're together again. I'll make that my job. To tell you both about your mom.

I listened with my mouth open, like some special-needs kid at group story time. I didn't remember Mom being "beautiful." She was older than Dad and she had short bleached hair, always raked back. Her blue eyeliner looked like it had been dug into her face, and no matter what she was doing she'd have a cigarette between her fingers. But Dad said she was beautiful. I wished to hell I could remember the beautiful part. And the swimming lessons. All I remembered was the screaming and the smell.

Beau read out five more letters. The word "love" came up a lot. I was glad.

"Did he put kisses on the bottom?" I asked. Beau showed me the page in his hands. Two kisses. I touched them with the tip of my finger.

"Are you finished with that?" he asked, noting my untouched pizza slice balanced on my knee. I nodded. He took it and started picking off the marshmallows.

I lay back on the carpet, trying to take it all in. I wanted to cry, I wanted to shout, and I wanted to grab hold of that bitch's scrawny neck and force her head down the nearest toilet. "He didn't forget one single birthday, Beau. I knew he didn't abandon us, I fucking knew it!" I yelled.

"Shhh," said Beau. "He DID abandon us, Paisley. He gave up the right to freedom when he robbed that hotel. . . ."

I sat up. I couldn't believe what Beau was saying. "We were poor. Dad didn't know what else to do. . . ."

"You're just quoting lines from the trial. He held a gun to a woman's face. Him and his friends deserved what they got. Whichever way you look at it."

I pouted. I'd watched that video over and over on TVArchivia before I got banned from the computer lab in whatever school I was in at the moment. Dad in his suit and handcuffs. His face creasing up when he talked about us. The judge looking at him above his half-moon glasses. Him being led away on the echo of "fifteen years." He didn't serve fifteen years; they let him out after eight. But we hadn't seen him since we were six. And now we were sixteen. That made ten years. I always was good at subtraction.

"He's still our family," I told Beau, pulling tufts out of the carpet.

A car door slammed outside, and Beau sprang to his feet and

meerkatted over to the window, looking for signs of the Skank. "I think she's back from the salon."

"Still terrified of her, I see."

"You know what she's like. If she sees the letters, she'll fire Connie. . . ."

"She won't do a damn thing with me here. I ain't afraid of no ghost." I looked at him. "What time's your curfew?"

"What curfew?" He licked his greasy fingers. "School then home. That's it."

Beau had the same haunted look on his face that he'd had as a kid back in Jersey. Whenever our parents were arguing. Whenever we hid in our tree house until Mom had passed out from shouting.

He was still at the window. "Oh, it's not her. It's Matt."

"Who's Matt?" I asked, carefully placing the letters back in the shoe box.

"The new gardener."

"The new boyfriend, you mean." I got up and joined him at the window. "So he's the latest tomb raider, huh? The stud. Younger than the last one. She spent any more of our trust fund lately?"

"No," he said. "Except the lake house. In Utah. I saw a picture of it in her desk drawer. Mirror Lake. She bought it a while back. It's pretty remote."

"Why the hell'd she buy in Utah?"

"For vacations, I guess. A retreat."

"Yeah, somewhere she can retreat for her week-long benders."

I tucked the box of letters under my arm. My eyes started stinging. "Why didn't he come get us, Beau?"

"Dad? Because Virginia wouldn't let him. He tried. Completed his parole, got a car, and drove all the way from Jersey. Says so in one of the letters."

I looked at him. "He came here? He didn't even know I was in boarding school back there?"

Beau shook his head. "He and Virginia had a fight. She got a restraining order, said he threatened her, tried to hit her, all kinds of stuff. It's all in the letters."

"She got a restraining order? What was he, some kind of wastoid?"

"No, he says he'd gotten his act together and came to get us. She was the one who called the cops, said he'd been drinking and wanted to hurt us. It wasn't true. But she told him that if he set foot inside the state, she'd have him back in jail."

"Bitch!" I yelled, pacing across the floor.

"Shhh . . ." Beau stuffed his hands in his pockets and bowed his head, his clean dark brown hair falling down over one cheek. "Look, she's had a lot of problems lately."

"Oh, what, California run out of Botox or something?"

"She checked herself into rehab a couple of weeks ago. Said it was the hardest thing ever . . ."

"I'll bet it was. Probably realized they didn't have an open bar."

"It's not just booze. She's got all these pills in her medicine cabinet. Just like Mom."

"Mmm. Well the apple never falls far, does it?"

Beau stuffed his hands down even deeper. "We've got to do something, don't we?"

"Uh, yeah," I said. "We've gotta find Dad. ASAFP."

I could tell Beau didn't want to do anything about it, but he knew I wouldn't let it go.

"But I got school and stuff . . ."

"Which you hate," I reminded him.

"Yeah, but—"

"But what?"

He sighed hard. "Well, all right, but we'll just bail, okay? Just run away and that's it. No need for revenge. You won't . . . do anything, will you?"

I looked at him. "Do anything?"

"You know. No Paisley-esque parting shots, like in Beverly Hills."

"That security guard had it coming, Beau. He'd been stalking us for weeks, up and down that mall. Just 'cause I got skulls on my backpack. Like that place wasn't already crawling with wannabe Goths."

"Yeah, but you made a laughingstock of the guy. Please, just this once, for me, can you not do anything to Virginia? She's not the type to forget it. She's not like the security guard. Our last gardener, Marvin, you know she sued him for sexual harassment?"

I sighed. "Yeah, you told me about that . . ."

"But it was her harassing *him*. She's got a mind all her own, trust me."

I laughed. "Yeah, a mind of her own but a vagina that belongs to the world."

"Paisley . . ."

"All right, all right. So what you're saying is, we should just disappear quietly?"

"Yeah," said Beau, suddenly enthusiastic. "We can go find him, and she'll never know where we are."

I put my finger to my chin and tilted my head like I was really thinking hard. "Yeah. Running away is good; I'm on board with that."

"Cool."

Then I went up to him. "But as for the no-revenge thing?" I squeezed his eager, pitted little cheeks. "I don't think so."

He deflated like a Bubble Yum balloon and went back to look out the window.

I was only thinking of one thing as I walked along the hallway to my bedroom. *We get out of here; we find our dad.* That was all there was to it. My bag was already packed from school, but I unzipped the side and threw out the textbooks—why the hell did I haul them all the way across the country, anyway?—replacing them with two clean push-up bras, my favorite holey fishnets, some ripped blue jeans, and some rock T-shirts. Springsteen, Metallica, Bowie. I knew it'd impress the hell outta Dad if I was wearing one when we met up. Like father, like daughter. Apples and trees again.

There are a lot of shitty dads in the world, and as an armed robber mine would probably rank among them. But he never hit or hurt us, never locked us in a closet. And when he held up those people in that hotel, he wasn't stealing their money to gamble it away on booze or drugs. He was stealing it for his family. He couldn't see another way out. He wasn't the perfect dad. Just *my* perfect dad.

I realized I'd used up the last of my cash on a veggie burger at LAX. I was pretty much broke.

I headed back into Beau's room. He had three neat piles of clothes laid out on his bed—one for socks, one for underwear, one for jeans. His toothbrush and toothpaste were wrapped neatly beside them in a white washcloth. He could totally rock the whole "white and nerdy" thing sometimes.

"How much money you got?" I asked him.

"Uh, 'bout seventy dollars. Why?

"I got about fifteen bucks in the world, that's why." I turned to leave.

"You seen my new razor?"

I turned back. "Uh, why?"

"I wanna shave before we go."

I just looked at him. "As if. Your balls even dropped yet?"

He squinted at me. I walked back into my room and slumped down on my bed. We wouldn't get far on eighty-five bucks. The lawn mower started up outside. I got up and looked out the window. Matt the gardener was walking up the edge of the small lawn, watching his own arm muscles tense as he pushed his throbbing engine along. He was good-looking in a comic-strip kind of way. But in the tradition of our grandmother's gardeners, he was probably screwing her, so that made him a total ass clown.

Still no sign of the Skank. A little lightbulb came on in my head as to how we could fund our yellow-brick quest for Dad. I went back into the hallway and tried the door to her bedroom. The sound of a car pulling up came from outside. The front door banged. Then came the throaty cough, a memento from twenty years of smoking and another twenty trying to give it up.

That was her.

BEAU

SIX

I poked my head out from the other end of the hallway. Footsteps at the bottom of the staircase.

"I won't be long. Help yourself to a beer from the fridge," came Virginia's voice. I darted back inside my room as Paisley darted back inside hers.

Seconds later, I poked my head out to see Virginia going into her room. I saw the shadow move around, heard the sound of drawers opening, her closet doors opening. Two *bangs!* as her high heels were thrown to the back. The *flip-flop* of her pool mules as she crossed to her en-suite bathroom. Water running, pounding the bathtub. The cloying scent of burning roses came wafting my way. This was her ritual after a long morning of doing nothing in Beverly Hills—she'd light all the candles around the tub and run the hot tap until the water was scorching. Then she'd go downstairs for a while to allow the water to cool and the candles to perfume the air.

She came out and shut the door. I pulled back.

"Beau? Are you home?"

It was all I could do not to answer. I bit down hard on my quivering tongue. She continued down the stairs. I stayed behind the door until I heard the distant sweep of the patio doors to the backyard. I went over to my window and saw her go outside, dressed in her red silk kimono and mules, barely hiding her white bikini underneath.

She was talking to Matt and twizzling a length of her long black hair extensions. When she had settled on her chaise longue for her pre-soak sunbathe, I heard a little rattle at the end of the hall and poked my head out again. Virginia's bedroom door was wide open, and Paisley was inside.

I was drawn to follow. "What are you doing?" I asked her in a forced whisper.

She was already rooting through drawers. "What do you think I'm doing? I'm funding our trip. Shut the door behind you."

"Are you crazy? She's already run her bath, she'll be back up here any second."

"I'm not scared of her." She was hunched over Virginia's dressing table, rummaging through crystal dishes full of trinkets and sundry bottles of antiwrinkle cream, bypassing them all in favor of the large red leather jewelry box. "And if I know our grandmother as well as I think I do, she'll be busy screwing the gardener in the cabana, which gives me just enough time to do what I gotta do and get out before she even notices. Ooh, that's pretty."

She bent down to search through the bottom drawers of the bureau, her blonde hair running down her back in waves like octopus tentacles.

"God, Paisley, please don't," I said, my rib cage contracting like a trampoline that she was happily jumping on. I edged back out the door, leaning my face against the frame. "We're so dead."

"Stop being such a wuss. Why don't you grow a pair and come help me?"

I tried to be strong and take a stand. *Do the right thing. Walk away. Just walk away.* But she was leaving, with or without me. And I didn't want her going off on her own. And I didn't want to stay here any longer if it meant she wasn't coming back. Counting down the days until my sister flew in from school was how I got myself through. So I did what I always do. I did what Paisley told me to.

Cautiously I moved farther into the room and stood by one of the four posts of Virginia's unmade bed. Paisley stood on the chaise longue beneath the window, which looked out on the back of the house and the valley below it, and began tugging at the Japanese silk drapes from Fukuoka. They wouldn't come off their pole. So she started taking things off the high shelves. Ornaments, candlesticks dripping in years' worth of hard wax, a clock, a diamond-encrusted snow globe with a little girl ice-skating inside. The chaise was draped in a black silk robe and several items of white lacy lingerie. Virginia's pink patent leather belt with its huge gold buckle shaped like a lion's mouth was curled up in the nook of the chaise. Paisley stepped all over them, leaving dusty marks.

"I've got some bubble wrap in my room. D'you want some?" I said.

She turned and looked at me in disbelief. "You would have bubble wrap for occasions like this, wouldn't you? Grab me a bag from the closet." She reached up farther, to a small wooden box at the very back of the top shelf.

"Bet you there's a stash in here. Maybe it's her emergency liposuction fund."

I made for the closet next to the bathroom, the flickering light from the candles around the tub catching my eye. Steam rose in little drifts above the motionless water. Everything gleamed. The gold taps, the deep white tub, the gold claw feet.

I remembered when it had arrived from Italy. Paisley and I had sat at the top of the stairs, swinging our legs through the banisters, watching the men hoist it up. It was just after we'd done an update on our story with Oprah.

I took out a black beach bag with little white flowers sewn onto it and threw it up to my sister, who was still standing on the chaise. She caught it and began filling it up until it bulged and the handles wouldn't meet. She stopped filling momentarily to admire the snow globe, giving it a little shake and watching the glitter float down on the small skating girl.

"Pais, I'm not kidding. She catches us, we're dead. We're beyond dead. We're history. Come on, Paisley, please, let's go. Put that down."

"I'll hear her coming," she said.

"No, you won't. You never hear her coming. And then all of a sudden she's there, like . . . like a crack in the window letting in a chill."

"Poetic, Beau."

I went to take the snow globe from her but she moved away.

"No," she said. "All this stuff was bought with the proceeds from OUR story. She got famous and rich because of US. This snow globe is ours. All these little knickknacks and trinkets are ours. That jewelry is ours. We're taking it back."

"All right, all right," I said, backing off and returning to the door frame.

"I'm gonna need a bigger bag," she said, throwing the snow globe down onto the silk bedclothes and marching out of the room with her swag.

The patio doors slid open downstairs.

"Shit, that's her," I said, edging farther back into the hallway and closing the bedroom door very gently behind me. Paisley came out of her room with her backpack and the swag bag and tried to get past me.

I blocked the way. "Paisley, we've got enough now. Let's just go."

"I'm not finished," she said, trying to get past me again.

"Look, I'll grab my stuff and we'll go out my window, okay? We can be gone before she even knows what we've done. Shhh. I think I can hear her."

"I'm getting the snow globe and then I'll follow you down. Go start the Fiero," she said, handing me both bags.

"What? You can't take her car. She loves that thing."

"Just do it."

And she disappeared back into Virginia's bedroom, leaving me standing there, dallying as usual. I checked for signs of anyone coming up the stairs, then ran along to my bedroom with the bags. I slid open my balcony door, my palms sweating on the handle, then stepped out onto the little balcony. Seeing no one around, I dropped my own backpack down onto the patio, followed by Paisley's, then yanked one of my bedsheets free, tying it around the handles of the swag bag and easing it down, too. Reluctantly I climbed over the balcony and let myself over and down until I hung by my hands on the railings. I dropped down onto the edge of the patio and stumbled backward, falling flat onto the grass. Getting up, I checked around to make sure I was still alone, then grabbed hold of the bags, running along to the front of the house to dump them beside Virginia's Fiero. My hands were shaking. I pulled the keys out of my pocket and fumbled to find the right one, then flung open the door.

I threw our packs into the back, tossed the swag bag into the foot well on the passenger's side, then slid into the driver's seat and started up the engine.

As I turned to look back toward the house for Paisley, I came face-to-face with Matt instead. He was crouched over, leaning on the open car door.

"Hey, Beau," he said. "I could have sworn I just saw you ripping off your grandmother. That didn't really happen, did it?"

I just looked at him. The engine was still rumbling. He stood up so his head disappeared above the car. "Out," he ordered.

I got out but left the engine on.

"I think you got some explaining to do, don't you?" he said, wrapping a thick, muscley arm around my neck. "Come on inside."

And he marched me back into the house.

PAISLEY

SEVEN

"Just do it."

I felt bad for ordering Beau around all the time, but I knew it was the only way he was ever going to do anything. He'd always been the same. If it were up to him, we'd still be in the womb.

I went back into the Skank's room. The snow globe glinted on the other side of the bed. I made my way around to grab it and saw that the drawer of the nightstand was slightly open. Once, when me and Beau were little, we'd been snooping around in there and found this book with color photographs of people doing each other over car hoods.

But the book wasn't in there anymore. Just a clean pile of lace panties. And on top of them, a shiny silver gun.

The handle was black, the barrel was silver, and I couldn't resist taking it out, molding my fingers around it. *Eclipse Target II*, the barrel read. I'd seen one in a movie, but it didn't look as beautiful as this one. This one shone. I touched it, held it against my cheek.

I'd heard her, the Skankmother, talking about getting a gun once when her circle of poolside bitches had come around for afternoon gin and sympathy. How the crime wave was getting worse, how she didn't feel safe walking in LA. How it was her right as an American to "bear arms and defend herself."

I didn't think twice. I tucked it in my skirt at the back and pulled my T-shirt down over it. Done. The cold metal against my skin made me shiver momentarily, but then it was warm and it stayed put against me as though it had always been there.

I closed the drawer and took the snow globe from the bed, holding it up to the window. The diamonds twinkled around the base.

I felt a presence behind me. Like a crack in the window letting in a chill.

"I see you're home, then," came the greeting. I turned. There she was, a cougar on two legs, almond-eyed. Expressionless. She'd had a boob job since I last saw her, and yet more Botox shoved in her face. The outer corners of her eyes made her look like someone was working her with strings from behind. Her silk robe was open to reveal part of her white bikini underneath.

"My my, Grandmother. What big tits you've got," I smirked.

She gave me the thinnest, coldest smile and closed the door behind her. "I got the phone call from your principal. What was it this time? Drugs, sex, or violence?"

"What can I say? I learned from the best."

I held the snow globe tight and headed for the door. She barred the way.

"Move!" I hollered. She just looked at me, clearly trying to frown, but the Botox wouldn't let her. She looked at the snow globe, then back at me. Then at her empty shelves.

"Oh, is that the game we're playing? You were stealing *my* car and *my* things and then running away, were you? Is that how I raised you, Jane?"

"Wrong, wrong, and wrong," I told her, brandishing the snow globe in my fist like I was about to smash her over the head with it. "Number one, that's *our* car. You bought it just after *we* got you on

Montel, remember? Number two, these are *our* things. And three, *you* never raised me or Beau. You just paid somebody ELSE to."

She sighed. "Is it any wonder? Your own mother couldn't bear to look at you. Your father went to jail to get away from you."

I moved in close to her and grabbed the door handle. The door opened, but she slammed it shut again. "You disgust everybody," she spat.

She always played the "absent parent" card in shit-uations like these. I'd never exactly gotten used to it, but we argued so often that I'd come to expect it.

"*I'm* disgusting?" I laughed. "At least I'm not some chronic slut who fucks her handymen." Come to think of it, actually I was. But I wasn't telling her that.

"Vile. My ears are not garbage cans, Jane."

"No, but your ass is. Get outta my way."

"No, you will damn well stay here and face up to what you've done."

"You think I'm gonna stay here for all eternity? You can't lock me up like a fuckin' prisoner. I'm not Beau."

She smiled, hands on her hips. "Where will you go, hmm? You don't have any other family, do you? You're sixteen. Face it. I'm all you've got."

"No, you're not. We're going to Dad's. We found his letters. Connie kept—"

"Dad's?" she repeated. She stared at me, wide-eyed like some weird bird. "Dad's what? Dad's flophouse? Dad's homeless shelter? They don't send ex-offenders straight to luxury mansions, you know, honey."

"Whatever. It'll be a palace compared to this shithole. Get outta my way."

"He hasn't even called you," she cackled. "What's wrong with this picture, Jane? Yeah, he wrote, but that was in jail. He had nothing else to do."

I gripped the snow globe so tight the diamonds pressed into my palm; I thought my fingers were gonna crush right through the glass. *Don't cry, goddammit,* I thought. *Fuckin' pussy. Think of Dad.*

Her words were like knives, but I just swallowed them down. "He came to see us as soon as he was paroled. You drove him away."

"And he never came back. The End. When he knew he couldn't get his little fingers on your money, he skedaddled out of here faster than you can say *gold digger.*"

"Liar," I said, going for the door handle again. Her face tensed and she slammed herself back against the door. We were so close I could feel her hot breath on my face. It stank like kerosene.

"You're in for a big disappointment if you think he's going to scoop you up in his arms like he used to. You're not his cutesy-wootsy babe in the woods anymore."

"Move your ass—"

"Think about it." She grinned, her eyes wide and black. "He didn't care about you enough to stay out of prison. And that's when you were children. Why would he give a damn about you now? Some monstrous little teenage . . . maniac?"

"Because he loves us. Remember love? It's in the dictionary, next to *lush.*"

She pressed herself harder against the door, all dramatic like a freakin' drag queen.

"All right, you can go. I'll *allow* you to go. But you're not taking your brother with you. You can go, Jane, but he stays. And *that*"—she said, clasping the top of the snow globe—"is mine."

I snatched it back. "My fucking name is PAISLEY." I turned to the window and pitched the snow globe, sending it smashing through the glass. There was a pause and a tinkling of glass, then it *boomfed* on the driveway below.

I turned back to her. She drew a full breath and glared, the way vampires always look at their victims right before they suck the shit out of their necks. She grabbed hold of my shoulders and shoved me backward against her closet. I grabbed her chin and forced it upward, then pushed her back onto the bed and bolted for the door, but she caught my foot with her freezing hands and held on.

"Get off me. Get the fuck off me!" I yelled, kicking, hoping to catch her face with my boot. She let go, only to tackle me to the floor and grab my head at the sides, slamming it down into the carpet. I wrenched away from her and stumbled to my foot. She got up, helped by the bed, her hair even more of a mess and one sleeve of her silk robe torn. I laughed, catching my breath before she lunged at me one final time and with one supreme push shoved me backward into her bathroom. She grabbed the door handle and pulled it shut.

I could hear her on the other side, propping a chair under the handle, panting.

"I've had it with you!" she shouted, all breathless and squeaky. "I don't know what to do with you. Now you stay in there until you damn well cool off!"

I lay half-slumped and all crazy-breathing against the tiled wall under the towel rack. I remember Mom saying the exact same thing the time she locked me and Beau in the basement. *Now you stay in there until you damn well cool off!* She couldn't handle us, either. The only light in Skank's bathroom came from the candles burning around the full bathtub. My mouth stung and throbbed like it had a little heartbeat. I touched my bottom lip. Blood. I yanked down some toilet paper from the roll to hold against it as I stood up and looked in the mirror. A cut. My right cheek was cut, too. She had caught me with one of her diamond rings.

"It's nothing, it's nothing, it's nothing," I whispered, stamping my foot on the tile floor, my whole face throbbing. "Stop-it-stop-it-stop-it-stop-it." I dampened the tissue under the faucet. My hand was shaking. I turned off the water and dropped the soggy wad in the basin. I sucked my lip and checked the mirrored cabinet above the sink again. I was gonna have a cool bruise. I could always guarantee a good scrap with old Skank. Most grandmothers taught their granddaughters to bake or sew buttons. Mine taught me how to fistfight. The girls at school were so weak. They always went for the hair or clothes. I never got hit by them like I did with her.

The cabinet was ajar. I opened it. I saw all the little pill bottles lined up on the shelf. Oxycodone. Vicodin. Fluoxetine. Hydrocodone. Tylenol. Ativan.

Ativan. I remembered one of the doctors overdosing on it on *ER*. Anxiety problems. I pocketed it.

I tried the door handle. Jammed solid. I sniffed, wiping my nose with my bare arm, expecting a trail of snot but seeing red. I wiped it on one of her pristine white bath towels and began kicking at the door, lightly at first, and then fuck-it fast. Faster and faster and harder and harder, until it started to weaken, buckling and chipping at the latch. Then it swung right out before me, knocking the chair into the center of the the empty room. Skank was gone.

I took two of the lit candles from around the tub and held them up to the Japanese silk drapes from Fukuoka.

"Fuk-u, Grandmother," I laughed. Damn right I'm a maniac.

Conducting my own little orchestra of fire up both drapes, I swung the candles back and forth, watching the orange flames flick higher up the fabric, smelling the burning silk, the heat fanning my sweaty face. Ecstasy prickled through my body, making my hairs stand on end.

"Oh, you need locking up, Paisley Argent," I said, throwing the candles onto the bed and striding across the room, slamming the door behind me.

There was no sign of the Skank. Outside, the Fiero was running. All our stuff was in the car, but Beau was nowhere near it.

"Fuck," I said, reaching through the driver's window to turn the engine off. As I looked back at the house, I saw Beau coming out, the gardener right behind him, his huge ham forearm clamped around my brother's neck.

"You must be Paisley," the brute said.

"And you must be Matt," I replied.

I looked up. I don't know what made me look up. A flickering. The fire had gotten as far as my bedroom.

"Can't let you do it. Can't let you take off with your grandmother's things."

The Skankmother appeared behind them in the doorway. She walked straight out, right up to me, and threw down a bundle of money at my feet.

"One thousand. That enough to get you gone?"

"That and my brother," I said, picking up the wad of bills. Thanks to Matt's headlock, Beau's feet barely touched the ground. He was trying to pry it away, but Matt's arm was big, wrestler big. He looked like Thor, only with girlier hair. The tendons flexed under his skin. My brother looked at me with his desperate brown eyes.

"I get it. You need Beau so you can still claim the money." It was all screaming back to me now. She needed one of us, and who was easier to control? "If I'm not coming back, he won't stick around."

"Oh, he'll stay." She glared back at me. "If I have to keep him under lock and key, he'll stay. Beau's a good boy." Matt tightened his grip. Beau closed his eyes.

"How much she paying you to do this, Matt? Or did she promise you a slice of our trust fund?"

Skank's eyes narrowed into slits. "Beau stays. You go," she said.

"You know there probably isn't that much left now, Matt," I warned him. "She creamed off most of it paying to send me away, and then there's the new furniture, the new tits. . . ."

"You better scram, girly," said Matt, tightening his grip on Beau's neck. Beau's face was getting redder and redder.

"She's blown through three million already. Probably more." I waited, looking from Skank to Matt and back again.

"Go," Matt told me. The Skank folded her arms across her big fake boobs.

"Beau, get in the car," I said.

"Mmugh?" he garbled.

"I don't think you heard me, Jane. Beau is staying here. But you can go. Be free." She ushered me away with a flap of her hands, like I was some little fly that wouldn't take the hint. "You don't have to wait until you're eighteen. I'm giving you your freedom right now. Take it. Go on. It's what you've always wanted, isn't it?"

"No. What I wanted was my dad back, you evil bitch."

She smiled at me, one of her huge stretched smiles with her big red trannylicious lips that looked like she'd been injected with Joker venom.

"Okay." I turned on my heel. I walked to the car. "Good luck putting the fire out," I called over my shoulder, getting in the driver's seat and slamming the door.

I started the engine and stepped on the pedal. *Skreeee!* I looked in the rearview mirror. The Skankmother was scurrying inside on her own screams and Matt had loosened his grip enough on my brother so he could wriggle free and run to the car.

I was rolling out of the driveway when the passenger door flew open and in scrambled Beau, breathless and gasping theatrically.

"My God, Paisley," he panted, reaching out to shut the swinging door and turning to look through the rear window. I shifted into gear and stepped on the gas.

"She should have known not to leave me in a room full of lit candles."

In the mirror, I could see the flames licking out of my bedroom window, lapping up at the milky afternoon sky like tongues. Splashes and sparks and debris flew out. It looked kinda pretty.

"Shit, Pais. You set it on fire?" Beau wheezed. "Oh shit, this isn't happening. This just isn't happening. . . ."

"Then let's pinch each other and wake up," I said, looking over at him. His hands were at his temples, like he was trying to massage away the last few hours.

"That's her home. She's gonna be pissed, she's gonna be so pissed!" he kept saying.

I kinda wanted to stick around and watch the old woman melt under the weight of her plastic skin, but we couldn't. I put my foot down and kept my head forward, leaving the whole sorry mess in the rearview.

BEAU

EIGHT

"Why do you call us the Wonder Twins, Dad?" I once asked him. I must have been around five, I guess.

"Because that's what you are. You and Paisley are my Wonder Twins. You took a long time to, well, come along."

"What do you mean?"

"Never mind. Point is, when we finally got you, we were real happy."

"Was Mom happy?"

"Yeah, Beau, she was. You know, there are these superheroes called the Wonder Twins, too. They're a brother and sister. To get their powers, they have to touch hands and say, 'Wonder Twin powers: Activate!' When you and Paisley were babies, your cribs used to be next to one another and when one of you would wake up, you'd stretch your arm through the bars to reach for the other one. Like if you touched hands, you'd activate your powers, too. It was the cutest thing."

"Do me and Paisley have superpowers?"

"You're both pretty super to me."

"Who cried most, me or Paisley?"

"You," said Dad, without even thinking. "But all we had to do was put you in the crib with your sister and you'd shut right up, every time. Like magic."

♥ ♠ ◆ ♣

So that was us as babies. The Wonder Twins. Better together. When we were found in the woods after we'd been missing for days, the news anchor who broke our story to the nation called us the same thing. Wondrous. Wonderful. Wonder Kids. They said we had kept each other alive. I didn't get what was so amazing about us until I read all the news reports years later. There was a spate of child murders around the time we got lost. Kids would vanish for a couple of nights and then their bodies would show up somewhere. Near the swings in a park in Elizabeth. Floating on a pond in South Orange. On the roadside near our elementary school. But we were found alive. Everybody just went nuts. And what with it being March and us being out in the open for three nights, alone. And us being six. We were little wonders. America loved us.

Now we were thieves. Arsonists. America wouldn't think us quite so wonderful now, that was for sure.

I folded Dad's letter and placed it back in its envelope in the shoe box at my feet. The Ficro thundered along the endless desert road, an hour and a half into our journey. It seemed to take forever to get to Paradise, just like tomorrow seems like next year when you're a little kid. I'd been biting my nails the whole way from Virginia's house, or rather Virginia's ruin. Because that's what it would be by now. Like Thornfield in *Jane Eyre*. Just charred remains. I still couldn't believe what had happened. We were on the run now, whether we found Dad or not. Virginia would have the cops onto us for this, make no mistake. My bitten fingertips were red raw, and throbbing like each one had its own little heartbeat.

"Such a boring road," said Paisley, switching radio channels. She had all the windows down and the warm gritty wind was whipping my hair up around my face. The whole ride out of LA, her white-knuckled fists had gripped the wheel and her jaw was tight and twitchy. When we got out on the open highway, she started to relax. Her hands slipped down, and she sang along to the mullet rock blaring out of the radio.

"It's a beautiful road," I told her. All right, it was still a running buffet of desert, but the sky was brightly blue in every direction as far as the eye could see, broken only by mini explosions of clouds. I looked at Paisley. The corner of her mouth glistened. It was cut and swollen. I reached out and placed a fingertip on it. She jolted away.

"What?" she frowned.

"It's bleeding again."

"Leave it. It'll scab over."

Pretty soon I felt a nudge on my arm. She handed me half a pack of peanut M&M's. I don't know where she got them from. I took them and popped a green one in my mouth.

"Wonder what those mountains are?"

"Who cares?" she said, scraping her hair away from her face.

I glanced toward the speedometer.

"I'm within the speed limit, Gramps," she informed me.

"What will we do for money when our money runs out?"

"Sell the antiques. Dad'll know some prison dudes who can fence the stuff for us. He's sure to. And he'll have gotten work at Caesars Palace and, I don't know, maybe we can get jobs there, too, as pool hands or something. I heard they got, like, five pools."

"Prison dudes? Like our old friend Eddie?"

"Yeah."

"I don't think Eddie's gonna be too happy about putting us up as well as Dad."

"We can rent somewhere. Between the three of us, it'll be fine."
She shivered and grinned. "God, I'm so excited. We're gonna see
Dad, Beau! At long fucking last."

She was watching the road, so I didn't need to smile. I couldn't
share her enthusiasm at all. I didn't like not knowing where we
were going. Not knowing where we were gonna sleep tonight.
Everything was so messed up. I rubbed my throat. It still hurt from
being half-strangled by Matt. The M&M was ready. I took it out.

"Bunny?" she said.

"Yeah. A good one, too." I held it out to show her. She smiled.
"How long will it take to get to Paradise?"

She squinted and pulled the sun visor down to shield her eyes.
"I don't know, another hour? Jesus Christ, it's hot." She put the
windows up and turned on the air-conditioning. Within seconds
the car was a refrigerator on wheels.

I stared through the windshield and watched the white lines
disappear beneath us. I wondered if this would be the road that
would lead to him. What his first words to me would be. What he
looked like. If he'd started to go gray. If he would hug me. If
he would cry.

My throat felt taut, as though Matt was still wrapped around it.
I coughed to try to clear the pressing pain.

"I seriously think that ape damaged my larynx."

Paisley rolled her eyes. "You're fine."

A song came on the radio, and she squealed and reached for
the dial.

"Oh, this is a classic. This can be our road-trip song. Dad used to
love this."

"Who is it?"

"The Boss, of course. Springsteen. 'Born to Run.'" She turned the volume up until it became distorted, and screamed her lungs out. "De-niw-niw-niw!"

It was my turn to roll my eyes. I leaned my head against my window. I wondered if the fire at our grandmother's house had made the news. If we didn't find Dad, I didn't know what Paisley would do. Dad had always been kinda like her version of Kryptonite. But a good Kryptonite. I only had to mention his name and her face would release its pulled tension, her eyes would soften. When we were little kids, she would throw tantrums all the time, especially if Dad wasn't home. She'd kick the walls and doors, and Dad was the only person who could calm her down. All he had to do was hold her hands and ask what was wrong, and she'd stop. One minute she was peanut brittle, the next she was a marshmallow. It was like flicking a switch. I didn't like to think about what she'd do if we didn't find him. She'd already burned our house down.

Paisley turned down Springsteen. "You can put that French crap on, if you want," she said. "Those two losers in turtlenecks. Noisy Blanks."

"Noir et Blanc . . . ," I corrected, feeling my head become heavier. "I didn't bring it." The air was cool and soft from the vents, and I drifted into nothingness, lulled by the gunning engine. The sun bounced off the hood of the car in little shimmers. I was with my sister and we were okay. It was all going to be okay. . . .

HONNNK HONNNK!

I woke with a jolt, opening my eyes and sucking in the drool that had run down my chin. A gigantic semi was passing us by.

"M—where?" I said, licking my salty lips.

"Back with us, sleepyhead? We're about twenty miles outside of Paradise."

I opened my eyes wider to focus. "How long've I been asleep?"

"A good hour. You missed all the fun. The traffic getting into Barstow was a real hoot. You got the last letter? I think it's, like, Chicks-with-Dicks Drive. Find the house number."

I fumbled around in the shoe box to find the envelope. "Uh, yeah, 659 *Dickens* Drive, Paradise."

She clutched my arm. "Oh my God, Beau. We're actually going to see Dad again. Can you believe it?"

"Now?" I asked, sitting up in my seat. "We're going there now?"

"What did you think we were going to do first, take in a show? Dad's the whole reason we're here."

"But it's, like, nearly dark, and we're tired, and we need to think about getting a room or something. We can go find Dad tomorrow."

But Paisley wasn't gonna quit so easy. "No way. Dad is here and I'm seeing him today. And God help anyone who tries to stop me."

We rolled through all these quiet little subdivisions, which looked pretty much the same as any other. The sunshine made everything look clean and happy. Kids were out on bikes, people in T-shirts and sandals were drifting around at their own pace. There were signs for golf courses, art galleries, craft shows, a farmer's market, a petting zoo, new apartment buildings. Everything looked so ordered and sanitary, like the town in *Edward Scissorhands*. Something just didn't fit here. Dad—at least the Dad we knew—definitely didn't fit here.

We started coming across street names that sounded like items on the Taco Bell menu: Escondido, Hacienda, Caliente. And then, after a wrong turn down Avenue del Sol . . .

"Dickens Drive, there it is, there it is, Beau," said Paisley, turning the corner and ogling out the window for signs of house numbers. Every house was painted a different color, pastel blue, pastel pink, pastel orange. "Six-five-six, six-five-eight. Where the hell is six-five-nine, Beau?"

"It's there," I said, pointing to a small house at the end of the cul de sac. "Six-five-nine."

Paisley pulled into the spotless yellow stone driveway next to an immaculate Ford and turned off the engine. She got out, slammed the door, and immediately went up to knock. I took my time. I still hadn't fully woken up. I still wasn't sure if I was just dreaming all this. And I still didn't know what I would say when I saw him. I'd kinda figured I'd think of something during the drive. But then I'd fallen asleep. And here we were. I couldn't think straight.

The heat outside our rolling icebox hit me like a sheet of hot plastic. It was late afternoon and the sun still showered down in pulsing orange waves. I followed Paisley to the door, hanging back a little, already wiping the sweat from my eyes. I didn't know what would be best, a hug or a handshake. A "How are you?" or a "Long time no see." I cleared my throat.

A black guy answered the door in a lemon shirt and navy shorts, like he'd just been called away from a barbecue. It was Eddie. Will Smith, but shorter.

I glanced at Paisley, who seemed unfazed.

"Hey, is Buddy home?" she blurted out.

The man glanced back inside the house and stepped out, closing the door quietly behind him. "Buddy?" he repeated.

"Yeah, Buddy Argent? He wrote us and gave this address."

"We're his kids," I cut in. "Remember? The Roosevelt Hotel? He said you'd put him up once he was on parole."

"Oh. Yeah. You're . . . Paisley and Beau?"

"Yeah, so is he here?" said Paisley.

"Uh . . . no."

"No?"

"I said he could stay here a couple of weeks." He looked over his shoulder at the house. "That turned into a couple of months, and I had to . . ."

"Let me guess, your wife was giving you static and you kicked his sorry ass out on the street."

"Look, I'd just gotten married and moved out here, I was trying to start over. And then Buddy shows up, asking to stay, and I let him. And he was here for a long time. But . . . I gotta get on with my life." He looked at me. "We wanted to start a family and . . ."

"What, did he keep walking in on you or something?" said Paisley, stomping away from the door and back to the car.

"It's okay. You don't have to explain," I said to him. "We just thought he'd be here, that's all. It's just kinda disappointing. Sorry to bother you."

Eddie smiled and then laughed. "Damn, Paisley and Beau! You two sure grew up since I last saw you. So y'all remember me? From the hotel?"

Eddie had been the inside man on the job, the concierge. He knew when people were checking in, going out for the evening, what they put in the safe. He laughed again and clapped his hands together.

"God, your dad never stopped talking about you two."

"Really?" I said.

"Yeah. All the time. You're what, fifteen now . . . ?"

"Sixteen."

"Sixteen! Yeah, Paisley was this little blonde hothead who always got her own way. And you were this quiet little dude, always smiling."

I raised my eyebrows and pushed away a sweat bead.

Eddie's smile disappeared. "I think Bud was under the impression that you two didn't wanna see him."

"It's a long story . . . ," I said, not wanting to elaborate further on the whole letters debacle. I stepped away. "Nice to see you again."

"Sorry I couldn't be more helpful," he called out. "Your dad talked about getting work on the Strip. Pal of ours works at a bar in Caesars Palace. You could try there."

"Okay, thanks."

Paisley was slumped in the driver's seat when I got in. It took me a minute to build up the courage to say anything.

"He said to try the Strip. Caesars—"

"I heard."

"We'll find him, Pais. It's just gonna take more time."

She started the engine and reversed out of the driveway.

"It's not gonna be like the woods," I told her, checking her reaction. I tried to sound optimistic. "We'll get to him. Whatever it takes. Okay?"

She just nodded.

PAISLEY

NINE

LAS VEGAS BOULEVARD,

AKA "THE STRIP,"

LAS VEGAS, NEVADA

Car horns blasted. Engines revved. Lights flashed. Music pumped from convertibles, tour buses, and ginormous Jumbotrons. It was full-on nighttime and we had hit a stream of traffic. This was it— the Las Vegas Strip.

On both sides of the street were these large looming hotels that looked like they'd been designed by children. We were stopping and starting the whole way down the street 'cause of the traffic, like a car in a board game when you keep throwing ones. But for the first time since we'd managed to escape from LA, I was glad. I wanted to take in all the sights, make mental notes of where we should go look for Dad and maybe have a little fun, too.

Beau was goggling it all like his eyes were kaleidoscopes. This big shiny bronze-colored building with *Wynn* scrawled across the top was definitely the hugest hotel, but then this sprawling Italian-style one came into view and that looked huger.

"Keep a look out for Caesars," I said to him, flipping the bird at a cab driver who was giving me the eye from the next lane. "Piss off, pervert."

Along the other side of the Strip there was a ton of construction going on, and presumably they were busy building even bigger and better and more wacky hotels to fill in the gaps between the others. Hundreds of tourists lined the sidewalks. We stopped at the lights and got a good look at them all, swarming like bees in a golden hive. Hawkers peddled overpriced bottled water from overflowing coolers. Guys and girls strolled hand in hand, some catching buses, others posing for photographs, laughing, pausing to admire and point things out. Everything was busy, everything was loud, everything was big, everything shone like cheap jewelry.

Beau brought his head back inside the car. "Pais, I just had a thought. We're not gonna be allowed in any of these places. They're casinos, and we're totally underage."

"It's cool. I got a fake ID."

"Oh. Great."

The computer equipment at ICA was pretty tech-tarded, but had the basic stuff to cope with this small task. "It was surprisingly simple. Me and these two other girls did it in Photoshop. Color printer, a couple of butterfly pouches, and a laminator. It got me banned from the computer lab, but it was totally worth it."

"It can't look very good. They'll know it's a fake from a mile away. Best case, they turn you away at the door; worst case, they call the cops."

"I made you one, too."

"You did?" he said, almost touched but still all paranoid android. I nodded.

The Paris Las Vegas hotel loomed over us, looking like some insanely ornate office building with its own Eiffel Tower and big blue hot-air balloon statue out front. That just blew Beau away. Next to the Paris was a giant Planet Hollywood hotel, and then we saw the MGM Grand with this gigantic gold lion out front.

"They got real lions in there, too," I told him. "I saw this documentary about Las Vegas on the plane. They got cubs sometimes."

He looked through the rear window. "If we can get a room at the Paris, that'd be way sweet."

"Not if you're gonna go all quoting Sartre and spouting how pathetically pleasing the place is the whole time. I don't think I can handle that, bro."

"Not pathetically pleasing, *aesthetically* pleasing."

I looked at him. "I know, Beau." I loved it when he corrected me. It made him feel all intelligent and high and mighty, and then all embarrassed when he realized I didn't need correcting.

"I wonder if they speak French in there," he said, then answered his own question. "Maybe not. They might have some French people working there, though. This is Vegas, after all. Anything's possible."

Another hotel was shaped exactly like the New York skyline, with an Empire State Building, Chrysler Building, Statue of Liberty, Brooklyn Bridge, and there was even a roller coaster looping around the outside of it. I could hear the screams of the passengers as it twisted and zoomed across the front. We had to stop again for some tourists to cross, but we could watch these fountains in front of the Bellagio Hotel dancing to "Hey, Big Spender," and on the trumpet parts the water shot up into the air.

"Oh my God, this place is awesome!" said Beau. I didn't think Vegas was going to be Beau's cappuccino, guessing he'd think it was sleazy and seedy, but for some reason he was really soaking it up. I leaned across him to get a better look out his window.

The car rolled on until the Strip became quieter, darker. The hotels became motels and the strolling tourists turned into bums sleeping on the sidewalks. I scoped a little pink motel right at the far end, illuminated by a tiny neon sign and a large green shamrock. *The Lucky Inn.*

We pulled into the parking lot. After everything we'd seen on the way, it was pretty disappointing. Beau just stared at me. He obviously had his heart set on a suite somewhere with valet parking and gold taps, but we just couldn't afford it. The buzzing neon sign and the dumpster with the cluster of derelicts rifling through it welcomed us to reality. I turned off the engine and went to get the bags from the back.

"You can't be serious," Beau said, shutting his door.

"The big hotels'll ask too many questions," I said. "We'll stay here so we can be more incognito." I handed him the swag bag and his backpack. "It's just until we find Dad. Then we can give him the antiques and he can pawn 'em and we'll be able to afford something better." I waited until Beau had turned his back before I reached through my window and stuck the keys back in the ignition.

There was no one in the tiny brown reception room when we walked in. It was all cheesy wood paneling, water stains on the ceilings, and chintzy pink drapes. A plastic Elvis figurine was wiggling his hips on the counter beside a miniature flashing sign saying *Welcome to Las Vegas*. Beau copped a glance through the window at the Luxor, then looked back at me and rolled his eyes.

A blonde woman appeared from a back room and came to the desk, glitterbag flashy and chewing gum like her mouth was mechanical.

"Hey there."

"Hey, do you have a room?"

"Got twelve of 'em. Twelve rooms, twelve vacancies. Queen or king?"

"Uh, no, a double, please," I said, offended, sifting through my wad of bills courtesy of the Skank.

She just looked at me. "You know, you're lucky to get a room. There's a big rock concert over at the Mandalay this weekend, and Britney's in town tomorrow."

"How come you've got twelve empty rooms, then?" I asked.

"Won't be empty tomorrow," she said.

"Whatever, how much for the week?"

"Five ninety."

"Five ninety?!" I cried.

"Like I said, Britney's in town. We're the cheapest on the Strip."

"I'll say," I muttered, peeling the bills from the roll. I slammed them down on the counter. She was lucky I was too tired to argue.

The woman teetered over to the back wall for our key and placed it on the counter. "You got no blow-dryer, and don't flush the toilet with the shower on 'cause it gets, like, extra hot. Okay, you're all set."

"Thanks bunches," I said, smiling my fakest.

Our room was basic to say the least. Two queen beds, draped in what looked like leftover gingham sacking. It stank of dog blankets, and the pleather headboards were spewing yellow foam at the corners. We each had a nightstand, and there was a small desk and chair with the Yellow Pages and a plain legal pad for notes. A sliding wooden partition opened to reveal a very small avocado-colored bathroom with a cracked shower door. There was a big warning sticker on the side of the tub: PROLONGED EXPOSURE TO WATER MAY CAUSE OSTEOPOROSIS, HEART DISEASE, AND BIRTH DEFECTS. Fu-larious.

"Well, there's a bed, so I'm happy," I said, throwing my backpack down on the floor and flopping onto the one closest to the bathroom. It looked kinda gray and hard, but it was so soft it felt like I was lying inside a loaf of fresh bread. Bedgasmic.

Beau stood by the window. "How much money have we got left?"

"I don't know. Take a look."

I threw over my jacket and he rummaged around in the pocket.

"There's, like . . . there's not even five hundred left!"

"Yeah, well. You heard what she said. Can I just get a little shut-eye, please?" I hadn't slept in, like, two days.

"Do we get breakfast at least?"

"I had to pay by the bath towel, Beau; what do you think?"

He dropped my jacket on the chair and went to the window. "Oh my God, Paisley . . ."

"What?"

"The car is gone."

"Huh?" I levered myself up. Beau had his hands on the glass and his mouth wide open.

"Our car, the F-Fiero, the goddamn car, it's gone! Oh my God. We gotta call the cops—"

"They work fast around here, I'll give them that," I said, leaning back down.

"Who?"

"Those bums we saw hanging around the dumpster. Musta taken it."

"You knew they were gonna take it?"

"We had to lose it, Beau. It's hot. Cops are gonna be after us. Skank may even come after us. We don't wanna draw attention to ourselves."

"How the hell are we gonna get anywhere? Now we're stuck here!"

"We'll find Dad by the end of the week. He'll look after us."

"Paisley . . ."

I turned over and tried losing myself. I could hear Beau sighing and padding around the floor. Zippers. Unpacking things. I heard his bed springs. Then a sigh. And pretty soon, a snore. I opened my eyes a little and turned onto my back, reaching down beside me to the shoe box. I pulled out a letter.

So how's my little girl? I guess you're not so little anymore. I always think that when I see you again, I'll be able to scoop you up in my arms like I used to when I came home from work. You'd come running downstairs to see me and jump from the bottom step. I remember the last time we saw each other; I tucked you in for the night. You reached up and hugged me so tight. If I'd known that was going to be the last time, I would've made that hug last longer. I love you, Paisley.

Dad xx

BEAU

TEN

The next morning we hit the Strip. It was hot in Vegas. "Day-am hot!" Paisley kept saying. Much hotter than LA. I was half-starved from the day before and wanted to eat something before my stomach started munching on my other organs, but she insisted we go straight to Caesars Palace to look for Dad. We split the difference. We went to Caesars Palace to eat.

The hotel itself took some navigating around. The place was enormous. It was obscene opulence times twenty, with extensions in the rear and fountains in the front. It was perfectly trimmed hedges and stretch limousines. It was marble pillars and gilt statues and people who smile at the right wallet.

I'd only ever heard about Caesars when there was a big concert on HBO or something, but to actually see it was unbelievable. The Forum Shops' entrance to Caesars was like a mall in itself, and we weaved our way through its maze of designer boutiques. The place was echoey and smelled of cinnamon and caves. There were a few tourists around, looking through windows and throwing coins into the huge ornate fountains that spanned the base of the escalators. We found this little café called the Stage Deli. I got the works: coffee, orange juice, supersize buttermilk pancakes with whipped butter, maple syrup, sausage links, bacon, eggs, and toast. And I ate every single crumb of it, aside from a triangle of toast that I insisted Paisley eat. She just ordered a fruit platter. Then we got into an argument over the tip. Paisley doesn't tip. She doesn't believe in it.

We walked through the main casino, where Paisley saw the sign for the concierge's desk. It was at the very front of the hotel in the massive pillared reception area that looked more like the check-in for an airport. A snaking line of tourists with large suitcases was already waiting and it was only, like, nine thirty in the morning. Out front, white limousines and cabs were pulling up one after the other, and men in burgundy uniforms were falling over themselves to load luggage onto gold carts.

The concierge wasn't at his desk. I rang the bell.

He appeared. A tall, thin, mustached guy with strangely tiny hands.

"Good morning, welcome to Caesars Palace, my name is Leon, how can I help you this morning?"

He'd taken so long introducing himself, I'd almost forgotten what we were doing there. Then I remembered.

"We were wondering if you could help us. We're looking for somebody."

"Are you lost?"

"No, we're just looking for somebody. An employee. We were told he might be working here."

"I'm sorry, but I'm not at liberty to give out information about employees. That's confidential."

Paisley broke in. "We just wanna know if he works here or not."

"No, that's out of the question, I'm afraid. If it's a matter of employment references, you would need to speak to our—"

"Look, jerk-off—" Paisley started, leaning into the desk.

I butted in. "His name's Buddy Argent. We're . . . friends of his. We just need to know if he's here or not."

"I'm sorry, son, but I am not at liberty to discuss employee information with members of the public."

"Don't 'son' him, you patronizing bastard!" Paisley shouted, marching off straight into the casino. She turned as she walked. "Fuck you, you know what? Fuck you!"

I turned to the concierge, my cheeks aflame. "I'm sorry. It's just really important that we find him. Thanks anyway."

He threw me an alarmed look and nodded, gesturing to the old ladies behind me to come forward. You had to know how to handle my sister, and if you didn't, you got your ass handed to you. I felt a little sorry for him. He thought he had power before he met Paisley.

I saw her amid a sea of tourists and flashing lights and the whir and woo of a zillion machines. Old women in baseball caps jamming slots with quarters and fishing out tickets. Guys with sunburns in Hawaiian shirts pummeling buttons and swigging beer. The whole place smelled strongly of sweat and decade-old cigar smoke. A blonde waitress sauntered over, draped in a toga.

"Sir, can I get you anything?" she asked me, hand on hip.

I shook my head, amazed she didn't even bother to card me. I attempted a smile, but I felt myself blushing and my head automatically dipped. She was too cute. I needed to get to Paisley.

I continued through the casino and back out into the mall, where Paisley had been heading. More tourists were milling around, and I could just see Paisley's head right at the end of one of the streets that made up one arm of the huge shopping complex in that part of Caesars. She was sitting cross-legged beside one of the marble fountains, staring up at the ceiling, which was painted to look like bright blue sky and clouds. This big godlike statue was in the middle of the monument, sitting on a throne and smiling with hollow eyes. Moldy green coins lay at his feet.

I could smell the stale water and chlorine as I got closer.

I sat down next to her on the balustrade. "Pais?"

"I know I overreacted. I don't wanna talk about it."

"Let's keep asking around then, 'kay?"

"Yeah."

I wanted her to look at me. She did. She jumped down and I followed her.

That day we walked the length and breadth of the entire hotel. There were six towers to the complex: Augustus Tower (where there was a spa and a couple of wedding chapels and some very snooty-looking restaurant where this waiter gave both of us the evil eye), Centurion Tower, Roman Tower, Palace Tower, Octavius Tower, and Forum Tower, where we had eaten breakfast. Paradise Eddie hadn't mentioned any one tower in particular, so we had to try all of them. Forum Tower seemed to be the hive of all activity, so we asked at all the bars and restaurants in there. No sign of Dad, nor anyone who knew him. Planet Hollywood let us sample chicken strips in their new barbecue sauce, so we stayed there and had lunch.

And then we kinda settled into the spirit of things. People were nice to us, so it was okay. Paisley was okay. Frustrated, but okay. And I was doing my best to help her forget about Dad for a while and just have fun. I didn't say as much, but I was having fun, too. We sat with some random kids, watching the fish in the huge aquarium while their parents were in a store. A boy and girl, about seven or eight. We gave all the fish names and little personalities, and me and Paisley made up a story about them going about their daily business under the water. I could have talked to those little guys all day.

But instead we covered as much of the Strip as we could, evading certain death on crosswalks and bypassing the many street sellers we came into contact with: guys touting water or show tickets; women wearing too much mascara offering discount vouchers for the monorail or the Fashion Show Mall; a giant M&M with legs handing out leaflets and posing for photos.

The following day, we headed to New York New York, where we walked through this casino that was supposed to be like an indoor Central Park but with slot machines. It even had street signs and fake stone pathways, and I kinda felt at home. Dad used to take us to Central Park sometimes to see the toy boats on the lake or the polar bears at the zoo. The hotel had a mock-up indoor Coney Island, too, upstairs from the casino, with this arcade and all these games. We found a dance machine and ate Twizzlers while stomping out a rhythm together, side by side. The song was called "Everlong," but I'd never heard it before. Paisley said she liked it. I kinda did, too. We even had a little audience watching us.

And I wonder,
When I sing along with you,
If everything could ever feel this real forever,
If anything could ever be this good again.

We did that same song three times. Our audience stayed for all three times. We were perfectly in sync. It was a good song. It sounded like us. Those lyrics were going around my head all day long.

If everything could ever feel this real forever,
If anything could ever be this good again.

Our audience even clapped when we finished.

We played at the arcade for about two hours, throwing balls into baskets, shooting laser tag, speed-racing in a Daytona simulator. I got thirty tickets for Skee-Ball and won some cotton candy and a monkey pencil topper. Paisley was pretty good at the three-point throw and won, like, fifty tickets, and she picked for her prizes two packs of heart-shaped stickers, a bag of Jelly Bellys, and a light-up popsicle ring that glowed through her cheeks when she sucked it. She managed to get seven of those stickers on my back and neck before I figured it out and had her peel them off me.

After a slice of pizza and a blue Gatorade from a vending machine in the lobby—the only slot we could actually play—Paisley rode the roller coaster that goes around and through the hotel (I wimped out and waited for her in the gift shop), and then she suggested we go to the other end of the Strip for the views.

By the time we reached the Stratosphere, this endless knitting needle pointing right up into the warm Las Vegas sky, I had just come around to the idea of going up to the observation deck. But I was adamant I wasn't going on the rides. I sat watching the casino from afar, from the under-21 "safety area," while Paisley got the tickets.

"Here you go," she said upon her return, handing me my ticket.

I looked at it. "Pais, my ticket says Tower and Big Shot. What does yours say?"

She showed me.

"Huh? Yours says Tower and three rides. Big Shot's a ride."

"Yeah, I asked if you could just go up, but they have this law and if you're going up to the tower you have to go on at least one ride. Otherwise you can't go up."

"I can't."

"Yeah, you can," she said, taking my arm and guiding me up the stairs to the security check. "I'll be there. We'll hold hands if you want. Big Shot's just this big donut going up and down on a stick, and you're strapped in."

"Yeah, but it's right at the top. It's, like, the tallest thing in the world!"

We joined the end of the security line.

"I did say to you I didn't want to go on any rides, Paisley . . . ," I kept saying.

"I know, but you have to. Come on. You might even, just maybe, enjoy it. Have a little fungasm maybe. Don't be afraid of it, Beau."

I fretted the whole time on line. She kept trying to reassure me, patting my hand and stuff, but I was really starting to sweat, especially when we were frisked and asked to take off our belts by security.

In the elevator, panic set in. "Paisley, I can't. I just can't. What if . . ." I leaned in to her. "What if I need to pee?"

"*Do* you need to pee?" she asked, prompting looks from others in the elevator.

"No, but it happens to people when they're scared. They pee."

I only stopped whining when we got out and saw the view. It was absolutely incredible. We were standing behind the glass and looking down on tiny little Vegas, laid out beneath us like a child's model built from matchboxes covered with sequins.

"It's so beautiful," I gasped, sticking a quarter in the observation telescope.

"Yeah," she said. "Can you see our motel?"

I swept the telescope around as wide as it would go. "No, I can see

Paris. We still haven't seen Paris. We gotta do that. Maybe tonight?"

"Yeah, yeah," she said. "I'm gonna get a slushie and then I'm gonna go on my rides. You want?"

"No thanks." I didn't take my eyes off the telescope.

"Aren't you gonna come watch me risk my life?"

"Yeah, I'll be there in a minute."

I watched Paisley on her rides from behind the glass on the other side of the observation deck. If I thought my sister was crazy before, I *knew* she was crazy now. There she was, spinning around on this big umbrella contraption, nearly a thousand feet in the air, dangling off the edge of a building. Who in their right mind puts three thrill rides a thousand feet up in the sky? And she wasn't even holding on! She was laughing. Waving! If it had been me, my knuckles would have burst straight through my skin from the sheer pressure of holding on so tight.

I met up with her when she came off, handing over her liquefying slushie. "*You're* Insanity, let alone the ride," I told her. "How could you do that?"

"Just gotta be done, Beau," she said, taking a big old slurp of her slushie. "When in Vegas . . ."

Next she did X-Scream, which was this little eight-seater roller coaster, stuck out on a limb from the building, that kept going up and down on its little track as though it was about to fall off the edge. I didn't open my eyes to watch her for most of it. I thought she was gonna come flying out and fall to her death at any second. But again she laughed and waved, and again I felt like the cowardly turd waiting for it all to stop.

I handed her slushie to her again when we met up. "Weren't you scared?"

"Nah," she said, panting, taking multiple sips, then getting instant brain freeze. She pinched her nose. "Piece of cake," she gasped, and stuck out her tongue. "Blue yet?"

I shook my head.

"Come on," she said, linking my arm and tossing her cup into a garbage can. "Now we're both going on Big Shot."

"Paisley . . ."

"I'm not scared, Beau. So you shouldn't be, either."

"Yeah, but I'm not you. I'm really not."

Paisley didn't hear any of my pleading, my fretting, my declarations of illness.

"Sorry, I'm a little deaf at the moment, Beau. Must be all the FUN I'm having!" she shouted in my ear.

We took the elevator up to the highest level of the tower and joined the line for Big Shot. A dude at the top was taking tickets. I stood in front of my sister. I put my hand back, and she grabbed it. I thought of the Wonder Twins, the real Wonder Twins. The superheroes, touching hands to activate their powers. I wondered if it would work for us, if just a touch of my hand could give me Paisley's courage. Then I realized how stupid that was.

"It's all right," she whispered in my ear. "You're gonna be fine."

"Okay," I kept whispering to myself. My palm was as slippery as a jellyfish.

We took our seats and buckled ourselves in.

"Do these bars come down? Why hasn't he come around to put the bars down? What if he's forgotten about this side of the donut, Paisley?"

"He's coming, look." And the guy came around to our side and checked our belts and pulled down the large red bars to hold us in place.

"Y'all ready for this? Sit tight," he said to me.

"Hell yeah!" said Paisley. "You wanna hold my hand, Beau?"

I shook my head, gripping the bars at my shoulders, tugging on them a little to check they were secure. I was belted, strapped down, locked. I couldn't fall out.

I heard the song from the arcade in my head again.

If anything could ever be this good again.
The only thing I'll ever ask of you,
Gotta promise not to stop when I say when.

We sat there, poised. I shut my eyes and breathed in. Once, twice, three times, waiting for it to start, waiting for the jolt, the surge, the screams.

"Paisley . . . ," I said.

"Yeah?"

"Are you scared yet?"

"No. So you shouldn't be, either," she said again. "This is gonna be great."

I opened my eyes for just a second, met her gaze, and nodded. And on my next intake of breath, the donut was released and shot *up and up and up and up* into the sky, way faster than anything ever, and right up to the top of the spire on the tallest tower in the whole wide world.

"WHOOOO-HOOO!" Paisley yelled. "Look, Beau, look at Vegas. Look, you can see everything! Look at the desert!"

"I can't open my eyes!" I screamed. "Oh my gaaaaahhhhhhhhhd!"

And down we went and then *whoosh* up we went again, lingering for a second at the top, where I briefly opened one eye, and then *schoom* down again, guts to the throat, eyes to the skies, and then *whoooooosh* up again, four times over. On the fourth time, I opened both eyes at the top and it was like the camera shutter came down. I only looked for a moment, an instant, but the view was enough to last my lifetime. Everything was so much smaller and more beautiful. I couldn't see the dirt or the depression or the gambling addicts. I couldn't see the pimps or the hos or the homeless. I couldn't even feel the heat. I just saw Vegas. And it was beautiful.

We gently came down and stopped, exactly where we had started.

I had my eyes shut again.

"You did it, Beau," my sister said. "You took your first ever thrill ride. Look at you, Jackass 3D!"

I opened my eyes. "Is it gonna move again?"

"Nope, we're done."

Then the dude reappeared and let us out, and I clambered off and promptly stumbled over to the railing and gripped on like the drama queen I am.

Paisley came over to me and put a hand on my back.

"I was really scared, Pais," I told her.

"I told you, you don't need to be. I'm strong enough for both of us." Then she asked, "Should we go check the Paris now? You can try out your French on some of the mademoiselles."

Still clinging to the safety rail, I shook my head. Sweat droplets flew from my face and the ends of my hair. "I need to cool off."

We knew from our extensive investigations at Caesars that it had, like, eight pools, so we headed back there and followed the signs. It did cross my mind that we'd be kicked out for not being guests or not having the right attire to be poolside, but there was no guy at the desk when we walked through to the pool area, so Paisley snagged us a couple of fluffy white towels.

And we chilled on chaise longues by the pool for the rest of the afternoon, eating jelly beans. Paisley got us a couple of ice-cold strawberry-and-banana smoothies from the poolside shake shack. I thought about when we were kids at Virginia's. We'd sometimes spend whole afternoons lying before the fireplace in the den with our sketch pads, a bag of jelly beans, and a jumbo pack of magic markers, drawing and decorating each room in our grandmother's house, down to the bricks—as though it really were our home. Being there by the pool at Caesars with Paisley was like being a kid again. And it felt great.

"Try lemon and cotton candy," she said, cross-legged on her chair, squinting in the sunlight. She had stripped down to her underwear. I was still in my T-shirt and jeans. I'd taken off my sneakers, though, and I was lying down. I had loosened up a little.

I pushed my shades back up my nose and felt two beans land on my chest. "Mm, yeah. Pink lemonade. That's good."

"I've got marmalade. Two tangerine, one lemon, and a lime." She tossed me two blueberries and a buttered popcorn. "Blueberry muffin. Flavorgasm, trust me."

I chewed the life out of them. "Yeah, that's the best." All possible combos were tested until only a couple of root beers and a strawberry daiquiri rattled in the bag and both our stomachs groaned from greed.

I looked over at her, and she smiled. Her nose wrinkled up, just like it did when she was little. She held up a blue bean to show me.

"Think any of these are magic beans?" she asked.

"Probably not. God, I'm so sleepy." The warm breeze on my face was bringing me to whole new levels of happiness. I could hear subdued chattering from the other sunbathers and swimmers around me, but nothing too intrusive. Little kids giggling and splashing in another pool a few yards away behind a pink-flowering hedge. More toga-draped waitresses sauntering around with trays of empty glasses. One came and took my empty smoothie cup. I pretended I was asleep behind my shades.

Then Paisley went and ruined it.

"We're kinda out of money."

"What?" I croaked, leaning up.

"Almost out." She sifted several receipts out of her wallet and went through them. Breakfast $35.75. Two Stratosphere tickets at $51.90. Chicken wings, steak fries, and two iced lemonades $39.04. Candy $46.71. Feminine care and shaving gel $18.78. Smoothies $18.00. Deuce tickets $28. More candy $48.63.

We worked out that we'd spent around $180 at the arcade and on snacks. Even so, I wasn't prepared for the total she gave me.

"We got . . . $32.19."

"Shit. We kinda went a little crazy, didn't we?"

Paisley started laughing. "Yep. So back to my original point. We're kinda out of money."

I leaned back. I thought I would be more worried than I was. I was so lethargic, I could have fallen asleep midsentence. "It's not funny. We'll have to get jobs."

"Yeah. That'll be easy. Two sixteen-year-olds with no skills, no references, and no home. Vegas'll be begging to hire us."

"We haven't found Dad yet, and we've got no money. What else can we do?"

"Are you getting in the pool?"

That was the last thing I heard her say. I must have drifted off. When I woke up, she was gone.

PAISLEY

ELEVEN

APOLLO POOL,
CAESARS PALACE, THE STRIP,
LAS VEGAS, NEVADA

Beau had eaten so many jelly beans he'd crashed on his lounge chair by the pool. Candy always had that effect on him, even when he was a kid. It didn't affect me at all, but it always put Beau into a sugar coma. I watched him snooze for a little while, his forehead creases disappearing, his dark brown hair falling across his face, his long eyelashes fluttering on his cheeks. The best part about Beau is that even though he is actually really beautiful for a boy, he has absolutely no fucking idea.

I went into the ladies' changing rooms, intent on just cleaning myself up, making myself look less underage, before I headed into the casino in search of bulging back pockets or short-sighted grannies with buckets full of quarters. I took off my faded Queen T-shirt, replacing it with a lonely white fitted blouse I found hanging on a gold hook by the sinks. There were other clothes around I could have chosen: a gold camisole, a pukey pink sarong, a psychedelic red and yellow shirt with big black buttons.

No. Go simple, Pais, I said to myself.

I bagged my boots and looked for another pair of shoes: There were silk mules, f-expensive-looking strappy sandals, red kitten heels. I went for stilettos, black with a silver heel. They were ever-so-slightly too big, so I stuffed the toes with toilet paper until they fit. Women staying at Caesars were either too stupid or too trusting with their stuff, and I didn't care which. Bags were lying around for the taking, but on inspection I found they were just pool bags, not purses, so no money. There were makeup bags lying around, too. I put on some blazing red lipstick and fired up my eyelashes a little. I've never really seen the point of perfume, but one of the bags had a little bottle, so I sprayed some of that on as well. It smelled like the Skank—lust and dead flowers. The shirt was a little tight and the heels a little high, but I ain't as fussy as Goldilocks. I checked my look in the mirror, pushed what little boobs I had up in my bra, and undid two buttons. I looked good. I shook out my hair. I looked older.

I strutted back through those wide marbled passageways like I was the new owner of the place. If I looked or acted sixteen years old in any way, shape, or form, they'd kick my ass outta there for sure. To my way of thinking, the dudes scoping for under twenty-ones would be so knocked out by my T&A they wouldn't think of carding me. *Think mature, think mature,* I kept saying to myself. *Be cool.* Back across the lobby, the wind from outside blowing my hair as the doors opened and closed, tourists goggling my fabulous bare legs–high heels combo: I had sunshine in a bag, and I knew it.

Without overworking the swagger, I ventured onto the casino floor. I bypassed the blackjack, craps, roulette, and mini baccarat tables, glided past the keno area, and hung around the slot machines waiting for someone on Wheel of Fortune, Megabucks, Blazing Sevens, or Jeopardy! to leave their purse or wallet vulnerable. I was trying to walk as steadily as I could. My feet were killing me and my bag was tugging on my shoulder from the weight of my boots. I checked coin trays, sizing up some redneck tourists who'd had a few too many, waiting for an opportunity to fleece them. A group of guys watched me from one of the tables. One of them, in a leather jacket, smiled. I was gonna be all, "Yeah, as if. Keep dreaming there, Leather Boy," but I didn't. I smiled back. *Might get a free drink out of it,* I thought. What was the harm?

A fat guy was leaning on the side of an Elvis machine as his girlfriend played. He was talking to a young couple. They were droning on about moving in together, and the fat guy was all like, "Been there, done that, divorced the bitch," and he sounded like the kind of guy you meet on vacation and can't shake off. He'd had hair implants, too, by the look of it. Bad ones. Total walking midlife crisis. I made a bet with myself that he had a Ferrari. I pretended to play a neighboring slot machine and listened in for a good ten minutes. The Midlife had no awareness of me, even though I did look badass delectable. He was too busy talking about himself. He didn't even notice that his wallet was teetering suicidally out of his ass pocket. Running out wasn't going to be easy in my heels, but I could do it. I knew I could do it without him seeing.

But his girlfriend ran out of quarters, so he had to dip into the wallet to get some bucks for her to change up, then tucked it back down deep into his pocket. Chance wasted.

I looked over at the guys at the table. They had moved. Another ship sailed.

I got bored real quick of fishing for loose change after that. I headed for the bar that overlooked the casino. I slipped as gracefully as I could onto a bar stool and ordered the most mature drink on the menu, an iced tea.

"Can I see some ID please, ma'am?" said the bartender.

"For an iced tea?"

"I'm sorry, ma'am, house rules."

It had to happen. I huffed and puffed around in my bag and found my wallet. I pulled out my Photoshopped ID and handed it to him. He looked at me. He looked suspiciously at it. He handed it back.

"Thank you."

Then he went off to make my iced tea. I scoped the bar. It was nearly six thirty and there were a few guys hanging around, sitting at tables. Mr. Suspicious returned with my tea and took my money and went to the register to get my change. It was loaded with cash. Good thing I'd left the Eclipse back in the motel room, or I might have just cut out the middleman, or at least the barman, right then and there.

The iced tea was pretty terrible.

By a quarter to eight, the bar was a little busier and more guys had gathered to watch some football game on a screen in the corner. I fixed my eye on some gray suit sitting at a table by himself. He looked like he'd been stood up. Black hair, shiny brown shoes, a gold watch he kept checking. Pretty soon I was getting longer looks in my direction. I could feel his eyes on my legs. I saw his wallet on the table. We exchanged a smile.

Then this bleached-blonde pigeon bagged my guy and they left. So it was back to square one. I was on my second iced tea. No other guys were alone. *Maybe I'm in the wrong bar,* I thought. Maybe there was a singles bar somewhere filled with desperation and big bucks. Eight o'clock came and I thought about going back to the motel. Music pumped. Looks were exchanged. Iced tea was sipped. I could feel my disappointment Hulking over into anger that I'd failed to reel in any big fish.

All I could do was sit, sit, sit, sit. And I did not like it, not one little bit.

"Can I get you a drink?" a voice offered. A man leaned against the bar.

I looked him up and down, just to appear distant. It was the guy who'd smiled at me earlier. He was okay-looking. Late twenties, I guessed, though I could have been wrong. If *I* looked twenty-one, he could have been way older.

"I'm solid, thanks," I said, caressing my iced tea.

"Come on, we can do better than that. Please. You look so lonely sitting there by yourself. It's my duty as a gentleman." He smiled.

"Okay. I'll have a Coke. Thanks."

He seemed surprised. "Sure thing." He scrolled through a wad of one dollar bills he got out of his brown leather jacket and placed them on the counter. I slipped down from my stool and teetered toward a table in a dark recess of the bar. *Yes,* I thought. *Just reel him in. Where's he putting the goods?*

Inside jacket pocket. *Damn.* He arrived with the drinks and settled them down on the table. He was wearing cowboy boots, gold-tipped.

"I hate to ask, but some idiot stood you up tonight, right?" he said.

"Uh, yeah. You could say that. I was just waiting for my knight in shining armor."

"And along came me," he said. He had oily skin and curly blond bangs that he flicked out of his eyes. He was good-looking in a young country-western-singer kinda way. Eyes were watching me from another table. I looked around. The other guys from his party were sitting around a plasma screen in the corner, and one by one they all looked away.

"They your friends?" I said, motioning to the TV threesome.

"Yeah." He leaned in. "Want me to introduce you?"

"Not really." I smiled. I felt his hand heavy on my knee.

"Is that okay?" he asked.

I looked down at his hand. "Yeah."

"You're really beautiful, you know."

"I'm not supposed to be here," I told him. "I'm not twenty-one yet."

He shrugged. "Hey, I'm easy to please." His hand moved up my thigh a little. I didn't like it.

"Like, nowhere near twenty-one yet," I said.

He ran his tongue slowly over his lip. "I had a feeling."

I got a gross feeling in the pit of my stomach.

"Ain't seen you around here much. First time in Vegas?"

I nodded, picking up my Coke. "You?"

"Nah, second home."

"Really?"

"Pretty much. Come here with a bunch of my boys once or twice a month. Play the tables, have some fun, then roll on home to Austin."

"Where's that?"

He finally moved his hand and glugged down half of his beer, gasping at the sheer heaven of it. "Texas. You?"

"Jersey."

He nodded. I looked at my drink. I sipped. There was vodka in it.

"There's vodka in this. I just said Coke."

"So you got more than you asked for. Come on, one drink's not gonna hurt."

I put my mouth on the edge of the glass and tipped it. I stirred it a little with the special golden Caesars Palace swizzle stick, took out a couple of the ice cubes, and pretended to sip it again. I hate alcohol. I hate what it does to people.

"What's your name?"

"Zooey," I lied. "With two *O*s." I'd read it in a book at school and thought it sounded cool.

"Zooey. That's a beautiful name. You want another one?"

"Another name?"

He laughed. "No, another drink."

"No, I'm good." I laughed, my eyebrows raised at the mere suggestion less than ten seconds into an already full glass.

"My name's Steve. So, Zooey, you here on vacation, or . . . ?"

"Yeah. Just having some fun, same as you."

He leaned in a little closer. He had long nose hairs. I could see the color of his wallet in his inside pocket. I just wanted to grab it and run outta there, but I had the damn killer heels on, so it wasn't an option.

"Look, if you want, we could hook up. I could show you around sometime."

"That'd be good," I said. It was my turn to lean in toward him. "You look like a man who knows where he's going."

He sank the rest of his beer, never once taking his eyes off me. He wasn't drunk enough, and I couldn't think how to get the wallet quickly and take my heels off *and* grab my bag all in one swift motion. It just wasn't going to happen. But I needed that money. Money = more Vegas = Dad.

He put the glass down and his eyes seemed to light up. "You know, it's funny," he said with a laugh. "I know we only just met, but don't you think we have a connection? Like we were destined to meet or something?"

"Kinda," I said. "So, you staying here at Caesars?"

"Yeah. You?"

"Yeah."

"I'll walk you back to your room," he said.

"No. I don't wanna go back just yet. I'd rather stay here. With you."

"Why don't we go up to my room? It's a suite. It's got a Jacuzzi." He exhaled, like he was a little nervous, and his breath hit my face. He smelled of leather car seats when your dog's been sick in the back.

He took my hand and stood up. His hand was big and covered mine. Had a strong grip, too. He handed my vodka and Coke to me. "You can take it with you. They won't mind; they know me here." We walked to the steps and he stopped. "I'm gonna get another coupla beers. Wait here."

I did as I was told. It was going too far, but I couldn't go anywhere else. Steve didn't strike me as the kind of guy who'd just put up with a girl running out on him. In any case, I couldn't run in those damn killer heels. I put the Coke on the rail at the top of the steps and plunged my hand inside my bag. I rooted around.

Steve looked over and smiled. I smiled back. He'd left me just long enough. I picked up my drink again.

"Sorry about that," he said, eventually returning with two bottles in one hand. "Gotta keep hydrated, know what I mean?" He took my hand and led me down the red carpeted steps toward the elevators, just as Caesar himself and a harem of scantily clad maidens walked by.

"Whoa, what's all this?" I asked Steve. He took my hand, squeezed it. I looked up at him but didn't shake it away. I smiled.

"He does this a few times a day," he said. "It's a different guy every time. Tourists love it."

Steve started to get a little huffy as tourist after tourist filed past us to get a closer snapshot of the Roman emperor. We then had a clear runway to the elevators, and there was one already open so we broke into a run—or in my case, a stumble. Damn. Killer. Heels!

He got me inside. Two couples were already in there with their suitcases, but we managed to squeeze in right at the edge and were mirrored on all sides. He pressed me back against the wall and it started to rise. The elevator, I mean. Though I did feel him against my stomach, at first nothing much, but as the elevator jerked and stopped at points where there was no one to be let in, he got harder. He pressed against me more.

He whispered in my ear that I was sexy.

The elevator shuddered and some of his beer spilled on the floor. He cussed. A gray businessman threw him a dirty look.

"Problem, pal?" he spat back.

The gray businessman's nook had suddenly stopped working and he focused on watching the floors flash by above.

"You're looking hot," I whispered to Steve and held my Coke glass to his cheek. "Want some?"

He moved his face around and I tilted the glass so he could sip. And he glugged half that sucker down. Which seemed to make him feel better. Made me feel better, too.

We got out of the elevator. Long pink-carpeted corridors stretched off into the distance like a spider's legs, and Steve led me down one, right to the end. Room 8037.

He took out his key card from the back pocket of his jeans and slipped it in the slot above the door handle. Then he allowed me to go inside first. As I walked past him, I got that pukey smell of his breath again. It made my stomach lurch.

If it was a suite, then Steve had been robbed. It was a shithole, and no bigger than our room at the motel. In fact it was smaller. Low roller, I realized. My bullshit shield had failed me.

Fuck.

He locked the door behind us and ushered me through to one of the beds. I looked at him.

"My friend Tommy's in the other one. This one's mine."

"Oh. You mind if I go freshen up?"

He shook his head. "I don't want you to go anywhere." He stepped closer to me and grinned so his bottom jaw stuck out and his eyes were wide. "I want you to stay here with me."

"I need to use the bathroom, silly," I laughed, pushing him away. "You can wait a minute, I'm sure." The puke breath was on me again, and now I could smell his BO, too.

He placed both hands on my waist, holding me close and diving in for the kiss. He kissed hard and cold. It was like being pushed into a wall.

I pulled back. "I want to use the bathroom," I kept saying, trying to push against his chest, slam my fists against him, but he just kept coming for me, and suddenly I was against the closet and he was unbuckling his belt and with one hand he held my neck, forcing my head back.

"You fucking stay there! You ain't going anywhere until you do what you came here to do."

"NO. Get off. Get off me, you sick fuck!" I shouted as loud as I could, even though my chest was being flattened.

This wasn't supposed to be happening. It shouldn't have gone this far.

Then I did something I haven't done since I was a child. I screamed. It was the scream I screamed in the woods when I was six, on the second day of looking for Dad.

It was the scream of lost causes.

BEAU

TWELVE

ROOM 2, LUCKY INN MOTEL,

THE STRIP,

LAS VEGAS, NEVADA

All the way back to our motel I racked my brain, trying to think if she'd told me to meet her anywhere. Nope, nothing. We were at the pool. Then I woke up and it was almost dark and she was gone. I'd been asleep for, like, two hours. Damn the jelly beans!

The clock beside my bed ticked over to nine fifteen. Everything was wrong.

"Where are you?" I said it out loud. I didn't know if I was hoping Paisley would answer back or send me some kind of sign as to where she might be. I had this unsettling feeling in the middle of my chest that something bad had happened. I was probably wrong. I was usually wrong. She would probably come into the room at any second and slump down on the bed. She'd gone up to the Stratosphere again or something, just for the hell of it. Hadn't realized the time. *Stop worrying, Gramps,* she'd say.

But as I watched the numbers on the clock roll over and over, my heart feeling more and more like a steak being pummeled by a meat cleaver, I knew I couldn't just sit there. I had to find her.

I caught the Deuce bus just outside the motel, but it was slow and seemed to stop every five seconds for more tourists to climb aboard and fumble around looking for loose change. I jumped off as soon as I could and ran the rest of the way to Caesars. I ran all through the mall, too, eventually finding the casino and the airport-like reception area and the concierge desk. I felt eyes on me the second I entered the casino. I was like this little alarm bell ringing, wherever I went, alerting the security to the fact that I was way too young to be anywhere near there. Two really thin waitresses asked me if I wanted a drink. They must have known I couldn't drink. All the security cameras must have locked their black eyes on me, my sweat patches, my red neck, my sixteen years of inexperience. Eyes everywhere.

Someone was in front of me talking to the concierge when I got to the desk, so I had a chance to catch my breath. The snooty Smile-Like-You-Mean-It guy who Paisley had been rude to earlier was gone, so I got a genuinely friendly guy instead, name-tagged Jamal.

"Hey, welcome to Caesars Palace, how can I help you?" he said.

"I've lost my sister," I said. "We were by the pool earlier and I fell asleep, and when I woke up she was gone."

"All right, what's your sister's name?"

It was then that I saw her, across the casino. I zoned in on a blonde leaving the bar with this tall dude with curly blond hair. They disappeared for a second behind a crowd of people in togas.

"Don't worry," I told the concierge over my shoulder, "I think I see her." And I set off again. What the hell was she doing?

Some guy dressed up in a white toga like Julius Caesar was passing through the casino, followed by a female entourage to rival that of most rock stars, so I had to wait for them to get out of the way before I could really get going. By the time they'd posed for photos and exited stage left, Paisley and the Curly had gone. One elevator was just closing with an old man in it. Another was broken. I stood outside the other four and watched to see where each one was going. They could be on any floor between seventy-one and eighty. I had to try them all. It would take me forever. I got out of the elevator and shouted along every hallway like a madman.

"PAISLEY! PAISLEY!" I waited a second. Some inquisitive doors opened but then closed. A couple of girls looked out of one door on seventy-five but otherwise nothing.

On eighty, I didn't have to make any commotion. I heard it myself, distant but definite. The worst sound I've ever heard. My sister screaming.

"PAISLEY!" I shouted again, and headed along one of the corridors that branched off the elevators.

I flew. I wouldn't have been surprised to look behind and see a trail of flames. I reached the end door and banged and slammed against it as if my life — or hers — depended on it.

"PAISLEY!" Eventually it buckled and swung open before me.

"Oh Jesus. Oh my God, Pais."

She sat on the far side of one bed. It took a couple of seconds before she looked around.

"Didn't know you had it in you, bro."

I walked toward her. She looked okay. She wasn't crying. I tried to catch my breath. It was then that I noticed the guy on the carpet, pants around his ankles. Unmoving. Mouth open. Dead.

"What happened? What did you do?" I panted.

She was counting money, distracted as she spoke. "How'd you find me?"

I bent over. I couldn't catch my breath. "I saw you . . . the bar. He's dead."

She got up. "No, he's not. I slipped him something. He's sleeping now."

"Heard you . . . screaming."

"Yeah." She gulped. "They took longer to work than I thought. Almost had to work for my money. But I'm okay."

"You sure?" I went over and stood in front of her. "Pais? Look at me, are you all right?"

She was still counting the money. She didn't look up. "I told you, I'm fine." She wasn't fine. She was breathing fast, and her face was bleeding.

"Tell me what he did," I said, crouching down in front of her.

"He didn't get a chance to do anything," she replied.

"What . . . what did you do to him?"

"Crushed up a couple of pills, put 'em in his drink."

I looked at him. Then at her. Then back at him. "You drugged him? You DRUGGED him?!"

"Yeah."

I couldn't believe what I was seeing. She had this white shirt on—wide open, exposing her black bra—and these black stilettos with heels that looked like medical instruments. And her face was bloody. And her hair was a rat's nest. And red lipstick was smudged all over her mouth. Talk about Beauty and the Beast: My sister was both.

"Oh my God. You killed him, Paisley. You're a psycho. You're a complete . . . psycho!"

She got up, the stack of money in one hand and a wristwatch in the other. "I told you, he's not dead. He's asleep. And our kitty's back up to twelve hundred and two bucks and a Rolex." She tapped the watch and held it to her ear. "I think it's fake, though."

"Paisley . . . we need to call the police." I glanced again at her open shirt. It was ripped at the buttonholes. "If he tried to . . ."

"I don't think our friend here would appreciate the cops getting involved. What with me being underage and all." She snickered, like she was laughing it all off. Water off a duck's back. But as she walked over to the desk and pulled out the drawer, I could see her hand. It was shaking. She fished out a piece of Caesars Palace stationery and a pen.

"I'll leave him a note. To explain."

I read over her shoulder as she wrote.

> To Steve,
>   If there's anything I can't stand, it's a pervert. If there's anything I can't stand more than a pervert, it's a liar.
>   And if there's anything I can't stand more than a pervert and a liar, it's a guy that smells as bad as you do.
>   Zooey, Age 16

I couldn't speak. I didn't know what to say or how to say it. She had it all planned out. All sewn up. A little orange bottle lay on the bed. I picked it up.

"Ativan? Where the hell did you get Ativan?"

She shrugged. "Virginia's personal pharmacy. I saw it on *ER* once. It's some kind of antianxiety pill. I thought it might help."

"Help who?"

"Me."

"You get anxious?"

"I get . . . everything."

"You . . . you could've killed him."

"Just a little bit," she said, and walked straight past me to drop the note on Steve's motionless body. "How sexy am I now, huh?" she muttered to him. I watched her shaky hand as it lifted to move her knotted hair back off her face.

As we left the room, Paisley pulled the door behind her but, thanks to me, it wouldn't close. By the time we reached the elevator bank, two guys in burgundy uniforms came bursting out from behind the automatic doors. They broke into a run down the corridor.

"What's going on?" Paisley called to them. "Hey, I think the people in eighty thirty-seven are having some kind of crazy party. It's lucky you showed up."

They just kept going, shouting back something about how they had everything under control.

"Suckers," mumbled Paisley as she stepped into the waiting elevator.

PAISLEY

THIRTEEN

DEUCE BUS STOP, OUTSIDE CAESARS PALACE,
THE STRIP,
LAS VEGAS, NEVADA

I saw you both on the news. It made me sick to think of you both in that children's home. And when I heard Virginia had taken you in, it nearly killed me. That woman is just bad. Bad to the bone. I knew she'd give you stuff, but she's doesn't have a maternal instinct in her body. She pulled a gun on me when I came to see you both, as soon as I was paroled. Bet she didn't tell you that. She said neither of you wanted to see me, that you were doing just great, and that if I ever came to the house again, she'd call the cops—tell them I'd been harassing you and acting all violent. That's why I write. I know she probably puts my letters straight in the trash. But I'll keep writing. Maybe one day, one of them will get through.

I was in a bad mood. I had almost been raped to begin with. Hey, that sounds like *A Christmas Carol*: "Marley was dead to begin with." And it's important to understand the fact that I was in a bad mood, because otherwise you cannot possibly imagine the wonder of what happened after that.

It was a few days after the whole Steve incident. I wasn't

speaking to Beau. He'd flushed my Ativan down the can. We were nowhere near finding Dad yet, and I was having a real heavy period. And even though we had some money now, I was in a pissy mood. It was a hot, hot day. One of those days when it's arid and dry and there's no air and you've nearly been raped and you can't find your dad and you feel sick from all the candy and the sun seems to hit you harder and harder the more you walk. I could feel the soles of my boots sticking to the sidewalk. I hated that.

We were waiting outside Caesars for the Deuce. Beau was sitting on the bench eating Jujubes. I stood leaning on the Plexiglas behind him. I couldn't wait to get back to the motel and deal with my underwear situation. Periods are a joke, seriously. I hate being a girl sometimes. I read once in one of those prim boarding school biology textbooks that you lose an "eggcup" of blood a month. I must be laying ostrich eggs. I was kinda glad to get it at first; I was way late and was worried I might have been sperminated by the train wreck of my life that was Jason. But I had dodged that particular bullet. My periods are always a nightmare, though. You'd think they would've come up with a solution to it all by now, all the cramps and the headaches and the mood swings and the misery. I guess they have. It's called death.

Anyway, this grizzly dude started walking up and down the line with this coupon book. He looked like a bum. As we waited, he walked up and down the line, again and again, his shabby white Reeboks flopping on the sidewalk like dirty worn-out diapers. His filthy toes poked through the front of one of them. His left eye was stitched shut like a pirate's, and he had on this T-shirt that read I Stayed, I Played, I Got Laid, and there was this naked woman sprawled out across his chest in silhouette. Made me wanna puke.

About the fourth time he came closer to us, Beau got up from the bench and joined me standing against the shelter. He took the slightest step behind me. I knew what he was doing. He was afraid Coupon Guy was suddenly gonna pull an audience-participation thing on him and single him out. Beau had always hated that. All that, *"What's your name, sonny?"* bullshit. Street entertainers. Magicians. Clowns.

"No smut here, folks. Get your coupons. Family fun. No smut. Pay no money," said Coupon Guy.

He walked up and down, up and down the line of tourists, back and forth, back and forth, badgering people as they walked by, shoving his books in their faces, saying the same thing over and over. The Deuce was taking forever to roll up.

"No smut here, folks. Get your coupons. Family fun. No smut. Pay no money. No smut here, folks. Get your coupons. Family fun. No smut. Pay no money," he kept saying, never deviating from the script, exactly the same tone of voice, up and down, taking his tobacco stench as he went and then bringing it back again.

The tourists would sidestep around him or pretend they didn't speak English. If I had a heart, I would've felt sorry for him.

"What is it, a hooker guide?" some jerk in sweatpants asked.

"No, sir, no smut here. Just coupons. Family fun."

"Why would I want it, then?" The guy shrugged, and two guys with him laughed like morons.

We ignored him for what seemed like an entire millennium, listening to his spiel surreptitiously. "No smut here, folks. Get your coupons. Family fun. No smut. Pay no money. Hey, buddy!"

For the splittest of seconds I thought he meant my dad, until reality kicked in and I looked behind us to where he had called, to see a similarly shabby guy with a beard and a red shirt, watching the news on the Jumbotron outside Caesars.

The bus pulled up and Coupon Guy went over to the other bum. The bus lowered a little and I stepped up, feeding my money into the slot. I took my ticket and waited for Beau. We scoped out a couple of empty seats and sat down. A fat woman fell up the steps, and some other tourists rushed to help her. I looked out and watched the two homeless guys rooting through a trash can together, pulling out wrappers and sniffing them. Red Shirt Guy thumbed through a paper.

"What are you looking at?" said Beau, leaning forward and putting his ticket in his back pocket. "Ugh, what are they doing?"

"What do you think they're doing, they're starving."

"God, how desperate do you have to be to go dumpster-diving?"

"Well, you're no stranger to trash cans, either, if I remember correctly."

Beau just looked at me. "Not by choice. Hey, look."

The bums were fighting now, shoving each other. Coupon Guy was trying to lay a right hook on Red Shirt Guy, but Red Shirt Guy was ducking, grabbing Coupon's waist, and trying to bring him down.

"My money's on Coupon Guy," I said. "He's way bigger."

Beau frowned. "That's really sad. They're probably fighting over a moldy pretzel or something."

"Get outta here, go on!" we heard Coupon Guy shout as Red Shirt moved away. Then he ran to catch up with him, and kicked his ass again. Red Shirt fell to his knees. Coupon Guy laughed and went back to his line of new tourists at the bus stop.

The doors wheezed shut and the bus started to move away. Red Shirt was walking alongside it for a second. I watched him. He looked up. The bus moved away from him. I saw his face.

Dad's face.

My blood froze.

"Oh my God, Beau." I shot up from my seat, climbed over him, and moved to the back of the bus, watching through every window as it rolled on, hoping to catch another glance. Tourists jammed the aisle, so I had to squeeze my way through, angering some old fart with a camcorder and standing on a kid's foot. The kid cried. The sun burned my eyes as it burst through every gap in the skyline to stop me from getting a closer look. He was too far away.

I called up to Beau. "It was him. The guy in the red shirt. It was Dad."

"Are you kidding me?" Then he started frantically searching out the windows for him, too, and hiking through the aisle to join me.

"You gotta believe me, it was him. It was Dad, Beau. I saw him. I saw him."

"All right, I believe you. But we're gonna lose him—"

"Stay back here and try to keep an eye on where he goes. C'mon, now!"

It was him. I knew it was him; I didn't need another look. I'd know my dad anywhere. Dad was like a brown bear, muscley and warm, and he had a smile that told you everything was gonna be all right. And even though Red Shirt Guy hadn't smiled and was smaller than I remembered Dad being, I didn't have a doubt in my mind.

I made it all the way up to the driver, but she was having none of my sweet appeals to stop the bus. "Miss, please step back and return to your seat while the bus is in motion."

"You gotta stop the bus," I said. "We need to get off."

"You can get off at the next stop."

"Where's that?"

"Up here, by the Bellagio. Now please step back, miss."

Beau joined me at the front. "He crossed the road."

"Keep watching him, Beau!"

"Miss . . ."

"Oh, keep your hair on, I'm going already!" I shouted, trying to push my way back through the tourists to my seat. They'd formed some kind of human shield, like cows do when they're being attacked by a bull (thank you, National Geographic Channel, for another piece of useless information), so it was much harder to get through. "Move out of my fucking way!" I shouted. The women tsked and tutted, probably 'cause there were kids around, but they got the hell out of the way.

The bus driver piped up then, spouting all this bus etiquette bullshit and how she could have me arrested for "abuse."

The Deuce came to a halt and the doors opened and before any of the cattle could do what they were threatening to do and stop me from getting off first, I rammed into them, crawling beneath legs and being as pushy as I could until my feet were on the sidewalk. Beau had stayed with me the whole way, and he took my hand and we broke into a run and didn't stop pounding the sidewalks and footbridges and plowing through shuffling tourists until we got to the walkway outside the Bellagio. We two-stepped it to the top of the stairs.

"Where'd he go?"

"This way," said Beau, panting all the way as we crossed over the bridge. I stopped to stare through the Plexiglas barrier for signs of the red shirt. I looked and I looked and there was no sign.

Then I saw him.

"He's there, he's going past Bally's."

So we raced along and down the escalator as fast as we could, past milling tourists and guys with more coupon booklets and so-called VIP passes. I caught sight of the red through a sea of people, and we kept on pushing through. I caught up with the red; it was the red of a giant M&M greeting people outside a store. I shoved past it and kept on running and running and running until we'd gone as far as the MGM Grand.

Dad had disappeared. Like a ghost.

I kept looking and looking, but he was gone. We stood there, spinning around, searching in every single direction for the slightest hint of a red shirt, but there was nothing. T-shirts. Hawaiian shirts. Wife-beaters. Baseball caps. Laughing. Joking. Tan. Happy. Strollers. Suitcases. Camera phones. The big gold lion.

We stood panting.

"Wow," said Beau, doubled over. "It was really Dad? Are you sure?"

And all I could do was nod. I started walking. I didn't know where I was going. I just had to keep walking.

BEAU

FOURTEEN

One of the dangers of being a kid is that you always believe you'll find what you're looking for right around the next corner. That if you dig deep enough in the sand, you really are gonna shake hands with someone on the other side of the world. That if you go to that end of the rainbow, a little pot full of gold will be waiting just for you. That if you strain hard enough on Christmas Eve, you can hear the tinkling of jingle bells in the sky. And kids take disappointment hard.

We had stumbled and crunched through the endless trees, over roots and dark soft dirt, walking and walking and walking forever, even though we were both exhausted and cold and out of breath and I was crying. Paisley had dragged me onward, convincing me the whole time that Dad was just around the next corner. And the corners were never-ending.

Ten years later, though we weren't in the woods anymore, but on concrete, with the full glare of the desert sun beating down on us like the lashes of a whip, it felt exactly the same: running after shadows that could have been Dad, and getting absolutely nowhere. I was ready for disappointment, anyway; I had been since Paisley saw him from the bus. I knew it couldn't be that easy, not after everything.

We went back to the Deuce stop at Caesars where we'd seen Dad watching the Jumbotron and rooting through the trash. We waited around, thinking he might come back. Paisley would have camped out overnight if she had to. But he'd obviously been spooked by Coupon Guy, and there was no sign of him. We walked up and down the Strip for hours, ignoring the dancing fountain displays and flashing lights, paying particular attention to the trash cans and bus stops, looking for red shirts and men with dark brown hair. But we found nothing.

I followed Paisley back toward the big gold lion outside the MGM Grand, and this time she went inside, along the red-carpeted walkways, past the gift shops and boutiques, until she'd led me to the glass-walled lion habitat. There was a little space between all the photo-taking tourists, and she stood at the window ledge and stared in.

I stood beside her. "So what do we do now? Do you want to go back to the Jumbotron, see if he shows up tonight?"

She didn't answer.

"Talk to me, Paisley. Tell me what to do next."

She just stared at two cubs playing with a blue ball. A voice-over was narrating their history and what they liked to eat.

I looked in at the cubs. "I know what you're feeling, 'cause I feel exactly the same way."

She pressed her head against the glass. "He's right here. He could be around the next corner." She looked at me sideways.

All I could do was nod. "Why don't we try the homeless shelters? Seems logical that's where he'd go."

She shook her head. "Dad wouldn't go to a shelter."

"How do you know? He's homeless; it's possible. . . ."

"He'd rather sleep on the streets. Trust me, I know my dad. He's too proud."

"You knew him when we were six, Pais."

She threw me a look. I swallowed hard but kept going.

"I'm starting to think we're not gonna find him," I said softly. "I mean . . . he's homeless. It's gonna be even harder to get to him now. I mean, you remember what happened last time. We were the ones who were lost, and we ended up on every TV station in the Tri-State area."

The blue ball bounced off the glass right in front of us, and Paisley backed away like it had suddenly become hot. Then she looked at me and started laughing. "Beau, you're a friggin' genius."

"Oh God, what?"

She turned back to the cubs and stared at them for the longest time.

"Pais? What is it?"

She looked at me. "You hungry?"

"Yeah. What is it, Pais, what's your idea?"

"Tell you later. Come on. What do you feel like eating? Domino's? Mickey D's?"

I shook my head. "I could manage something sweet. A donut, I guess."

"Donuts. Yes, oh yes, this is gonna be good," she said, clinging on to my arm and practically dragging me all the way through the front entrance. "Let's go to Doh-Nutty's."

"That's not the best donuts. The best donuts—"

"I don't want the best donuts, I want Doh-Nutty's," she said.

"Okay," I said, a little wary of my sister's newfound vigor but hungry all the same and, as always, happy to follow her wherever she went.

So we walked to Doh-Nutty's, along the same side of the Strip as the MGM and just around the corner from our motel. There were only four and a half other people in there at the time: a white guy with long dreadlocks sat in a booth nodding his head before a plate of balls, which on a second look I could see were donut holes. A fat woman eating a plate of crepes sat beside a stroller. Her baby looked at me like it was saying, *I don't know why I was born, either.* A couple in the corner were *Lady-and-the-Tramp*-ing on a churro.

Paisley put her shades on, nudging me.

"Hey, look," she whispered. "They're feeling each other up under the table."

I looked, more fool I. She giggled and studied the lit-up donut menu above the counter.

"Yes please, what can I get you?" said the sweaty, harassed guy behind the counter. As far as I could see he had no reason to be so stressed. It wasn't exactly busy.

"Can I get one of every single donut, please?" asked Paisley.

"Every single one?" the guy repeated.

"Every single one," she said, smiling. "In fact, let's make it two of every kind." She looked at me from behind her shades and whispered, "Follow my lead."

"What?" I said, still a little distracted by the couple in the corner. I came around to discover my sister had a sudden desire to be morbidly obese.

The guy started shoveling donuts into shallow white boxes labeled with the brown and green sunshine emblem of Doh-Nutty's.

"Two of every kind for the lady," he said, looking up at Paisley and giving her the most unctuous of smiles.

Paisley smiled back. "So how's business?"

"Pretty good," the man replied. "You know who comes here for her donuts?" He motioned to the huge billboard across the street picturing some diva in a sparkly dress.

"I thought she'd gone low carb!" said Paisley in mock shock. "Or gluten-free. Or was it a juice fast?"

"Not anymore," said Doh-Nutty, shoveling a couple of Double Chocolate Fudge Melts into an almost-full second box and closing the lid.

"Wow," said Paisley. "Then she musta gone back to the trusty two-finger upchuck. Good publicity for you, though."

The man nodded and smiled, scooping up two Blueberry Whites with sprinkles and two Glazed Maple Creams for the next box.

She nudged my hand. Her eyes glimmered, cheeks flushed with excitement, just like when we were kids.

"Put your sunglasses on," she told me.

"Why? What are you doing?"

"There you go," said the man, placing three Doh-Nutty's boxes on the counter. "Thirty-two donuts plus tax comes to $36.75."

"Cool," she said, fumbling for her purse. "But I think I can do better than that." And I watched as her hand dipped inside her bag and pulled out this shiny silver gun. She pointed it right at Doh-Nutty.

Doh-Nutty stared at her in horror, his little ball of chewing gum falling out onto the counter with a *thud*.

"No, please!" he begged, moving backward and fumbling with the key on the cash register. The drawer popped open and he rummaged around, handing a wad of bills to Paisley.

The white Rasta in the corner stood up but made no attempt to come forward.

"It's okay. We don't want the money," Paisley told the man. "We'll just take the donuts."

Doh-Nutty fumbled some more with the register and then backed away with his hands up.

Paisley nodded to me to take the boxes and looked up at something behind the counter.

"Is that a camera you got up there?" she asked the man.

He nodded.

"Can you get sound on it?"

He nodded again, more vigorously.

She looked up and blew the camera a kiss. "We love you, Dad!" she called out. And as she opened the door and pushed me out with the donut boxes, she turned back to Doh-Nutty and said, "When they ask you what happened, tell 'em the Wonder Twins did it. You got that?"

"W-wonder T-twins," he stammered.

Then she smiled at him and walked out as calmly as she had walked in, shoving the gun inside the waistband of her skirt. And I walked beside her, staring, waiting and hoping I was dreaming, trying to keep up and desperately holding on to the three boxes of donuts.

I did this all the way back to the motel. On the way, we saw another homeless man searching through a trash can. Paisley gave him the top two boxes of donuts with her compliments. Then we walked inside the motel with the last one.

She went straight in and shut herself in the bathroom. I set down the one remaining box of donuts on my nightstand and turned on the light. I heard the toilet flush. Then she came out, sat on her bed, and began looking through the TV guide.

"Is that Goldie Hawn movie on tonight? The one where she falls off the boat and gets amnesia? I love that movie."

"YOU HAVE A FUCKING GUN ON YOU?" I yelled at her. "HOW LONG HAVE YOU HAD A FUCKING GUN ON YOU?"

"God, turn off your CAPS LOCK, Beau." She sighed. "I knew you'd be like this."

"How do you expect me to be, Paisley? I mean, am I dreaming? Is this some kind of sugar-induced absurdist nightmare? That's a real-assed gun, and you just pulled it on a guy selling donuts!"

"Yeah, but not 'cause I wanted to hurt him. I just want to get us on those Jumbotrons. Like the one outside Caesars. Anyway, it was your idea."

My mouth was too energetic to find the right shape for my words. I paced the room. "My ide . . . Wha . . . ha . . . what was my idea?"

"You said when we were lost in those woods, we ended up on every TV station in the Tri-State."

"And . . . ?"

"We're lost again, Beau. We can't find our dad." She stood up. "We need him to see us. To see that we're okay. He doesn't even know we love him. Skank has poisoned his head with all her crap. I want him to know we care."

"How is pointing a gun at someone going to show him we care? Did you see how scared that guy was? Jesus Christ, Paisley. You're not *Scarface*!"

She put her hands on my shoulders, and I shook her away. She grabbed on to me and I tried shaking her off again, but she held on.

"Listen to me, Beau, dammit."

I stopped.

"There's no point breaking your crayons over this, okay? This makes sense. We get ourselves on those screens, on that screen outside Caesars where we know he hangs out, Dad will see us. He was watching it before Coupon Guy started on him. We get famous, we'll be one step closer to finding him."

"We'll be one step closer to prison, Paisley. Can't you see that?"

"God, when did you become such a prude?"

"I don't know. Maybe the same day you slipped down into the moral abyss?"

She started to protest again, but I didn't care what she had to say. There was no excuse. She was making us another crime statistic. And I didn't want to be what everyone expected me to be. I didn't want any part of it.

She sat on the end of the bed and just looked at me.

"Can't we just keep going down to the Jumbotron and see if he shows up?" I sighed.

"Too hit or miss. And we'll probably always miss. This way, we can really put ourselves out there. We get a snappy little slogan, maybe even costumes. We rob a few small-time places—donut shops, candy stores, coffee bars. That ice-cream place off the Strip that we walked past the other day. Places people don't expect anyone to pull a gun on them. We're polite, we don't hurt anybody, we take the shit, we leave our message, and we go. And then we come back here and wait for it to hit the news."

I didn't say a word.

"Maybe we could graffiti that giant M&M outside the store or something. Kidnap him for a ransom. Ten million M&M's or Big Red gets it." She laughed.

I didn't laugh.

"I know how you feel about this, Beau," she said. "You don't wanna hurt people. You don't wanna rob people. You don't wanna be one of those clichéd troubled teens. Like me."

I started to say something, but she interrupted.

"But we'll be doing this for one reason: to find Dad. Or at the very least to let Dad find us. We can get our message to him that we're okay and that we love him."

"By putting a gun in someone's face and stealing their livelihood," I told her slowly. "No, I'm not doing it. No way. There has to be something else we can do. Where the hell'd you get it, anyway?"

"Skank's nightstand."

"It's Virginia's?"

"Yeah, and it's not even loaded. Today is the first day I've even taken it out of the motel. I don't know, I just . . . wanted it with me today. I thought it would come in handy after Steve the Texan pervert. And it did, didn't it? Besides, I gave away the other two boxes of donuts to that bum, didn't I? That was a kind thing to do. Steal from the rich and give to the poor."

I got up and went to the window. "That Doh-Nutty guy wasn't rich."

"No." She got up and stood beside me at the window. "But when we're famous, he'll get some good publicity out of it, and we can pay him back that way. His place'll be jam-packed. He'll be busier than a one-legged man in an ass-kicking contest."

I shook my head. "Oh man. This sucks out loud."

And that was when she started to get angry. "Put it this way, Beau. You can stay here and keep working your whole Jesus of Suburbia thing if you want, but I'm going. I am doing this. You're either with me or you're not."

"Not," I said, turning away from her and slumping down on my bed.

"Fine," she said. I pretended not to watch as she adjusted the gun in her waistband, then pulled her shirt out over it, grabbed the keys from the desk, and headed out of the room. The door slammed behind her.

After a couple of seconds, I sat up straight and looked around. I could feel my heart thudding. She had really gone without me. *Stay put,* I told myself. I leaned against the headboard and just breathed for a while. I picked up the remote and flicked on the TV. There was a Dennis Quaid movie on and I tried losing myself in it, but it was pretty bad. I switched it off and felt for stubble on my chin. I took my new disposable razor out of my drawer and shaved over it, just in case any hairs came through later.

I got up. I went into the bathroom and checked the mirror. My hair was an insane asylum of knots. I needed to get it cut. I had a little cluster of zits on my chin and bacon grease stains on my T-shirt. I turned out the light and went back to bed.

"Shit," I said. I got back up. "Shit," I said again and went to the door. My hand hovered over the handle. "Shit."

I walked out into the bright sunlight. And Paisley was standing right there, waiting for me.

"Took your time," she said.

PAISLEY

FIFTEEN

HEADING NORTH ALONG THE STRIP,
OUTSIDE BILL'S GAMBLIN' HALL,
LAS VEGAS, NEVADA

It's just like in that song. People really are strangest when you're a stranger. Everyone does look ugly when you're on your own.

I couldn't remember who sang it but I knew my dad used to say it was a classic. And it was so true. I hadn't had one nice thought since we'd lost Dad in the crowds. I hated everything. The cowboy fathead who stood right in my path to gaze at the pirate ships in the water. The dwarf in front of the mall who called me "babe" and asked me if I wanted a bottle of cold water. The woman in the baseball cap who handed me a flyer for a strip show. The skinny blonde with her phone on a diamond chain and her heels the height of pencils who looked like she was headed for a strip club audition. She was pole-thin. I looked down at my stomach. We had only been in Vegas six days, but there was a definite new bulge that hadn't been there when we'd arrived. I pulled my T-shirt out over it, regretting the half-eaten pack of M&M's in my bag. And the Rainbow Twizzlers in my pocket. And the giant Peppermint Patty.

After checking out the Caesars Palace Jumbotron area for Dad again, we headed for the mall next to the Treasure Island hotel complex. I had decided we needed uniforms.

"You mean a more cohesive statement of fashion sense while we rob people left, right, and center?" Beau had said. The whole way there he laid his guilt trip on me. He was right as usual, and I needed to feel better about what we were doing.

"You know, I'm not fully on board with this whole robbery thing, Paisley. . . ."

"Yes, Beau," I sighed, trying to yes him to death till he shut his pie-hole.

"I mean, it's just such a—"

"—brilliant idea of yours, Paisley?"

"—such a long shot. Think about it for a second. If we get caught, we could do time. Juvey. Or prison for real, Pais. You know what they do to guys like me in prison."

"That was in the olden days. They're more like summer camps now. You might get to do canoeing and stuff."

"I don't care, I don't wanna find out. I don't wanna get caught."

"We're not gonna get caught."

"How do you know? Something could go wrong. Someone could get shot."

I was sweating. "Beau, for the eighth time, it is not loaded."

He squinted in the sunlight and screened his eyes with his hand to look at me as we walked. "How do you know they're not going to hit back? Everyone carries a gun these days. What if they pull a gun on us, what's the big plan then, huh?"

"So the guy who works part-time at Licky's Ice Cream Parlor is gonna pull his Glock out on me just 'cause I don't pay for my soft serve? Gimme a break, Beau. I told you, they won't be expecting it."

"You don't know for sure."

I knew one thing for sure: I had about one nerve left, and he was getting on it. But I couldn't help noticing this tiny little sting somewhere inside me. Beau was right, and I knew he was right. And him pointing out all the itsy-bitsy things that could go wrong had kinda weirded me out. If I was on my own, I wouldn't be thinking twice. Beau made me think twice.

"We'll cross here," I told him, stopping at the light.

"If you say so," Beau mumbled.

The mall was a little farther up the Strip on the other side of the street, and by the time we got inside, I had managed to steer the conversation over to what outfits we were gonna wear in order to rob people.

"Jeans and T-shirts just make us look like your average teenage thug," I told Beau. "I've been thinking about maybe a black-and-white theme, to pick up on the whole Eclipse thing of the gun."

"Genius," he mumbled, looking down at his feet as we went up the steps to the huge mall entrance.

I looked at him. "It is, actually. We wanna get noticed, we gotta wear stuff that stands out. Jeans and T-shirts just won't cut it. Bonnie and Clyde had an image."

"We are NOT Bonnie and Clyde, Paisley. We're not carrying guns, you are."

"Whatever . . ."

"And Bonnie and Clyde killed people. We're not gonna kill people. And anyway, their image wasn't an image, it was just how people dressed in the twenties."

"Thirties," I corrected.

"How do you know?"

"It was one of Dad's favorite films. It's one of mine, too."

Beau looked away. I just wanted to shake him and say, *Look, we're doing this whether you like it or not, so just DEAL WITH IT.* But I didn't. Somehow I reined in the old Paisley tendency to shout first, ask questions later. I ignored the urge and tried to bolster my argument instead.

"Look at those guys who climbed the Lincoln statue. Remember that story? The dads who wanted to see their kids. They got their message across. They were dressed as superheroes. We gotta have a 'thing.' An image."

Beau pushed the door and went in first. I heard him mumbling again, but I chose to ignore that, too, before steam started shooting out of my ears.

I thought a mall in Vegas would be different from one in LA or Jersey, but it wasn't. I don't know what I was expecting. Maybe more casinos, maybe some circus act on a high wire, zebras on skates, or a roller coaster weaving in and out of the stores. But there was none of that. It was like every other mall you ever saw. Cool relief from the heat, all white and marbled. Cleaning people who swept up your candy wrappers the second they hit the floor. Hip-hop pumping out of electronics stores where happening hot guys checked out the merchandise with blonde bobble-heads with *Juicy* written across the asses of their velour sweats. Chain bookshops or generic clothing stores lulled customers in with soft jazz and cream faux suede couches. Naked gold mannequins and snakeskin purses in the windows of Neiman Marcus and Bloomingdales told me I shouldn't even darken their doorsteps, while Nathan's Famous and KFC were ready to welcome me with open arteries.

The mall entrance was on the third floor. We stopped at the

balcony overlooking the second-floor event area with its fashion show runway.

"Okay, meet you down there by that runway thing in two hours."

"We're not shopping together?" Beau asked, looking mildly hurt.

"No. I'm gonna trust you to get your own stuff."

"But I don't know . . ."

"Black-and-white theme, Beau. Use your initiative. Here . . ." I riffled through my pocket and pulled out the wad of cash left over from chumping Steve, the Texan pervert. I handed Beau roughly half of it. "Black and white. Stylish. Cool. Go with that. Okay?"

He had this heavy brow thing going on and wandered off, turning back to me, confused, as I shooed him away.

"Two hours," I called out. He didn't look back again.

I needed to not be with him. He was pissing me off to the nth degree with all his guilt-tripping. I wanted to be on my own, figure out stuff in my head. I wasn't stupid. I knew what we were doing was risky, not to mention a long shot. Even if Dad *did* see us on the Jumbotron outside Caesars, how the hell was he gonna get to us? I just wanted him to see me, even if I couldn't see him.

I went down to the first floor to a store called Little Madams, and they had just what I needed. A sleeveless white sheath dress that buttoned at the shoulders. I already had on my long-sleeved black T-shirt, so I slipped the dress over it and took my skirt off. My fishnet thigh-highs and black Doc Martens set the whole thing off, and I picked up a pair of white-framed shades from a little display case beside the cash register. I paid for it all and still had tons of money left. I mooched around the first floor for a while to kill time. Checked my e-mail on a display netbook in the Sony store. Mostly spam. Tried some lip balms in The Body Shop. And just wandered.

It was kinda boring without Beau. Even though he irritated my ass off sometimes, I felt wrong without him. Like in school. It was just wrong when he wasn't there. I went into a bookstore to check out the novels in the teen section. A blonde girl about my age with black streaks in her hair was checking them out, too, with her dad. He was going to treat her to one. They all seemed the same to me, though, so I left.

I headed next door to this pet shop, lured by the sound of yapping puppies. There were other animals around, too, birds in cages, white mice on wheels, kittens all nestled into their mom in a small sheepskin pod, but I just sat and watched these little pups, about ten little yellow guys in a large glass case. There was one lying down in the corner, not yapping at all. His head rested on his outstretched paws, just looking up at me, his brow peaked as if to say, *What are you lookin' at?* I'd plagued the life out of my dad for a puppy when I was little.

I thought to myself, *Go on, buy it. What's stopping you now? No Dad to stop you, no school ties anymore. Buy that sad chubby one in the corner. Pull the Eclipse on the salesgirl and demand that dog. It'd be something to love.*

But it didn't feel right. *We're on the road. We're planning robberies. We have to be fast on our feet. It wouldn't be fair. He'd be a big responsibility.* Who was that talking now? They weren't my thoughts. Must have been Beau's creeping in. Or Dad's. Or they *could* have been mine. I didn't know anymore.

I got out of there and made my way to the runway area and a nearby smoothie cart. All Shook Up, it was called. I bought a Blueberry Hill Power Pulp and sat down on the marble seat to drink it and wait for Beau. The Eclipse felt awkward in the deep front pocket of my new dress. It didn't like it when I sat down. It needed to be straight against my body. I put my green jacket on and zipped it up in case the gun fell out.

Scatt's House was directly across from the bench, so I had no choice but to focus my attention on it. Scatt's was this supposedly übercool clothes store for preppy assholes, and half the stuff looked like it had come from a thrift store. I guessed it was made to look like that: distressed. I was distressed just hearing the music they were playing. Some rapper shouting. Not my kind of music. I liked the stuff my dad used to listen to. Timeless rock bands. Classic guitar riffs. Melodic geniuses. I didn't give a shit about gangstas and bitches and bling.

There was a topless male model in stonewashed jeans just outside the entrance, welcoming people in with squirts of cologne. It was a while before the smell hit me, but then I got it. The dry, clean, aftershavey scent of lemons and drywall. I inhaled and closed my eyes. I knew that smell. I inhaled again. I felt funny. Like an open gate waiting for water to come rushing through. And right then it all came pouring back through me.

Me and Beau were in the basement of our house in Jersey. We were about five, I guess, and Mom had locked us down there. We always seemed to be doing stuff that pissed her off. I remember we'd hidden her purse once, and we both got hit across the backs of our legs when she found it in the washing machine. Another time she chewed us out for drawing on our newly painted bedroom door, and she dragged Beau across the room by his arm until he'd cried. I yelled and yelled back at her, but she kept hitting him. I got so angry I pushed her. Not hard, but enough. She fell back against the door.

It was real dark in the basement, and stank of mold and mildew and old broken furniture. Beau was scared of the dark—had been for, like, forever—so for a while we just sat together on the bottom step and held hands. I remember not wanting to move into the darkness in case I fell down a hole. I told Beau I wasn't scared.

Anyway, Dad came home early. He called out for us.

"We're here, Dad, we're down here!" we yelled out, and then we heard him jiggling the lock. We ran to the middle of the stairs, and he was there at the top.

He ran down to us and squished us both tight.

"Oh, guys, I'm sorry," he kept saying. I can still hear it. He sat down on a step, me on one knee and Beau on the other, and looked at our faces. His tears were streaming down, even though he was smiling.

"How long you been down here, kiddos?"

"I don't know, Dad," I said, hugging him again.

Beau put a little hand up to his cheek and smoothed away a tear. "Naughty tear, you go home now," he said, and wiped it on his jacket.

Dad laughed. "Is that right?"

"That's what you always tell me," Beau said.

I buried my face into Dad's stubbly neck and clung on. And there it was: the smell of aftershave. The dry, clean smell of safety.

My straw slurped against the bottom of my cup. I tossed it into a nearby trash can and went on over to Scatt's House.

The half-naked cologne model spotted me through the little clique of schoolgirls who had gathered to worship at his impressive pecs. The smell was stronger. I couldn't get enough of it. "Would you like to try some, miss?"

I looked at him. "Uh, isn't it for men?"

"No, it's unisex." He sprayed the cologne on a white card from a distance, then handed it to me. It wasn't exactly the same smell. It wasn't exactly Dad. But it was close. And I loved it.

"On sale. Ten percent off. Today only . . ."

"No thanks," I frowned, walking past him into the store. I didn't want him thinking I was one of his groupies, though I did want to buy a bottle. Just a little tester size that I could smell whenever I wanted.

I sought out a salesperson and walked right up to this short woman folding pink T-shirts at a table full of folded pink T-shirts. The shouty music was deafening and the place reeked of the not-really-Dad cologne the model was spraying.

"Excuse me, what's the name of that cologne . . . ?"

She didn't even look at me, just kept on chewing her gum and folding her T-shirts. "We don't have anything black here."

"What?" I said.

She still didn't look at my face, she still kept on chewing. *Smack smack.* "And you can go tell your little Goth friends outside that if any more of you come in here looking for their wrist slitting outfits, I'll call security."

"Oh . . . ," I said, totally stone-faced.

"Mm-hmm," she smirked, looking me up and down before going back to folding her T-shirts. *Smack smack.*

Okay, so I *was* wearing black fishnets and combat boots, but my dress was white and my jacket was green. And my hair was blonde. How fucked up is that? And anyway, how rude was she? If I *had* been a Goth, I would've bitch-slapped her good and plenty.

I decided to leave, turning around and mumbling about her being in the wrong job, when I stopped. I couldn't let it slide. I turned back. "What's up with the attitude?"

She actually looked me in the eyes then, still smacking her gum. "All day I've had kids coming in here asking for black this and black that. I'm tired of it." *Smack smack.*

"I'm wearing white. And I don't wanna slit my wrists. I just want some of the goddamn cologne that Brad Pitiful is spritzing out front, if you don't fucking mind."

Her face dropped like a bag of wrenches. I followed her eyes. My green jacket had shifted. My gun was sticking out of the pocket at the front of my dress.

I smiled. "This what I gotta do to get some respect around here?"

She stared at me. She gulped something down. Her gum.

"Now, where's the cologne?"

She didn't take her eyes from the gun and stepped backward, scrabbling around for a small box on a display table near the cash register. The T-shirt she had been folding dropped to the floor. She handed a box to me. "Take it."

I took it. "Thanks. Try to be a little more fucking helpful next time, huh?"

"Please don't . . ."

"And ask your manager about getting some black stuff in here. Seriously. If that many people are asking for it, maybe you got a little gap in your market." I motioned to the cologne. "Thanks bunches."

So I strode out, giving the model a dirty glance as I did, and went back up to the third floor, feeling mighty pleased with myself, bolstered by the Eclipse once again. As I reached the top of the escalator, I saw Beau coming out of Dude Wearhouse.

He looked unbelievable. Like some kind of model, strutting out of there with his jacket slung over his shoulder and one hand in his pocket. Confident. Deadly sexy. Ugh. He was my brother! But he looked absolutely not like my brother. To kick things off, I could actually see his face, because he'd got a haircut. It was slicked back and flicked out a little behind his ears. He looked super-stylin'. White shirt, black vest, black pants. New Chuck Taylors. His skin glowed. We're talking *GQ*. We're talking rock star.

He spotted me at the top escalator and headed up.

"Oh . . . my . . . God," I said, smiling. "What did you *do*?!"

He smiled back. "What do you think? Is this what you had in mind? I tried to be mostly black but my shirt's white. I got some new white laces, though." He looked behind him in a store window to check his hair.

"Beau, it's so . . . not you." I couldn't think of what else to say. He put me to shame a little, what with my thrown-together-in under-five-minutes ensemble from Little Madam's. And I already had the black fishnets, so all I'd really bought was my white dress and the shades. He'd had an extreme freakin' makeover and then some.

"I got the full prom king treatment at this salon on two. And the guys in there"—he raised a shopping bag in the direction of Dude Wearhouse and chuckled like a little kid—"fixed me up with a three-piece suit and tie. I kinda spent a lot, though."

"That's okay. I kinda spent a little." I pulled him aside to the balcony so I could keep an eye on what was happening down below at Scatt's.

"You look cute, Pais. Real cool."

I patted his hair at the front. It was rock solid. Then I paused and wrinkled my nose.

Beau sighed and put his bags down. "Go on, get it over with," he said with a smile.

I loved how well he knew me. I rolled up his shirt sleeves and loosened his tie a little. Then I tried to mess up his hair a bit in the front.

"Hey!"

"It's okay, it's just a little *too* Jersey with the gel. It needs to be less rigid, more just-got-out-of-bed. There, *now* you're übercool."

"How übercool?" he pressed.

"Sub-zero," I said, which he seemed happy with. He turned to check his reflection again in the window.

"Hey, what do you think of this cologne?" I asked him, opening the box I got from Scatt's and spraying a little into the air before him.

Beau sniffed. "It's okay."

"Remind you of anything? Of anyone?"

He shook his head. "No. It's good, though. Can I?"

I handed it to him, a little bummed that it didn't remind him, too. A security guard ahead was speaking into his walkie-talkie and looking around.

"You've been busy," I said, slipping off my green jacket and folding it into one of my bags.

"Yeah." He smiled, picking up his bags. "I got these cheap canvas totes from Hot Topic. They've got rock band names on 'em, but it doesn't matter. . . ."

"You don't like rock bands. What do you want those for?" I rooted blindly in my purse for an elastic and tied up my hair.

He stared at me like some alien had landed on my face. "For the swag. To put what we steal in."

"Oh yeah!" I laughed. "I didn't think of that, Beau. Good lookin' out." I put on his brand-new suit jacket over my white dress.

"Nah, that doesn't look right," he said. "Take it off."

A security guard ran past me at that moment. He had his two-way held up to his ear and I heard this scratchy but distinct voice say, ". . . long blonde hair, green jacket . . ." He headed for the escalator.

I guessed he was on his way to Scatt's House. I made a beeline for the exit, and Beau followed my lead.

"So you're finally on board?" I asked. "No more questions and freak-outs and giving me shit over doing this?" I said, glancing behind me as we walked.

"I'm not on board, no. It's still harebrained. I just figure that if we're going to do this, we should be prepared."

"Good. See, your old Boy Scout days are paying off at last." I could see the automatic doors of the entrance up ahead; the white marble walkway, the sunlight from outside blinding, like it was the gateway to heaven.

"The lady said I looked sexy."

"What?" I said.

"In Dude Wearhouse. She said I looked sexy."

I looked at him and snickered. He blushed.

I picked up the pace, glancing over my shoulder again. "Where are your sunglasses?"

"Right here," he said, putting all his bags in one grip and grabbing his shades out of his front pocket with the other. Totally black. Totally cool. "Why are we going so fast, Pais?"

"Put them on," I told him, pushing down my own white frames from the top of my head.

"Why?" he said, a little out of breath now. "Are we going to hit up another store? Now?"

Another security guard ran straight past us, followed by a third.

I glanced over the balcony to see the first one heading into Scatt's House below. The exit was in sight, and the light from outside was dazzling.

"Yeah. But not here. We'll try someplace off the Strip."

"I thought you wanted to do M&M's? Or that candy store on . . ."

"Beau, we gotta get out of here. ASAFP. I did something."

Beau's face darkened like a little cloud had appeared above his head.

"Paisley? What did you do?"

And then I grabbed his arm and we started running.

BEAU

SIXTEEN

I wasn't listening. I was too preoccupied with running as though my life depended on it. Sweat streamed off me, and my new white shirt was soaked on the back and under the armpits. My side ached. I thought I was gonna cough up blood.

"I saw it on YouTube," Paisley panted as we ran. "The fathers who hung . . . this banner at the Lincoln Memorial." We were clear of the mall and heading toward the very far end of the Strip, our shoes pumping on the sidewalk, dodging tourists, looking behind us, running faster.

"What?" I heaved, a biting pain in my side. I had to stop and bend over. Little droplets fell from my forehead onto the sizzling hot sidewalk.

Paisley stopped, too, but stayed upright, her hands on her hips. "No sign of them. We're okay. But . . . do you see what I'm saying? 'We are the Wonder Twins, tell Buddy we love him' is too long for a slogan. I'll forget half of it."

"So . . . we need to shorten . . . our slogan. Is that . . . what you're saying?"

There was a line of stores behind us and a bus stop with an old dude in a coat huddled up in the corner. A tacky souvenir shop, a tattoo parlor, and a wig-maker's.

"We could make a banner," she suggested. *Pant pant.* "Something written down. Spray paint?"

"We can't spray paint people. I draw the line at vandalism."

"Oh, you draw the line?" she mocked, wiping her forehead.

"Yes. We're not causing any more . . . damage than we have to."

She muttered under her breath, and then did a double take at one of the shops. "There's a Kinko's."

"Huh?" I grimaced.

"A copy place."

"You wanna print flyers or something?"

"Why not?"

She started walking toward it, and I pulled her arm back. She tugged it away, frowning at me. I let go. "People will just think it's a publicity stunt."

"Well, it is!" she said, and walked on.

As it turned out, though, we didn't get flyers. Paisley had a better idea. We got stickers. About the size of a credit card. White with black writing, saying WE ARE THE WONDER TWINS. Two hundred of them.

"We'll just slap these on the counter each time," she said, peeling one off its backing and attempting to stick it to my forehead. With all the moisture it just dropped off. "So all we have to say is . . ."

". . . tell Buddy we love him." I nodded. I got it. It was either a genius idea or the longest shot in history. We'd hold up these small stores, unsuspecting little places selling stuff no armed robbers would ever wanna rob. Yet all of these places would have security cameras, potentially scaring off kids and anyone else trying to pull off sly little five-finger discounts. Paisley would do her thing, and we'd run off without paying, leave the sticker and the message about Dad, and then go into hiding and wait for the heist to hit the news.

The ice-cream place was just around the corner from the copy shop.

"So, take two?" I said.

"Yeah." She pushed her shades up onto her head, hiking her tote bag up to her shoulder.

Inside General Custard's it was hustly and bustly, and there was an explosion of color from the walls, floors, and tables. It smelled of burned sugar and body odor, and the song playing was scratchy with a hint of maracas. I wondered if the woman behind the counter would even hear us telling her to "Stick 'em up" over all the noise.

An endless line of people stood waiting to order. I joined it behind Paisley, who didn't seem in the least perplexed by the people or the noise. She waited her turn, hands clasped before her, studying the overhead menus. They had every flavor in the world: butter pecan, strawberry, cookies 'n cream, peach, cherry, chocolate brownie, rocky road. There was a choice of hot fudge, chocolate sprinkles, whipped cream, nuts, and marshmallows, whatever you wanted on the top. Two little boys at one of the tables were inhaling foot-high shakes.

There were some girls sitting at the counter by the window, scooping out ice cream from little blue cups and huge waffle cones. I thought one of them was checking me out, but I wasn't sure. I thought maybe she was waiting for someone. She had red hair. I saw her glance over at me.

I asked Paisley, "You see those girls over there by the window? No, at the counter. Don't look. Are any of them looking my way?"

She peered over my shoulder. "No," she said nonchalantly, going back to looking at the menus. "Why? You got a chubby for any of 'em?"

"No," I said, feeling my cheeks glow. "One of them looked over when we walked in."

"Probably waiting for her boyfriend."

Zzrak! The electric fly killer claimed another victim.

"That one on the end, with the red hair. She looked at me. Twice."

I looked slowly behind again. We caught each other's gaze, and she turned away.

Paisley saw it, too. "You're right. She is checking you out. Why don't you go and put the moves on her?"

"You think I should?"

"Sure. Now that you've had your makeover, your junk's bringing all the girls to the yard."

We were next in line to be served, behind a woman who must have had fifty kids out waiting in the car. She spent, like, sixty bucks. I had a wedgie but I didn't dare try and pluck it out with the redhead watching. I looked back at her. We locked eyes again. She smiled. I smiled. Wow! I couldn't believe it. I'd always imagined having a girlfriend and doing stuff that couples do together. Not gross stuff. Stupid stuff, really, things couples take for granted or don't even think about. Holding hands. Sharing a milk shake. Giving birthday presents. I'd never had that. But I could see it all happening with this girl. I could see our future like a rainbow-colored bubble in the air. *I'd be such a good boyfriend,* I thought. I prepared myself to go over to her, checking my hair, straightening my clothes.

Paisley spoke to me through gritted teeth. "Stop fidgeting. You gotta be cool now. We need to make a good impression for the news."

"She's cute. I should go over," I said. "I'm gonna go over and just say hi."

Paisley elbowed me in the stomach. I *oomphed* and bent forward to relieve the pain. "You're not going anywhere," she said. "We got work to do."

"What the hell, Pais?" I groaned, guarding myself in case she did it again. I looked back. The redhead was still there, smiling into her ice cream. She'd seen me *oomph*. She was laughing at me. "I can't go over now. She thinks I'm stupid."

Paisley turned and brought her face up close to mine. We were exactly the same height. She said it slowly and quietly. "We're about to commit armed robbery, and all you can think about is picking up chicks. What's wrong with this picture, Beau?"

Zzrak! Another one bit the dust.

Our grandmother would say exactly the same thing to me all the time. *What's wrong with this picture, Beau?*

"That really hurt, Paisley. Totally embarrassing . . ."

"Can you please just shut your pie-hole and keep focused?" she said. "We can see about getting you laid afterward. You've waited sixteen years, what's another hour?"

I gave her my filthiest look. "Paisley . . ." She paid no attention.

Waiters rushed out from kitchen doors with double triple quadruple chocolate sundaes and Belgian waffles dabbed with melting balls of ice cream. The guys all kinda looked the same, and the way the woman behind the counter was ordering them around gave me the impression they were her sons.

"It's getting busy in here," Paisley noted. I didn't say anything.

The waiters ran around the tables, filling coffee cups, clearing dishes, flinging themselves in and out of the swinging doors, taking orders, while others banged and shouted in Spanish in the kitchen beyond. One dude hurried through wheeling a large refrigerated box, ushering the line of customers out of his way.

"Jeez," Paisley whispered, leaning back toward me. "Now they gotta do a heart transplant as well."

I didn't laugh. She always did that, pissed me off then tried to act like nothing had happened and make me laugh. She could say some pretty hurtful stuff, and I never deserved it. Like just then. She knew how much I hated even mentioning that I was a virgin. I wore my inexperience like an albatross around my neck. I hated even saying the word *virgin*.

"You ready?" she whispered back to me.

I didn't answer.

"Beau?"

"Yes," I spat back. My chest had begun to throb. The woman in front paid and moved away with her eight gallons of ice cream. I knew what was gonna happen next. I looked behind for the redhead. She was gone.

"Next, please!" barked the short, sweaty server lady.

My sister stepped up. "Yeah, can I get four buckets: one chocolate brownie, one pistachio, one French vanilla, and one mint."

"Any toppings? Marshmallows? Chocolate chips? Jimmies? Nuts?"

"No, but can I get rainbow sprinkles on all of them, please?"

The woman was on it before Paisley had finished speaking, sliding back metal doors on freezer cabinets, clattering plastic buckets, hollering into the back for help. A short man with pit stains and two large moles on his face appeared and started shoveling out the ice cream with the strength of a construction worker. The four buckets were placed on the counter. The ice crystals sparkled like daylight stars before the woman flung some rainbow sprinkles on and snapped the lids down shut.

"Forty ninety-five," she barked.

Paisley reached into one of her front pockets, muttering that she could never find her wallet when she needed it. The woman shifted around on her feet, her palm flat out for the money.

Paisley pulled out the Eclipse. "Ta-da!"

The woman froze.

"Beau, take the buckets."

I'd frozen, too. I couldn't get used to seeing her with that gun. It was pointed directly at the woman's chest.

"Nobody move!" Paisley ordered, sweeping the Eclipse around the whole place, back and forth like she was scattering sugar. "Nobody say anything or do anything."

A girl screamed at the window counter. A baby hollered. An old man gasped. One waiter sank to his knees. Some kids our age in a booth were recording it on cell phones. Another waiter approached us, and it looked for a second like he was gonna be the big hero and wrestle my sister to the ground. Paisley zoned in, and he stopped in his tracks.

"TAKE THE BUCKETS!" Paisley yelled. I grabbed hold of the plastic handles and fumbled around for the canvas totes I'd bought. The buckets just fit inside them, two apiece, but they were heavy. Seriously heavy.

"Done," I said, and backed out of there, pulling the door open and standing with my back to it to wait for Paisley.

She was doing her talk-to-the-camera bit and had a sticker at the ready. She ordered the woman to put her hand on the counter, and stuck it on top. Then she backed away, stopping to blow a kiss to the kids with the cell phones. They smiled in stunned awe.

"ANGELO!" the woman screamed.

"Okay, go, GO!" Paisley shouted, pushing me out and stuffing the sheet of stickers, minus one, inside her dress pocket. Outside and along the street we ran. I looked back. The short man with the moles was running after us, shouting, calling us names in Spanish and cursing. I heard *"Policia,"* and I picked up my pace, encumbered somewhat by all the bags.

Paisley stalled to take one of the totes from me, shoving the gun inside, and we started running again.

"Jeez, they're heavy."

"What did you expect?" I said, looking back for signs of Angelo. He was distant, but he was still in hot pursuit. "What the hell do we want with four gallons of ice cream? It's all gonna melt before we eat it."

"It's not about the ice cream, Einstein!" she yelled, overtaking me. The lid had come off one of the tubs in my tote, and ice cream was leaking through the fabric, streaming behind me in vanilla ribbons. We were headed back down the Strip toward our motel, crossing roads without warning, paying no heed to the cars that had to brake hard and honk at us, nor to the tourists we had to shove past, wetting their legs with our leaking bags. My chest heaved, my feet hammered the steaming concrete, my head ran with sweat, my mouth poured with *sorry*s and *excuse me*s.

Boomph!

I didn't see it until I was on the ground. Well, *we* were on the ground.

"Oh my God, Beau!" my sister laughed breathlessly as she U-turned and grabbed my arm to help me up. The giant red M&M lay there on the ground, its legs floundering. "Get up," she said, still laughing as she pulled on my arm. My legs were in shock; I couldn't stand up. People had gathered around. A blonde woman in a yellow M&M shirt came running out of the store to see what was happening. She bent down and put her hand on me, asking if I was okay.

"He's fine," Paisley chuckled as I finally got to my feet. "Come on."

"I'm sorry!" I yelled back, still grasping my bags of melted ice cream.

We had to get off the Strip. We were too conspicuous. Paisley found us a nice dirty side street to run down, which she swore would lead to the back of our motel if we followed it all the way to the end. We dragged our sorry asses down this street that the flashy Vegas hotels don't want the tourists to see. Broken glass, concrete blocks, cardboard boxes, and the odd mumbling drunk lined our route.

Paisley slowed to a walk. We had just about reached the back of our motel, and I stopped to bend over and relieve yet another stitch in my side. I wanted to throw up. I gagged a little, but there was nothing. So I just spat.

"That was a little close for comfort, sheesh!" she puffed, coming to a halt. "Reminded me of that part in Indiana Jones when he's got to grab his hat before the stone block comes down on his hand. If that Angelo had gotten *his* hands on you, you'd be toast, bro."

She threw her totes down by some trash cans and stepped up onto a pile of empty cardboard boxes to climb the wire fence.

I dropped my bags on the ground, too. "Paisley, that whole thing was shit."

She turned around, one leg on the top of the fence. "That whole thing was . . . fu-larious! That M&M did not see you coming."

"You're not listening to me. This ends now."

"What does?"

"This whole effed-up situation. You pulling guns on families. Kids. Old people."

"Not guns, Beau. *A* gun," she panted, straddling the fence and then jumping down to the other side. I scowled at her through the holes. "What's up with you?" she asked blankly. "You keep doing this brow thing. . . ."

"I'm pissed, Paisley. If you can't see that . . ."

"I told you what we were doing. I gave you an out; you didn't take it. You're in this up to your neck now."

"Not this. I didn't sign up for pointing guns at kids, Paisley."

"I didn't point it at the kids."

"No, you pointed it at their parents."

"But did you see those kids with their cell phones? We'll be all over YouTube this time tomorrow!"

"I don't care, all right? I don't fucking care."

I looked away from her. I'd heard a siren in the distance. I looked back. Paisley had barely raised her eyebrows. She turned and started walking across the lot to the motel. Then she stopped. She walked back to the fence. I hadn't moved.

"What, are you embarrassed because you tripped over an M&M?"

"No, I'm not."

"Then it's about that girl, isn't it? The redhead. You're pissed because you wanted to hook up with her and I wouldn't let you."

"I don't wanna talk about it."

"I think we've got to."

"Paisley . . ."

"Beau, she was a cooze. Let's leave it at that."

"Wha . . . ?" I couldn't see straight, I was so mad. "I just wanted . . ." I kicked the stack of boxes again and again until my foot went straight through the side of one.

Her eyebrows arched up. "All better now?"

I pouted. "Leave me alone."

She hesitated, then came closer to the fence. "No."

I didn't know what to say. I was just grabbing at words as they came to me.

"I just . . . It's so damn . . . All you can think about is Dad, Dad, Dad. Finding Dad. Gotta get to Dad. Even if it means we terrorize people. Steal their stuff. I hate it. I hate this."

"There's no alternative."

"Yeah, you made that pretty clear."

Paisley sighed, scuffing the broken glass and crumbs of concrete at her feet. "Don't you wanna find him?"

I didn't answer. I thought about the redhead. "I didn't sign up for this. . . ."

She scratched her head and laughed. "Why did you come with me, Beau? You thought about that? What was the alternative? Staying in LA as Grandma's little house elf? Getting beat up by kids at school? Shutting yourself in your room, reading weird French books and writing poetry? Hiding away?"

"Well, you pretty much burned all those bridges for me anyway!"

"You could've gone off on your own. I didn't force you. You willingly came along with me."

"Yeah, more fool I."

"Beau . . ."

"I just wanna be normal, Paisley. I want . . . a girlfriend. I want to go to a good college. Study. It's all I've ever wanted. Just . . . simplicity."

"Yeah, well you're shit outta luck, 'cause you're my twin and I hate simplicity."

I backed away from the fence and folded my arms.

Paisley hooked her fingers through the wire diamonds of the fence. "If you had gone over to that redhead, she would've ignored you, laughed at you to her friends, and you would've walked away feeling like the biggest loser in the world. She was a butter face anyway."

"A what?"

"You know. Okay body, but her face . . ."

"Seriously, Paisley . . ."

She pressed her forehead against the wires. "Maybe General Custard's will make the news and we won't have to do any more stings. We can get on that screen and Dad'll see us and somehow we'll get to him."

"How? How are we gonna get to him? All right, so he might see us. What then, huh? What do we do then?"

"He'll know we love him. . . ."

"SO?" I shouted. I didn't mean to. It just came out. "He won't know where we are, and we'll be on the run. The longer we keep doing this, the more people who'll be after us. We'll have to leave. Go on the road. And we'll never find him."

"I have to let him know that we still care," she said, her finger going around and around inside one of the wire holes in the fence.

I thought about Dad's letter. The one I kept in my back pocket.

Beau, I still think of you as this quiet little boy.
You're probably totally different now. I'd give
everything just to see your face. Just to know how
school's going. I remember you were so good at
reading, even at five years old, and I wonder if you
ever tried out for Little League. You were a great little
pitcher! I think you took after me. Your brown eyes and
dark hair. It's the Italian in us Argents, or "Argentos,"
as we were known once upon a time. Paisley takes

after your mom's side—blue eyes, blonde. We had the
best of both worlds with you two . . .

"All right, so it's a shitty plan," Paisley was saying. "But it's the
only one we've got. And when we get on TV, then it'll be over. We
can go out somewhere and celebrate. Whatever you want. Make
some friends."

I couldn't help smiling. The idea of Paisley making friends was
just funny. I tried not looking at her, but it didn't help.

"What's so fu-larious?" she said, all offended, pulling back
from the fence. A little wishbone-shaped crease appeared between
her eyes.

"Nothing," I said, stacking the boxes again to climb over the
fence. It took me a while. I wasn't as nimble as my sister, and I was
struggling. She offered to help me down, but I didn't let her.

She stood there, one hand resting in the front pocket of her
dress. "Still best sister?" she said. We always argued the same way.
Like a mini volcano going off and then nothing, nothing but ashes.
She never apologized, just always said that. *Still best sister?*

"I guess," I said to her, keeping a little distance.

PAISLEY

SEVENTEEN

THE SHOPPES AT MANDALAY PLACE,
SOUTH END OF THE STRIP,
LAS VEGAS, NEVADA

Our next week in Vegas was hard and fast. It had to be. If all went according to plan, our black-and-white uniforms would soon have us sticking out like two zebras trying to get into a parrots-only party, so the idea was to do as many holdups as possible, then ditch our outfits. We bought another week at the Lucky Inn and mapped it all out.

And then we just did it.

We hit the Chronic Chocolate Company, Jellies from Heaven, a couple of chichi cupcake places, Cookie Lookin', a churro stand, and another ice cream parlor, all on different blocks jutting off the Strip. We'd do one a day, and when we were done we'd head back to our motel the long way around, through the back alleys, and lay low until the next morning. We steered clear of all the obvious places, like M&M's World and Krispy Kreme, figuring they'd have super-duper alarm systems and automatic door locks, and only did one store on the whole Strip—Mandie's Candies in the Mandalay Bay mall.

The joint looked like Candy Land on acid. Fluorescent pink throughout, it had this annoying little squirrel mascot everywhere with speech bubbles coming out of its mouth saying stuff like, *Try 'em, you'll like 'em!* and *Don't forget to brush your teeth!* The store was near the back entrance to the complex, and the nearest security guard was stationed at the far end of the neighboring casino, so by the time whoever was on staff had rung the alarm, we'd be long gone. It was an easy raid.

Claire the Candy Girl was pink, too, and sweet-natured, and helpful, and the store was empty, probably because it was eight thirty in the morning.

She got all upset when she saw the Eclipse, so I tried to make her feel at ease, I really did. "My, that fudge smells yummy. Can I get a bag of that, too? Fresh, though. Don't try to stick me with yesterday's leftovers."

She helped us shovel little white bags full of chocolate-covered peanuts, raisins, and raspberries; Jujubes; Lemonheads; Laffy Taffy; Tootsie Rolls; Mike and Ikes; Rainbow Twizzlers; Dum Dum Pops; soft chunks of rum fudge and caramel squares. We got Pixy Stix in cherry, grape, and orange; Swedish Fish; gummy worms, gummy cola bottles, and gummy bears that looked like little rubber jewels; wax lips, Gobstoppers; Pop Rocks; bubble gum. We got fun-size Kit Kats, Snickers, Milky Ways, Butterfingers, Reese's Peanut Butter Cups, Peppermint Patties. Licorice shoelaces in black, green, and yellow. Containers of flavored hot chocolate mix labeled *The Best in the West*, and for good measure sweet Claire even threw in a couple of T-shirts saying *Mandie's Candies*. Pink for me, blue for Beau. Guess what, Beau didn't want one. I stuffed it down his rock n' roll tote bag anyway.

"It's free, Beau, just take it," I told him.

"Yeah, except it's not really."

As Claire was putting all the little white bags into two big white bags, a tear fell from her eye and splash-landed on the counter.

Beau headed for the door.

I leaned in. "I'm not gonna hurt you," I told the girl. "You're doing great. Would you like a sticker?"

She looked at me, then nodded. I told her to put her hand out, and pasted it down on top. "There," I said. "Tell Buddy we love him." She gave me the customary look of confusion, and I followed Beau out of there with the bags.

On our way out the back entrance, we bumped right into this shock-headed rock dude in shades. I dropped one of the candy bags.

"Sorry," he said, scratching his head behind his ear. I thought I recognized him. I think he was famous. He had on a sleeveless vest, and there was a really cool tattoo of a burning rose on his shoulder. It reminded me of the rose tattoo mom had on her ankle.

He picked up the candy bag I'd dropped and handed it back to me. I didn't feel like being nice.

"Get a guide dog!" I snapped at him, pushing past. I didn't even hear Beau apologizing on my behalf like he usually did. I don't think he said one word.

I felt bad then, and I didn't know why. I'd been in a pretty good mood while we were robbing the crap out of that candy store. But now I felt all at sea again, and that ain't easy when you're in the middle of the desert.

It was the final day of our planned heists. Outside Sin City Bakes, west of the Mandalay resort down Ali Baba Lane, I had another flashback, like the one I had about Dad when I smelled the cologne. This time it was about Mom. The front of the cake shop was full of the most unreal specimens I'd ever seen. A three-layered carrot cake with tiny little frosted carrots dancing in a chorus line all around the edges. Huge chocolate cream cakes with roulette wheels made out of spun sugar on top. Sparkling fruit pies, their lattice crusts cut to form the shapes of diamonds, spades, clubs, and hearts. Someone had worked damn hard on making every single one just perfect. And in the back was the wedding cake section. A "Love Me Tender" special with an Elvis statuette on top, standing with a prayer book before a little plastic bride and groom. Another cake, designed like two big red dice, had *Take a chance on me!* written across the top in swirly icing. Others were made to look like huge poker chips or horseshoes. One like a cowboy hat, another like the MGM gold lion.

The cake I zoomed in on was at the bottom of the window in the corner. It was on sale, I guess because it wasn't as popular as Elvis: a one-tiered angel-food cake with pink frosting, covered in tiny marzipan strawberries.

It was our sixth birthday, one of the few days I remember our mom being our mom, not just some psycho drunk woman—at least at the start. Mrs. Wong's kids came over, and so did some other randoms from school. Dad wasn't there, so Mom was in charge. She managed to make us peanut butter and jelly sandwiches like we'd asked, and she even baked a cake. We helped her frost it, and put on the letters that spelled our names, and stick a big "6" candle right in the middle.

Me and Beau played in the backyard with our friends, wearing our Princess Leia and Luke Skywalker costumes, and we looked supercute. There was a photograph of us dressed like this somewhere, but I guess all that stuff got left behind at the Jersey house. Mom had tried doing the Leia buns in my hair, but she couldn't get them to stay put so I just had pigtails instead. We got some really cool presents from our friends. Beau got a microscope, and I got this Barbie hair accessory kit with a mini hair dryer and stuff, and a Moo Box that made everyone laugh when I kept turning it over — the way kids do, taking a good joke and stoning it to death. I ran inside to show Mom.

She was in front of the open drapes in the living room, head back, downing the dregs of a glass. She poured herself another. The banner above the door frame had come down at one end.

"You two opened your presents already?"

I nodded.

She went over to the mantel and put down the glass. "What'd you get?"

"Barbie hair stuff. And this . . ." I tipped the box upside down and it made the moo noise. Mom didn't laugh. She just nodded and picked up the glass.

"And Mikey got Beau a detective kit with an invisible ink pen. . . ."

"Go cut the cake now," she said, looking at me over the top of her glass.

"Dad says we're not allowed to touch the knife drawer."

"Dad's . . . not . . . here . . . is . . . he?" She said it very slowly.

I hesitated. I shouldn't have, because she started yelling.

"JUST GO AND CUT YOUR GODDAMN CAKE!"

I ran into the kitchen. The back door was open. Everyone was gathered under the tree, around Beau's microscope. I went to the knife drawer and took out the largest one I could find. My hands were shaking so much I had to use both to hold it. I cut everyone a raggedy little sliver and set them down on seven paper plates.

I cried when our friends went home. I get the same feeling every birthday.

"So are we doing this place today, too, or what?" said Beau from the doorway, where he was putting on his sunglasses.

"No," I said. "I don't wanna do any more today." And I started walking back down Ali Baba Lane. It was hot. Damn hot and damn dirty. Flyers and candy wrappers clung to the soles of my shoes as I walked. About a block down was a thrift shop, and we took the bags of candy and chocolate in there and dumped them down on the counter. The place was big and jumbled, like a garage sale, but gray and stinking of moldy vegetables. I held my sleeve up to my nose and breathed in the almost-Dad scent I'd sprayed there.

We approached the desk. "Can you take these to some homeless shelter, please?"

"Sure," said the little hobbit guy, standing on tiptoe to peer inside the bags. "Ooh, candy. All this? Thank you."

He'd lucked out. *He'll be dipping into that candy the second we leave the store,* I thought.

Beau piped up. "Is the homeless shelter nearby?"

"Yeah, there's one not too far from here. Between Paradise and Pebble. Would you like it all to go there?"

"Uh, yeah," Beau said. And I could see the cogs whirring behind his eyes. "You know what, we'll take it ourselves, if that's okay."

"Oh, well, if you're sure. . . ."

"Yeah. Thanks anyway."

On the way out, Beau was suddenly Beau again. After days of pissing and moaning over the robberies, he was almost giddy.

"This feels good, Pais. This actually feels like a lead. There's a shelter less than a mile away from where we saw Dad. He could easily be there."

"He's not there, Beau, I'm telling you. He wouldn't be." I rummaged around in the Mandie's Candies bag for a Dum Dum Pop and pulled off the wrapper. Lemon.

Beau put his arm around me and squeezed, like that would inject me with some of his glee. I'd gone all emo since since my birthday cake flashback at the bakery. I didn't miss Mom; it wasn't that. But that night, our birthday night, Dad had come home after work, and he took us out for pancakes and we played kickball in the street. And it made everything okay again. That's why I'd forgotten Mom's outburst; Dad made me forget it. He was like magic. The thought of finding him in some homeless shelter with all these rejects was disgusting. But the thought of *not* finding him there made everything feel so much worse.

It was a long walk to the shelter, but I knew we were getting closer to it because there were progressively less and less tourists and more and more homeless people. Men bundled in blankets lying in doorways. A guy with no legs lying on the sidewalk by an upturned wheelchair. Some crackhead having a fight with an invisible man in an alley, screaming at the top of his lungs. He was a kid, the crackhead. About our age.

Typically grim and grimy, the entrance to the shelter looked like the box office of an old movie theater. A woman in a Plexiglas booth was reading *People* magazine, all dolled up like she was Cinderella in some shitty-assed pumpkin carriage. She looked up. She had large eyes and even larger eyelids to cover them, caked in glossy purple eye shadow.

"Women's check-in is at four forty-five; men's at six o'clock," she drawled. I took it she thought we were checking in.

"No, we're here to donate some candy," Beau said, holding up one of the bags to show her. He was sucking on a Dum Dum Pop, too. He'd gone for strawberry. "And we're looking for somebody. Our dad. He might be here."

"You don't want beds? If you just want a meal, dinner's served at seven. . . ."

I pulled out my Dum Dum Pop. "No, we don't want beds, or dinner. We just wanna make a donation and see if our dad's here."

"You can't just go in, miss. Women's check-in is at . . ."

I scowled at her and nudged my brother to the side so I could speak through the hole in the Plexiglas. "Four forty-five, yeah, you already said so. I don't *want* to stay here. I *have* a bed for the night." I breathed out, trying to get rid of the poisonous anger that was building up in my lungs. I tried again. I even tried smiling. "Do you have a list of inmates or whatever you call 'em? Could you just look up a name? Please?"

Beau nudged me back and leaned in to speak.

"His name's Buddy Argent. He might be under Michael Argent, though. If we could find him, you wouldn't need to put him up. We'd take him off your hands."

He smiled all genuinely at old Purple Eyelids, which actually stirred her into action. She started tapping on her keyboard and hit the space bar, looking briefly again at Beau. I watched him. There was a small but definite bat of eyelashes. He was playing her like a piano. I'd created a monster. But it was working.

"Yeah, here you go, Buddy Argent. Bed thirty-seven."

Beau looked at me. I looked at Beau.

"Oh. My. God." We both stood there, white sticks in our mouths, mirror images of each other. *Suck on that.*

Purple Eyelids swiveled her chair around and produced a long chain from her pocket. One end of the chain was tied to her belt; there were keys on the other. She found the right one to unlock her little booth. She didn't even say thanks for the candy, just shoved it inside and locked the booth up again.

"Follow me."

She took us through these double doors into what looked like a high school gymnasium, littered with metal-framed beds. On the bars at the end of each bed dangled collections of cherry and vanilla Magic Trees. They didn't make the place smell any better. It just smelled like cherry-flavored ass crack. Grizzled men in baggy sweats on stained mattresses looked up at us briefly before going back to sleeping, scratching, playing cards, talking with each other, talking to themselves. I saw torn football jerseys, T-shirts, patchwork blankets. One old guy in a Red Sox cap was puking into a blue bag. I looked for the red shirt. I didn't dare get too excited. I'd been there before, preparing myself the whole way from LA to Las Vegas. I kept hope at bay, pushing it off me like a puppy who just wanted to lick my face.

The beds weren't numbered, so I don't know how she knew where bed thirty-seven was, but soon she brought us to it. On the far side, next to a door marked WOMEN'S/FAMILY ROOMS, she came to a stop. A man was lying curled up with his back to us, like a big baby, wrapped in a muddy gray raincoat.

"Hey, number thirty-seven, wake up," said Purple Eyelids, kicking the metal leg of the bed.

The man turned over and saw her. Then he saw us. It wasn't Dad. I threw my Dum Dum stick on the floor.

"I'll give you a couple of minutes," she said, smiling at Beau and leaving.

The man was wearing a green baseball cap, and he turned it around backward. "Who're you?" he garbled, still half asleep.

"We're Buddy Argent's kids," said Beau. "And you're not Buddy Argent."

I was still slaloming down Mount Disappointment. I knew who the guy was, though. It was Coupon Guy from the day we saw Dad at the Deuce stop. I remembered the gruff voice and the stitched-up eye.

Coupon Guy sat up on his bed. He was fat for a bum. He had a real-assed belly on him. I kicked at the brown paper bag placed down by his bed. There was a stack of those coupon books behind it.

He leaned up on one elbow. "Lookin' for Buddy, princess?"

"Yeah, what have you done with him?" I said, all annoyed and foot-stampy, like he'd hidden my teddy bear and I wanted it back.

"I ain't done nuthin' with him, princess. I was just borrowin' his name."

"Why couldn't you use your own name?" asked Beau.

"'Cause I done that once before in here, and they threw my ass out."

"Why?"

He tapped his nose as if to say, *That's for me to know.* "What do you kids want, anyway?"

"What do you think we want? We want our dad!" I yelled in his face. Beau stepped in and held me back. My hand went to the Eclipse tucked safely in my dress. Beau's hand went on top of mine to stop me.

"Then I can't help you. I ain't him." He grinned. Across the far side of the room, there was a clanging of metal. "Now, if you don't mind, I'm gonna wash up for dinner." He started to untie the luggage straps that were holding up his pants. "Unless there was something else . . . ?"

"Do you know where he is?" said Beau. "It's important. . . ."

"I might," he said, getting up. He was about two feet taller than us and that gigantic gut deserved its own zip code.

"Forget it, Beau. I don't want this mooch's help," I said, turning to leave.

My brother grabbed my arm, force-whispering, "Paisley, he knows Dad. We can find out where he is, get a message to him. We need this guy. He's our best bet."

I shook him off.

Beau looked back to Coupon Guy and attempted a smile. "If you could tell us where he is or how we could reach him, we'd be grateful."

"How grateful?" He stroked his chin and pulled at the spiky hairs.

Beau shrugged. "I don't know. What do you want?"

Coupon Guy looked at me with his one good eye. Then he looked back at Beau and scratched his chin. "Oh, I don't know. Some dead presidents maybe?"

Beau nodded. "We have a little money. We could buy you dinner; you could tell us what you know."

Coupon thought for a second. Then he tied up his pants again and buttoned his coat. He smelled so strong of so much stuff. Cigarettes, gasoline, cabbage, whiskey, piss. If I'd had a lit match, I would've thrown it at him and done everyone else in the place a favor.

"Money, dinner, and I'll tell you where you can find him."

Beau nodded. He picked my Dum Dum stick off the floor and put it with his, tossing them into a nearby bucket that served as a trash can. "Cool. What's your name?"

"Well, my name's Trenton. Trenton Anthony Ford. And you are?"

"Beau Argent. And this is my sister, Paisley," he said.

Trenton's eye zoomed in on me. I could feel my nose twitch up in a sneer. "Well, Paisley and Beau," he said, picking up his brown paper bag, "buy me dinner, I'll tell you what I know."

We went to this yellow diner a little farther up homeless avenue and Beau got the Early Nerd special: a hot pastrami sandwich with Swiss cheese and a chocolate shake. Trenton ordered a double short stack with bacon, eggs, sausage patties, syrup, and whipped butter. I had to sit directly across from his saggy old bunghole, so I just ordered a coffee.

"What's Dad doing now?" Beau asked. I kept my mouth shut for once as he asked Trenton all the questions. They got along like my grandmother's house on fire. But my top lip kept doing this little Elvis thing whenever Trenton's eye caught mine. I sat with my arms folded, leaning against the back of the booth, my stomach churning at his table etiquette.

He had egg hanging from his chin. "We hang out. Shoot the shit." Every time he said an *s* word, he sprayed pancake crumbs across the table.

Beau nodded in understanding. He had eaten half his sandwich and pushed the plate over to me as a hint that I should eat something, too. I pushed it back. He hunched over his shake and started popping bubbles on the top. "How'd you end up on the streets, Trenton?"

His brown paper bag was on the floor under the table, out of the way. I wanted to know what was in it.

"Little woman kicked me out. I fooled around and got caught. You know how it is."

"Did Dad talk about us?"

"Oh yeah. All the time. Talked about you two and your mom. Said you were the most 'portant things in the world to him. I saw him a couple of days ago."

"Yeah," I said, slowly pulling the bag toward me with both feet. "We saw him from the bus. You were giving him shit, and he took off. We couldn't catch up with him."

"Do you know where he went?" Beau asked.

Trenton shrugged. "He's around. Doesn't come in the shelter. Doesn't think he deserves to."

That was so something Dad would say. He'd much rather live out in the open and sleep on park benches than admit he was destitute and go to a shelter. I bent forward, feeling around for the bag.

Trenton continued eating his pancakes. I hadn't touched Beau's sandwich or my coffee.

"More coffee?" asked the waitress, appearing with a pot full of it. I looked at my cup and then at her. She just waited.

"I'm good. Thanks!" I said at last. Duh. She had a lot to learn if she thought I was gonna leave a tip for a lukewarm mug of grounds.

I continued with my undercover bag-opening attempts. Trenton was more focused on his plate.

I looked down. The bag was open. I couldn't see much. Something white. Something silver. Candy wrappers. A beer bottle. A lighter. A roll of quarters. A roll of yellow police tape. Daredevil action figure still in the packaging. Something silver.

He was still talking to Beau. ". . . shit outta luck," I heard him say. "No one's gonna hire an ex-con with no fixed address, are they?"

I reached down into the bag. Tentatively at first, and then I had my fingers on it. I pulled it up, like a little crane pulling up a wreck from the ocean floor.

It was my mom's necklace.

I would know it in a mountain of jewelry. I used to play with it when she was unconscious. I remembered not being able to open the clasp. I held it tight in my fist.

I pushed the bag back slowly across the floor.

". . . my bet is he's still hanging around Caesars trying to get work."

I flashed back to last week. Coupon Guy and Dad arguing at the bus stop. He'd robbed him. He'd robbed my dad. That's why Dad wasn't coming back to the Jumbotron. Trenton had told him to stay away from his turf.

I leaned forward, my eyes so sore it felt like they were being scored by a steak knife. "Did he talk about our mom?" I interrupted.

"Yeah," he said. "Just how much he missed her and still wanted her back."

"He seen her recently?" I said

Beau looked at me. Trenton shook his head, slurping up a dangling, chewed lump of sausage. "He wanted to get back in touch with her, though. Thought they could give it another shot. For you two . . ."

I dipped my head and thought. I came back up. "Did he say why he left us?"

Trenton shoveled another heaped fork into his face, probably to buy him enough time to think up another lie. Then he just said, "Sometimes dads just leave . . ."

I smiled, though I felt tears finally falling from my eyes. I couldn't hold them in anymore. Everyone has a limit. This was mine. This was definitely mine.

"Kiss me, Trenton," I said.

"Huh?"

"Kiss me. I like to be kissed when I'm being fucked."

Trenton looked at me. My bullshit shield was tingling all over. I shot up out of the booth and lunged at him.

"YOU FUCKIN' LIAR!" I shouted right in his ear, plunging

his head down into his butter-soaked pancakes. "You evil . . . fucking . . . leech!" And with every syllable I dunked him again. And again. "How d'you like me now, 'princess'?" I shouted, and each time I pulled his head up, there was more crap stuck to it.

It took every muscle Beau had to pull me off of him, then I marched out of there, the heat of the day bombarding my face after the air-conditioned coolness of the diner. I left Beau trying to stem the waitress's concerns and probably leaving twice what our bill came to. I kept walking, right to the end of the block, taking insanely deep breaths the whole way. The tears kept coming and coming and coming.

I soon heard quick footsteps running up behind me.

"PAISLEY!"

"Fucker!" I shouted. "I should have choked him. BASTARD!" I shouted back up the street. "God, why are people such assholes, huh? Why, Beau? Why do we keep getting dicked at every single turn?"

"All right, calm down. It's okay . . ."

I stopped. "He doesn't know Dad any more than he knows Mom. Didn't even know Dad was in jail." I shook my fist. "And he obviously didn't know the truth about this."

Beau looked at me, grabbed hold of my hand, then gently pried open each one of my fingers and lifted up the necklace. The chain tickled my palm as it went.

"Where did you get this?"

"From his bag. It's the necklace from Dad's letter. It's Mom's necklace."

Beau's eyes were going all soft, and he started leaking tears, too.

"I always thought it opened. I can't open it. Stupid fingers."
I wiped my cheek.

"Uh . . . I think you gotta slide it," he sniffed, fumbling and
rubbing the locket until unexpectedly it split open into two, like
scissors' blades. Two little sections. A little child's face in each
one: Beau one side; me, the other. Both grinning to show the little
gaps in our top teeth.

"That was Dad's fault." Beau smiled, his tears trickling down
over his lips as he spoke. "Too much candy."

Another memory flashed into my mind. Of me, tugging and
twisting at that tooth and getting all covered in blood and spit.
And of Dad, holding my head and reaching in to pinch it straight out
with his finger and thumb

And of the dollar Mom put under my pillow that night.

I leaned over to Beau and put my head against his, and we looked
down at the locket in his hands. And we both just cried and cried.

BEAU

EIGHTEEN

ROOM 2, LUCKY INN MOTEL,
THE STRIP,
LAS VEGAS, NEVADA

We went back to our motel. Neither of us wanted to do anything else. Paisley threw up. I didn't know if it was all the candy we'd been living on or the shock of finding Mom's necklace. Probably both. I was feeling a little sick myself. Our room looking like the refuse pile from Wonka's factory wasn't helping, either.

After I'd passed it back to her, Paisley hadn't once let go of Mom's necklace. The chain was coiled around her hand, the pendant gripped tightly in her palm. She came out of the bathroom and we lay on my bed with the bottle of cologne Paisley had picked up at the mall. She swore it smelled like Dad. We sat our stuffed toy owls, Two Wit and Two Woo, between us. We talked into the night about everything. Stuff we didn't usually like talking about. The times O'Donnell and his gang had kicked the shit out of me at school. This Jason guy at Paisley's school in Jersey, whom she said meant nothing to her but who I could tell had broken her heart. Well, maybe not her whole heart, but he'd definitely bitten a chunk out of it.

I guess unless you knew Paisley really well, it was hard to tell when she was hurt. She buried stuff kind of deep down and pretended it didn't matter. But I knew. It could just be a look, a shrug, a fake smile. But I could see it. She talked about her counseling sessions. And I told her what had *really* been bothering me about the robberies—it was starting to feel like we were little again. Like we were in kindergarten or something. It was just like in that song from the dance machine.

And I wonder
When I sing along with you
If everything could ever feel this real forever
If anything could ever be this good again.

I was beginning to enjoy myself.

I couldn't hold the gun without shaking, and I couldn't demand money from store clerks. But just watching my sister, yelling at her to run, us fleeing each scene, pushing past tourists and vaulting over chain-link fences to race back to the motel and eat candy on our beds. Even falling over that damned M&M. I felt part of something exciting again. I felt like I was a kid again.

"You better hope me and this O'Donnell guy at your school never cross paths. Because if we do, I'll probably kill him."

"Yeah. And I'll probably let you."

We talked about being lost in the woods when we were six.

"I don't remember much about it," I said. "Do you?"

Paisley was staring up at the ceiling, chewing on some blueberry gum she'd pocketed from the Mandie's Candies heist, the chain of the necklace wrapped around her fist. "Bits and pieces. Waking up and just seeing leaves. All these leaves. Trying to find open sunlight. And this really tall tree that I couldn't see the top of. I remember going to pee behind it, and when I got back you were crying 'cause you thought I'd gone somewhere without you."

I laughed. "Yeah. Always the wuss."

"No. You were a kid. We were both scared."

"I don't remember you being scared."

She looked at me and stopped chewing her gum. "Yeah. You know me. Wouldn't give a fuck if I had a bag full of 'em."

I looked at her. She had the oddest twinkle in her eyes.

She looked back up at the ceiling. "I remember finding the Wonder Gummies in my coat pocket. We ate them that second morning. And I remember just walking and walking and my legs aching 'cause we never got anywhere. And just being so tired. But I knew we had to find Dad. And that if we found him, we'd be heroes. We'd find Dad, and he'd save Mom, and everybody would love us."

"You really thought we'd be heroes?"

She nodded. "The third night I gave up. You had fallen asleep, but I was wide-awake, by myself. I snuggled up to you in this little burrow I'd made out of twigs and stuff, and I just drifted off. We must have kept each other warm."

"Just like Hansel and Gretel," I said. "Except now we're leaving a trail of stickers, not bread crumbs."

"I guess."

"I don't remember being found at all."

"You were pretty out of it," she said, levering herself up and hawking her gum toward the little trash can across the room. Amazingly, it went in. She took another piece from the nightstand and began devouring it. "I remember opening my eyes and seeing this giant above me with the longest legs, that stretched up and up into the trees. I thought it was Dad at first. But he said, 'My name's Officer Worley. You two are gonna be all right.'"

"What happened then?"

"These two women cops got us orange juice that tasted like warm medicine, but it was the best drink I ever had in my life. Then we were put in the ambulance. They were saying all this stuff like, 'Oh my God, I can't believe we found you,' and 'You two are all over the news. Everyone's so happy you kids are okay.' I just remember wanting Dad. And him not being there."

She took the top off the cologne and sprayed a little into the air. She sniffed and put the top back on.

"If he hadn't been in jail, he would have been at the country club. You were right to go there, Pais."

Paisley held out Two Woo to kiss Two Wit.

"You know what I finally realized?" I said.

"What?"

"You remember when Dad would take us into the city? And we'd go to The Roosevelt and we'd play with Eddie and go up the stairs and eat candy and stuff . . . ?"

"Yeah," she said softly.

"They were casing the joint. Him and Eddie. And those two other guys."

Paisley sat up and hugged her knees to her chin. I thought she was gonna call me a douche for even considering such a thought. But she bit her bottom lip, then said, "I try not to think about it. I always tried to believe he took us there 'cause he wanted to show us the places he worked. He did it for us, though, Beau. To get money for us."

"Always sticking up for him." I smiled.

She smiled back. "Like he was sticking up for us," she said, then blew out her cheeks and spat her gum in the direction of the trash can again. This time it missed.

"Great," I said. "I'll be picking that one out of my socks all day tomorrow."

She chuckled. "So did Hansel and Gretel make it back to their dad?"

"Um, yeah. In some versions they just find their way outta the woods and make it home. Others, they have to cross a river on a white duck."

"A white duck, huh?"

"Yeah. A white duck carries them across the water on its back."

"How come you know the different versions?" Paisley said, lying back down.

"I read 'em all. I went through a little phase of being kinda obsessed with it. I thought it was us. Because it was. We are those kids in that story. . . ."

"Tell me it," she said, closing her eyes. "Especially the part when Gretel pushes the witch in the oven. I wanna think happy thoughts."

And as I told my sister the tale of Hansel and Gretel, the stress went out of her limbs and the wishbone crease in her forehead disappeared and she became heavy beside me. This time it was me who couldn't switch off my brain as easily. I stared at the walls for a while before carefully reaching out to the nightstand for the remote. I pressed POWER.

Someone was being sexy and dramatic and probably a vampire on The CW. On the History Channel it was the biography of some saint. Discovery was in the ocean. Disney was something colorful and unfunny set in a diner. On HBO some faux-hawked rock band was screeching live from Mandalay Bay. The nightly news was just starting on ABC, CBS, and NBC. Breaking news on CNN was the president's meeting with the latest British prime minister. I clicked to Fox. Two old guys debating: One of them loved it; the other thought it "deplorable and dangerous."

I switched to *Fairly OddParents* on Nickelodeon. Paisley stirred and propped herself up on her elbows.

"What time is it?" she garbled, rubbing her eyes.

"Almost seven. Wanna go get something to eat?"

She nodded, a little blonde firework party dancing on the back of her head. "I need to take a shower first."

The bathroom door closed. I sat up and reached for the half-bottle of blue Gatorade that had been on my nightstand for a few days. I winced at the warm syrup as it trickled into my mouth. I twisted the lid back on and threw the bottle over to the trash can under the desk. It missed. I lay back again, feeling my eyes go heavy. I heard the water go on. I turned over on my side and shut my eyes, my ass pressing down on the remote. *OddParents* turned into the news. It got louder, too, and before I could find the remote to turn it off, I heard . . .

"*. . . Police still don't know who the duo might be or how old they are. They say they could be anywhere from sixteen to twenty-four. The pair are shown here on a surveillance tape holding up a Las Vegas candy store. . . .*"

That's when I looked up.

"*. . . known only by their code name, the Wonder Twins . . .*"

"HOLY SHIT."

"*. . . fansites have already been launched in their honor, all trying to decipher their curious message, 'Tell Buddy we love him.' Anyone with any information is being urged to contact the Las Vegas Police Department at the following number . . .*"

Paisley came running out of the bathroom, all sudsy and wrapped in a bath towel, stinking of vanilla. "What the hell . . . ?"

I pointed at the screen like an idiot, jumping up and down on my knees, barely able to get the words out. "It's us. It's us; we're on TV. We're on ABC!"

"You have GOT to be kidding me!" she yelled. "Oh my God!"

The next news story was about premature babies.

"Try another station," she said. I hopped through the news

channels. The mortgage crisis. Afghanistan. The World Series. Promising cancer research. Iraq. And then . . .

". . . *though it is still unknown why this M&M representative was knocked to the ground in such an unprovoked attack. . . ."*

"Oh my God, Beau! That's the M&M you floored! He's being interviewed on CNN! We did that; we made that M&M famous!"

". . . *Welcome back to Headline News. Police in Las Vegas are investigating a series of robberies of donut shops and candy stores . . ."*

"WHOA!" squealed Paisley, jumping on the bed. I turned up the volume.

". . . *The duo, known as the Wonder Twins by the strange calling card they present at every crime scene, have been caught on security cameras in stores along the Las Vegas Strip. Holding this sales assistant hostage at the Chronic Chocolate Company, the female of the duo is heard shouting the words, 'Tell Buddy we love him,' before applying a Wonder Twins sticker to the assistant's hand. The duo leaves every scene with ice cream, cookies, or candies before disappearing. They're believed to still be at large in Las Vegas, and between sixteen and twenty-four years old. The public is warned not to approach either member, they are armed and dangerous, but if you see them, contact Las Vegas Police at this number . . ."*

"I can't believe it," I said. "I just can't believe it!"

No other channel was carrying our story, or if they were, we had missed it. Two of the biggest national news shows were, though. NATIONAL news!

"Okay. Okay," I said, pacing the floor, trying to be decisive but having absolutely no idea what to do. I stopped and bit my nail. "What do we do, Pais?"

She was staring blindly at the TV screen, a little in a daze. "I need to rinse my hair, get dressed." She snapped out of it. "We gotta get down to the Jumbotron. See if he's there. See if he's seen it!"

I could feel my face fall. Of course: Dad. He was the reason we were doing this. Not just to get on TV, to find him. Didn't I want to find him? Yeah, of course I did. I think. I liked it being just us for a while, together again, no friends or grandmothers or schools getting in the way. I didn't know what I wanted. It felt good to be on the news, though. Really good. I looked cool in my shades, in my suit. I looked good.

We couldn't wear our uniforms to go down to Caesars. Now that we'd made the news, we had to go incognito in case any cops were around. Paisley suggested we wear jeans and our Maudie's Candies T-shirts instead. I said this was kinda like advertising our crimes, but she wanted us to look the same, and I didn't argue anymore.

A lot of people were milling around under the Jumbotron, waiting for the bus, coming back from the volcano or the pirate battle, or heading to the Bellagio for the eight o'clock dancing fountains. Buying bottled water or monorail tickets.

We looked and we looked and we waited, but Dad didn't show up.

The news was still on, and we sat on a bench for a while watching it. It wasn't the same footage as before. This time, they named us.

". . . This just in on the breaking story of the duo dubbed the Wonder Twins, caught on security cameras holding up candy stores and ice cream parlors in the Las Vegas area over the last two weeks. We can now confirm that these two candy bandits are none other than twins Beau and Paisley Argent, who some viewers may recognize as the Wonder Twins who first made headlines ten years ago when . . ."

"'Candy bandits,' yeah, I like that," my sister repeated, grinning.

"They know who we are now," I said. "They'll know all about us."

They were talking about Virginia.

". . . The twins' grandmother, award-winning soap opera actress Virginia Creed, identified them from security camera footage. She also verified that the 'Buddy' the teen robbers refer to is their father, Buddy Argent, who has been in prison since the twins were six years old. In a further twist to the story, Mrs. Creed claims the twins stole one thousand dollars from her before setting fire to her house and also stealing her car. . . ."

"She gave us that money!" I practically shouted, forgetting for a moment that we were surrounded by hundreds of tourists.

"God, when's she gonna fuckin' flatline?" Paisley muttered. Then she chuckled. "She must be so jealous. We're more famous now than she ever was. She's gonna pin everything on us so the cops ratchet up the charges. Any unsolved murders in Vegas recently?"

That was like asking if the sky was blue. I turned back to the Jumbotron.

Virginia appeared on screen. The news crew was filming her back at the charred remains of her house. She was trawling through the wreckage.

". . . I brought them up. I gave them a good home and love and care . . ."

"Liar," said Paisley.

". . . and this is the thanks I got." She started to cry. *"Now I'm living in a motel with my partner, Matthew."* Matt appeared stage left. He held her hand and rubbed it.

"'My partner, Matthew'?" Paisley parroted. "And here I thought they just hooked up in her pool house. I didn't realize they were *partners.*"

". . . They've stolen my money, ruined my life. I don't know why. I think they've gone completely crazy. So many teenagers do nowadays." She looked into the camera. *"It's not surprising. I don't think punishment is the answer, but they need to know that what they're doing is wrong. They can't do these things to people. They can't do this to me."*

I couldn't stop looking at the screen. It froze on her face for a couple of seconds, a glitch in the broadcast. The look in her eyes sent a quiver straight down my back. It made me more afraid of her than I'd ever been.

The news anchors were back in the studio, talking about that week's football games.

Paisley was still looking around for Dad. "What about him?" She nudged me, pointing to a huddled mass in the shelter of the Deuce stop. The bus pulled up and the mass got to its feet, and we saw it was a black guy wrapped in blankets.

We both turned around and went back to watching the news briefs. Tourists on their way to and from shows along the Strip would pass by every so often, laughing about *Spamalot*, carrying posters or Cirque du Soleil programs. Some drunk and disorderly. Or bemoaning large losses at blackjack. Then a small gaggle of teens about our age appeared and stood under the Jumbotron. Our bulletin came on again and they cheered.

"We love you guys!" they shouted at the screen. They booed at Virginia.

Paisley looked at me. I sank down a little in my seat. She pretended to look at something else. Both of us were still listening.

"We totally should get T-shirts," one of them said as they walked past.

"Yeah, a ton of people have asked for them on the site."

I looked at Paisley and smiled. "Wow. Did you hear that? They must host one of the fansites!"

"Wait, there are fansites?" Paisley said.

"Yeah. I think you were still in the shower for that part."

"How can we check them?" She grabbed my arm and pulled me to my feet. "They have computers at the Fashion Show Mall. In a store. You know, display models. I checked my e-mail on one the other week while I was waiting for you."

"The mall?" I said. "Where you pointed a gun at a woman in a clothes store and scared the crap outta her? Won't that be like returning to the scene of a crime?"

She shrugged. "Wanna check the Internet or not?"

Hey everyone, it's Nancy Nightmare here, official President of the Argent Army website. This is the place to come for the absolute latest info on what the twins are up to, and THE place to come for your official Argent Army T-shirts. Due to overwhelming demand, we even have awesome new Team Paisley and Team Beau shirts, available in either pink or blue, and wristbands with a variety of slogans, including "Tell Buddy We Love Him" and "We'll Just Take the Donuts." So hurry up and order yours now. They're going fast!

"Unbelievable," I laughed. I cruised in and out of fansites set up in our honor, read through countless message board threads, and after a while became so brainwashed that I wasn't sure who we were anymore.

"What?" said Paisley, coming back over to the computer where I was standing. I was quicker with computers, and she was better at fending off sales attacks from overdiligent store clerks. She'd already tried out a new digital camera, MP3 player, and 3D TV, but she kept circling back to check what I'd learned.

"Does that say, *ever since the fire*?" said Paisley, loitering. "We've had fans since then?"

"Yeah, apparently local LA news picked it up. Then there was a Facebook group, A told B, B told C; you know how it is. Once they found out it was"—my voice dropped to a whisper—"*us* doing the robberies, the whole thing just snowballed. The kids love us!"

"What about *Perez*? Did we make *Perez* yet?" she asked, nudging me over. I'd minimized the two celebrity gossip pages I had opened. I maximized one of them again to show her. We were all over it.

"Cool!" she shrieked.

A store nerd came scurrying over. Paisley turned and asked him which was their biggest TV.

> What dreams have you had about the Argents? What presents would you buy them? Where are they: the latest sightings! The "We Hate Buddy Argent" thread. Help celebrate National Beau and Paisley Day. What would you do to show your love for them? Baisley: fan fiction.

"Ugh. That's disgusting."
"What?" she said, coming back to me.

> Black or blond: What's the best hair color for Beau? Screen shots from security camera film. Is Beau Argent gay? Is Paisley Argent gay? Paisley and Beau: early years news footage. Who is Buddy Argent? They're looking for their dad! What places would you like to see them rob? What animal is Beau most like?

"Ooh, this I gotta see," she said, taking over the mouse and clicking on the link.

NANCY NIGHTMARE: I think he'd be a little koala bear 'cause he's so cute and he's got little sticky-out ears ever since he got his hair cut. LOL.

"Shit. Do I?" I said.

WONDER GIRL: No it has to be a puppy bc of his brown eyes. I swear his eyes are sooooo beautiful I could just drown in them! It's like he completes me.

"Give me a break," Paisley said, and went back to the clerk and the TV she swore she couldn't leave the store without.

I clicked on the eBay link at the bottom of the page.

Now available: Own the cutlery used by the Argent twins at Denny's. Starting bid: $1,700.

"Seventeen hundred bucks? Holy crap!"

I clicked on the discussion board "Argent Angst."

LITTLE MISS BOSSY: I just had the worst day ever. My mom's been crying a lot lately since my dad left, and seeing Beau and Paisley doing their stuff makes me so happy. Paisley's so the girl I want to be. And Beau is just so amazing. I just wanna hug him. . . .

NANCY NIGHTMARE: Aw, I feel bad for you, Little Miss B. But I know what you mean. Beau and Paisley are awesome. I wish we could help them get their message across.

CLUELESS: It's really hard for me. Since my dad died, I feel like there's no one who understands what I'm going through.

I see people way older than me who still have their dads, and I'm so jealous. Sometimes I wish other people's dads would die or just leave, and I feel guilty for thinking that but I just want someone to feel the way I do. When I saw on the news that they're doing all this stuff to find their dad, I thought it was so cool. Beau and Paisley know exactly how I feel. They'd do anything to find their dad and so would I.

TWINZ ADDICT: OMG, I know what you mean. I'd do the same thing if I thought my dad gave a rat's ass about me. LOL. Sometimes the only way people will listen is if you effing make them listen. I wanna go with them!

BUNNY BOILER: Srsly you guys, I don't think I can live much longer without Beau Argent being my husband. He is the most beautiful person in the whole world.

There was a little yellow blob with hearts coming off the top, followed by a line of smooching red lips.

Paisley returned. "I didn't buy the TV. Not big enough. Find anything else?"

"Oh my God. People love us, Pais. I'm serious. We are in demand. Some of the discussions are weird, though."

"What?"

"They're talking about me and you, like as a couple."

"We are a couple."

"No, like a . . . sex couple."

"What?!"

"Yeah, I know."

Paisley grimaced like she was trying to swallow her fist.

". . . and some of these girls are talking about doing stuff to me and they're, like, thirteen."

"So? I know girls, like, eleven and twelve who've done it. It's no biggie."

"Oh, okay, I'll put that on the website, then. *Have sex, preteens. It's no biggie.*"

"Stop being so judgmental. Get that smug twitch out of your eyebrows."

I looked back at the screen. "For real, these guys love us."

Paisley peered at it. "They're mostly girls," she said. "And it's mostly you they're loving. As far as they're concerned, I might as well be a piece of shit. They all think you're adorkable. I can just see the spread in *J-14*. Wait till they find out you read books."

"It's more than that, though," I told her. "It's like we're helping them. Look at some of the stuff they're saying. This one girl's dad just lost custody of her, and she's looking at us and we're helping her."

"How?"

"Because she's gonna stand up and fight for her dad. She says she's gonna run away and go find him."

"Whoa. That is pretty weird," said Paisley. "I've never helped anyone before."

"Yeah. The message boards are going insane."

"Let's leave them a message," she said.

"Really? What do you wanna say?"

I set her up and she nudged me out of the way again and started typing.

Dear Fans,
Keep Wondering . . .
Luv, P & B

"There," she said. "What do you think?"

"Sweet, Pais. Pretty sweet."

"Why, thank you."

"But we gotta do more."

"What?"

"We gotta do another one. Robbery. To keep our profile up."

"Well, there's turning worms and changing tunes and then there's you, Beau."

"Just one more. My way. Then we'll lay low."

"If you want. I still got the Eclipse on me. . . ."

"No. No Eclipse. No outfits. My way," I said. "Not so aggressive, not so rude. We've got a little fame now. We can trade on that."

She held up her hands in mock surrender. "Fine. Do it your way. Where, then?"

I logged off. We walked out together. The mall directory was right outside. We stood looking at the map. "Cornucopia," I said. "Popcorn shack. Top floor."

PAISLEY

NINETEEN

CORNUCOPIA, FASHION SHOW MALL,
THE STRIP,
LAS VEGAS, NEVADA

"Hey, can I help you?"

My big, macho brother stepped up. "Yeah, can I get one salted, two sour cream and chive, one caramel, two chocolate, and one cheese, please."

"Cans or cartons?"

"Cans, please."

"Tiny, small, medium, large, extralarge, or super-duper?"

"Uh, tiny, please."

I threw Beau a look as if to say, *Why bother?* but he got his money ready.

"What are you doing?" I whispered. "We're not gonna pay."

"I'm just throwing him off the scent."

"I'll say. What'd you get cheese for? I hate cheese popcorn."

"I don't plan on eating it."

The Corn Dude got seven little cans ready, which looked like see-through paint cans, and went over to the huge glass machine behind him. It buzzed and hummed and there was this little fountain in the middle of it, spewing out fresh popcorn. At the bottom were the five trays for the five different flavors they sold. Somewhere deep inside that machine, those popcorn kernels were given their flavors, then sent to the right tray. The Corn

Dude kept looking back at us as he opened the chocolate tray and scooped out enough for two tiny cans.

He came back to the counter. His badge said his name was *Corn Dude — Danny.*

"Hey, you guys were on the news."

"Oh, you recognize us, do you?" said Beau, turning to look at me.

"Yeah. Shit, you guys are way cool!"

"Yeah?!"

"Yeah! Wow. Can I get an autograph or something — or, no, wait — one of those stickers? Please? Wow, this is awesome." He continued shoveling out our order, but chuckling, barely taking his eyes off us.

"Sure," said Beau, reaching into his back pocket for the stickers.

I stopped his hand. "Beau, you can't do that. We only give stickers to people who deserve it. People who we've robbed."

"Yeah, but this guy seems nice. He might give us a discount."

Corn Dude Danny wiped his palms down his white apron and held his hand out. Beau peeled a sticker from the paper and pressed it down.

"Cool. Thanks, man. Hey, could I get a kiss from you?" he said to me.

"A kiss? Why do you want a kiss?" I looked at Beau. "No, you can kiss him."

Corn Dude Danny laughed. The machine behind sent out another rush of popcorn to the empty caramel tray.

"Just kiss him. Call it public relations," said Beau.

I looked at him, my hands on my hips. "So we can't rob people anymore, but you're more than happy to pimp me out to any mook that comes along, is that it, Beau?"

"No, it's just a little give and take. . . ."

"I can't let ya have all this stuff for free, though," said Corn Dude Danny, stacking up our cans. "Sorry. It's, like, company policy." He chuckled again. I felt a little sorry for him. He had, like, no teeth.

"But isn't it good publicity? Us being here?" said Beau.

"I guess," said Corn Dude Danny.

"Kids are going batshit crazy for us. You said so yourself that we were on the news," I added.

"Yeah, but I need this job."

I turned to my brother. "Whatcha gonna do now, Beau?" I said. "Danny don't wanna play with us."

Corn Dude Danny rang up what we owed on the cash register. "So that'll be sixty-eight ninety-five."

Beau huffed and got out his wallet. "Well, that's not gonna get our message out there, is it?" he said.

"No," I said, "but this is." And I pulled the Eclipse once again from my waistband and held it out in front of me, pointed at the glass popcorn machine, my finger poised on the trigger.

Corn Dude Danny stopped laughing. Beau dropped his wallet. My finger pulled back.

PEEOW! PEEOW! CRASH! WOOMPH! The glass exploded and a fountain of popcorn came flying out, ricocheting off every wall. Corn Dude Danny ducked behind the counter. It was still raining popcorn as I grabbed the cans and bolted for the door.

"I knew you wouldn't let me handle it!" Beau shouted, running along beside me.

"What did you expect?" I laughed.

We ran out of there into the near-empty mall to the sound of ringing bells and the smell of burning popcorn. The once again fashionably late security staff were nowhere to be found, so we booked out of the nearest exit and made our way back along the Strip into the dense tourist cluster of Treasure Island. Another pirate show was in progress, and we lost ourselves in the crowd.

"Jumbotron!" I shouted out to Beau. He caught up with me at the fountain outside the entrance to the Forum Shops, where we sat on a bench to catch our breaths.

I looked over at him before he even had the chance to say anything. "Yeah, I knew it was loaded."

He leaned forward and shook his head, still out of breath.

"Aren't you going to start yelling at me? Tell me I could have taken someone's eye out? That a little shard of glass could have severed an artery or something?"

He leaned back, still breathing hard, prying open one of the chocolate popcorn cans and picking out a couple of pieces. He shoved them in his mouth and shrugged.

"I'm sorry I put you through all this, Beau," I said. He offered me the can and I took a handful. "I know you wanna be one of those kids who doesn't run with the crowd, and you wanna go to Paris and read all your French books and stuff."

The lights on the big screen illuminated his face. "It's okay."

"No, it's not. I know it worked, this whole weird, psychedelic, scary, gun-toting adventure of mine. But I'm sorry you had to be a part of it, okay? It's my thing, not yours; I know that."

"Pais, you do know we're gonna have to leave Vegas pretty soon. Cops aren't gonna have to search for long. Especially now that you pulled the trigger."

"I guess."

"We need to go pack our stuff."

I nodded. "What about Dad?"

Beau put his arm around me and squeezed. "We're okay as we are, aren't we?"

I looked at him. I knew what he wanted me to say, so I nodded.

The news was still going. We were on. I looked back to see grainy footage of me flipping the bird to the security camera in the Chronic Chocolate Company.

". . . Tonight, we take a closer look at the twins whose story is once again captivating America. I'm right here in Las Vegas where the Argent twins, once America's sweethearts, are now known to have embarked on a candy crime spree. I'm Amanda Peace, and that's all coming up on Peace of the Action."

"Ugh, can't stand that cooze." I opened a can of caramel corn. There she was again: smirky face, thick bangs, perma-tan, talking about us through her nose like she could smell the shit we were up to our necks in. At the ends of her sentences she'd dip her head and look intently into the camera as if to say, *This is serious, everyone. This is soooooo serious.* Like she even *cared* about those stores we'd robbed. Those "decent, hardworking families" I'd pointed the gun at. Or us. Very least of all, us.

After commercials for the Diaper Genie and Oreo cookies, she reappeared.

". . . Las Vegas law enforcement officials are desperate to apprehend the sixteen-year-old brother and sister duo who have been dubbed the twenty-first century Bonnie and Clyde. And although they are wanted for a string of crimes including arson, car theft, and robbery, many young people see the twins' exploits as heroic. The Argents have become modern-day celebrities, gracing the covers of the current issues of Teen Times and Face It. Like Bonnie and Clyde before them, the duo perpetrates their crimes in an era of severe economic difficulty. And they've become nationwide celebrities because of it. Cell phone footage of their raid at an ice cream parlor right here in Vegas has already registered over one million hits on YouTube. Internet sites have been set up in their honor, web forums are inundated constantly with messages of support, and, believe it or not, items alleged to have been used by the twins in various restaurants have even been posted for auction on eBay. . . ."

Our photos came up again: the grainy black-and-white one of me flipping the bird at the Chronic Chocolate Company, and one of Beau, full color, at General Custard's.

Amanda Peace spoke to some teenagers hanging out at the base of the Stratosphere.

"They're just so cool," said one girl with red cheeks. "And it's not like they've hurt anyone. I don't think they'd be doing it if they didn't have to."

"It's not like Mickey and Mallory," said a black-haired boy. "Beau and Paisley don't kill. They're not sadistic. They're just cool."

"And Beau is really sexy," said an older woman with a lip ring, laughing.

Out the corner of my eye I could feel Beau looking at me as he stretched out on the bench like a cat stretches after sleep. He was smiling.

The governor came on TV. He had a total stick up his ass.

". . . The LVPD expect to capture the Argents within the next twenty-four hours. The net is closing in on these lawless juveniles. Everybody knows what they look like, thanks to the overwhelming media coverage, so they'll be easy to spot now. And I repeat: If you do see them, do not confront them yourself. They are armed and dangerous. Notify the nearest law enforcement officer instead. By tomorrow, the twins will no longer pose a threat to the residents or the tourists of this city—of that I have no doubt."

"Asshole."

"Everyone knows where we are, Pais. . . ."

"Yeah, well. Maybe we *should* get caught. Maybe that's the quickest way to find Dad."

"Or the quickest way to jail." Beau looked at me. He looked down at Mom's pendant around my neck. "It looks good on you, Pais."

"Thanks," I said, offering him the caramel popcorn.

Then there she was in billions of pixels, Granny Dearest. The old Vaginasaurus herself, once again against the backdrop of the toasted remains of her house.

"*. . . I've lost everything, Amanda. I just don't know why they would do this. They set fire to my house; they stole my car, my jewelry, valuables. I brought them up well, gave them everything I could. Jane was sent to private school and . . . they had a good life after the trauma of losing their mother. I don't know what I'm going to do now. . . .*"

"Squeeze a little harder, Skank, you might actually produce a tear."

"She must be massively pissed off at us," said Beau.

"At me," I said, digging around for popcorn in Beau's can.

"What do you mean? I was there, too. I'm an accomplice."

"Yeah, but you're Golden Boy. She'll hang me out to dry. And once the cops find out about my expulsions and . . ."

"I'm not Golden Boy."

"Yeah, y'are. She's always loved you. You're the one who never makes any waves. You don't even tell her when you get beat up at school."

"That's not true."

"Oh, really? You've told her about O'Donnell and his crew and what they do to you? The head-flushing and the spitting and the locker graffiti?"

"No, of course not."

"That's why she kept Dad away. She'd sell me down the river in a heartbeat, but she'd never let you go." I closed my can and opened a sour cream one. "She ever try anything, you know, sexual?"

He looked at me from under his hair. "Paisley . . ."

"I'm just asking. It happens. Something-Ophelia. I heard about it. Like necrophilia, but when old women get horny for young guys. She's already bagged the infant gardener. She ever get you alone and . . . ?"

"You are unbelievable! You're twisted. Have you ever thought that maybe she just prefers me because you're the difficult one? You're the one who 'doesn't take any of her shit,' whereas I'm 'the doormat.'"

"Well you know what they say, a boy's best friend is his grandmother."

"Shut up."

"Aw, Beau. If I'm outta line, just tell me to fu—"

"Fuck off," he spat.

"All right." I smiled. I always appreciated him more when he told me to fuck off. I did need to be told. I would've told myself to fuck off if I thought I'd listen.

"Come on," he said, leaving his popcorn cans on the bench. "Let's go back."

I did the same and got up. I followed him through the flood of people who were headed for the on-the-hour dance of the fountains outside the Bellagio. They looked just like they did at the end of that George Clooney movie. All these huge bursts of water from all over the pool were shooting straight up into the black sky on the beats of the music. It was amazing. Hundreds of people had gathered all around the pool to watch, and all the best spaces at the front were taken. I wanted to get closer. I went to see if I could push through.

I peered over, jumping up to see if I could see somewhere we could stand, and turned around to tell Beau where to head to.

But he had disappeared.

BEAU

TWENTY

She came toward me like a tiger stalking through long grass. Except the long grass was a crowd of tourists. And the tiger was my grandmother.

I turned around. "PAISLEY!" I shouted. I didn't know if she heard or saw me. Matt gripped one of my arms, Virginia the other, and together they dragged me through the rest of the tourist mêlée. I wriggled and writhed to be free of them, but the more I squirmed, the harder they held on. I didn't stop, though. It wasn't like before, outside the house with Matt squeezing my neck. There, I didn't dare breathe for fear of what he might do to me. But this time I kept on pulling and pushing and making it as hard for them to take me as I could.

Neither of them said a word, all the way to the motel. They didn't ask me where we were staying, they just knew. They must have been trailing us. In the parking lot, Matt manhandled me, searching for the room key. I squirmed in my grandmother's grasp, shouting for help, hoping someone might hear and come over.

"Gimme the key or I'll bust it open. Your choice," said Matt. I just smiled at him. He busted it open.

Once inside, Virginia pushed me face-first onto my unmade bed as Matt started binding my hands together with rope. The same rope he used for marking off planting areas in our grandmother's garden.

She bent down so her face was level with mine. "Where are my antiques?"

"In the closet," I mumbled, burying my face in the bedsheets.

She went over to the closet and pulled one of the handles, immediately spying the beach bag. She pulled it out and searched inside. "Good. It's all here."

"You don't need to tie me up," I said, as Matt wound the rope around and knotted it tightly, checking that my hands wouldn't slide. Then he did the same with my feet and left me on the bed. I lay there, my wrists and ankles throbbing with the rope pressure. "You've both got what you came for. There's only me here."

Virginia walked back over to the bed, slowly swinging the bag. "This is just the down payment, Beau. YOU'RE what we came here for. . . ."

"Me?"

"Uh-huh. We're going to the lake house, Matthew and I. And you. We're going to live there. Just the three of us."

"What, you're gonna hold me for ransom?" I didn't understand it. "No one's gonna pay for me. You know we don't have any money. We can pay you in jelly beans. We got plenty of them," I said, my mouth getting my ass into something it seriously couldn't handle.

She grabbed a fistful of my hair and yanked my head back. Upside down, her features looked all distorted, like a melted clay pot. She raised her eyebrows and chuckled, like Jack Nicholson in *The Shining*. "Well don't you suddenly have so much to say! You were always so eager to please me, Beau. What happened since you've been away on your little adventure?" She came down closer to my face so I could feel her breath on my skin. "If I have to lock you up for the two whole years, you'll stay—"

"Two *years*?"

"Well, eighteen months at least."

My follicles screamed in agony. I thought my eyes would pop out of my head. She gave me a look, right up close, like she didn't know if she was gonna kiss me or hit me. "Then you'll get our fund." Her eyes gleamed at the thought.

"Yes," she continued, "once I've got that, you'll be as free as you want to be. We've got a long time together, boy. I suggest you make nice. I may even throw in a little cash bonus for good behavior."

She would have let go if I'd said something nice, something palliative. But I didn't have it in me to be nice to her anymore. That old Beau was gone. Well, I hoped he was gone, anyway. "Paisley will kill you for this."

Her mouth screwed up in a knot. "I don't want to hear that name again."

"She will. She'll know where you're going and she'll find you and she'll kill you. You don't know what she's capable of."

Matt scoffed and took the bag from Virginia, heading outside to the parking lot.

Virginia gripped my hair harder. My eyes bulged. "You don't know what *I'm* capable of. And I have a pretty damn good idea of what your sister can do. I watched my home burn to the ground, remember?"

She finally let go and shoved me back down onto the bed.

My scalp throbbed. "Is that what this is, a revenge thing?"

She reached behind me and picked something up. Two Wit. She didn't take her eyes off me, but clutched the owl with both hands and started pulling it, until the stitching ripped apart at the neck and it was two separate pieces of useless white stuffing. She took a handful of it and crammed it in my mouth. Then she took Two Woo from Paisley's bed and, still looking at me, did the same again, except she threw all of the stuffing behind her into the trash can.

"Where's my gun?"

I didn't answer.

"Where's my gun, Beau?" She came over to the bed and stared down at me. I lay on my back looking up at her, still with a mouthful of stuffing. I laughed in her face. She slapped me hard and some of the stuffing came out. I laughed again. She hit me again, twice as hard and this time with nail digs for good measure. I laughed again, though my eyes were running with tears.

She pulled the rest of the stuffing out of my mouth and yanked me upright on the edge of the bed, gripping the sides of my face in her claws. "Where . . . is . . . it?"

"You know where it is," I said.

Matt came back inside and closed the door. "You ready?"

She nodded. "Take him."

Bundling me over his shoulder, Matt took me out to his pickup. There was a large blue tarp over the back, folded over to one side. I didn't know what Virginia was up to, but she hadn't yet come out of our room.

Matt threw me down on the bed of the truck. I lay next to a pile of old tools and a lawn mower on its side. He took a roll of duct tape out of the pocket of his hoodie.

My heart was hammering so hard I didn't think my breath would make it out of my chest. I just said it before I could edit myself.

"You won't see a penny of that money. Think about it. If she's doing this to her own grandchildren, what's a two-bit gardener mean to her, huh?"

He tore off a length of tape and plastered it over my mouth. Then he looked at me, as if weighing something up. I gulped. The last thing I remember was the fist coming toward my face.

PAISLEY
TWENTY-ONE

LUCKY INN MOTEL,

THE STRIP,

LAS VEGAS, NEVADA

I made it back to the motel, all pissed at Beau for going on ahead without me. The door to our room was hanging off its hinges. And something was burning.

I ran inside. In the middle of the orange carpet, a fire was burning. And the fuel was Dad's letters.

"Oh shit!"

I ran over to the little burning mound to try and stamp it out, but the flames were too big. And it was still spreading. The carpet was catching, the skirt thing on Beau's bed was catching. I saw the mess all over the room: My clothes all torn up and scattered around the floor; my backpack empty, dumped beside my bed. I scrabbled around and found the one letter of Dad's that I had kept separate, in the front pocket of my backpack. I opened it. It was okay. I folded it up and put it inside my bra. The closet was wide open. I ran to it and saw that the bag of antiques was gone.

"Fuck!"

All our stuff was gone, except for a stack of Wonder Twins stickers on the nightstand. I grabbed them.

The fire was all along Beau's side of the room now, right up to the drapes, which caught within seconds. There was no way I could get out the way I came, not without burning up myself. So

I had to go through the bathroom. I stepped up onto the sink and sized up the window for my head, shoving the stickers down into my boot. I could just squeeze out. The catch caught on my belly as I writhed and wriggled and squirmed like a caterpillar to get outside, landing with a *flump* on the grass. Inside, something exploded.

The window banged shut behind me, but I didn't look back. I got to my feet and just started running, filled with a rage so painful I could have torn off limbs. I didn't know where I was going, I just ran.

All hope plummeted like a bird shot down. All my stuff was burned. Dad's letters were burned. Beau had vanished. I just knew the Skank had taken him. She'd done it, and she'd do more if she didn't get what she wanted. No matter how hard I ran or how deep I breathed to control it, I couldn't stop my own tears. I stopped in a sheltered doorway, some defunct record store just off the Strip, trying to stifle the huffs caught in my throat. I breathed hard and heavy, *in, in, in* then *out, out, in, out*. I stood back against the wall, feeling the cold tiles against my hands. I was sweating; my hair had become stuck across my face as I ran, but I didn't move it away. I didn't know what to do. I couldn't hold it in any longer. I sobbed.

I sat in the doorway until two bums came stumbling along, shouting that I was in their spot. They were still shouting at me when I began running back along the Strip. What was it about that fucking block that kept me coming back to it? Dad, that was what. I'd seen him there, I knew I had. I watched people walking along, hand in hand, on vacation, smiling, laughing, taking photos, sipping drinks through curly straws. Families. Little girls with their dads. I watched groups of guys strutting past with calling cards for hookers. More hunched-up homeless shuffling along, holding their hands out for spare change. I watched drag queens shimmying past on their way to a show, acting like the whole world owed them a favor. None of the faces I saw was Dad's, and that made me hate them all. I hated the world. It was all so dirty and loud and complicated. Everything was fugly. Everything was wrong.

I didn't stop walking for hours. I moved around unseen in the crowds. I didn't know what to do: I had no money, nowhere to go, I hadn't found Dad, and—worst of all, I now realized—I'd lost Beau, too.

I was totally lost.

My chest felt like it was being crushed, like a piano had fallen on it or something. The pain squeezed and squeezed and there was nothing I could do about it. I thought about hamsters. Hamsters get on their wheels when they're stressed out, right? I needed to just keep walking, run if I had to, run it all out of me.

I ran down the Strip, weaving in and out of tourist clusters, and finally stumbled into some bullshit gift shop. I bummed up and down the aisles with no intention of buying anything. Thumbed through magazines without even reading them. Picked up packets of crap I couldn't even identify through the water in my eyes. As I came to the last aisle, I scoped the shelves displaying the Scotch. There were so many kinds, but only one that meant anything to me. One particular bottle came into focus. Black-and-white label. I grabbed the bottle and walked to the entrance. Then I ran like a bitch. I could still hear the alarm screaming as I reached the Jumbotron outside Caesars. I sat down on the bench, watching for police or security guards—nothing. Nobody. Nobody gave a shit about me, and I gave a shit about nobody. I twisted off the lid of the bottle and brought it up to my nose. It smelled disgusting. Like the living room the day we found Mom. Like my grandmother's breath when she was shouting. My stomach turned over at the thought of drinking it.

I sat there with the open bottle between my knees and watched the screen. We were on again. Two old dudes were debating the effect we were having on teen America.

". . . It's a sorry state of affairs if these are the kinds of role models we are producing for our younger generation. . . ."

"They don't want to be role models, Glenn. They're doing this because they've lost their way, that's all. They're lost souls. Society has failed them. . . ."

When in doubt, blame society. I put the bottle to my lips and swigged. I held it in my mouth. I spat. I tried it again. I held it in my mouth for longer. I tried swallowing again, but my damn throat wouldn't let me. I spat it out and heaved into the trash can. On my third swig, I swallowed. I shivered. It was disgusting. But I needed it. I needed it to forget where I was. Who I was. I understood Mom. For once, I understood my grandmother. I felt the swig going down my throat, into my stomach, like a little rush of liquid Band-Aids traveling to all the places in my body where it hurt. My heart. My stomach. The pain deep inside my body that no doctor could ever get to. The more I drank, the less it hurt me. Beau being gone. Dad being gone. All my criminally insane efforts to find him a total bust.

Whatever.

Whatever.

Whatever.

What-fucking-ever.

I laid my head on the arm of the bench and watched our news reports on repeat. Pretty soon I closed my eyes.

And when I opened them, the Jumbotron was still twinkling above me. They were looping the old dudes. Same shit, different news cycle: "Bad role models. Lost souls." The crowds hadn't thinned out, either. Moms and dads and kids and friends and grandparents and boyfriends and couples and bums and brothers and sisters and guys in red shirts. Guys in red shirts. No, not guys, *a guy* in a red shirt. A guy standing there, watching the screen. Watching the Jumbotron. Watching *us*.

He had his back to me, hands in his jean pockets.

I thought I was dreaming. I thought he'd disappear like a ghost. Like the day we saw him from the bus. But he didn't.

I sat up. He was still there. I stood up. I came up to his shoulders. He was still there. I was wobbly on my legs, but I walked up to him. He didn't turn around, just kept on watching the screen. Now it was the governor again, talking about the manhunt for those dastardly Wonder Twins.

I reached out and put my hand on his back. I still thought he would disappear even as my hand touched his shoulder blade. He twitched.

He turned around and looked at me, frowning at first like he was gonna tell me to fuck off. And then he really looked at me. And he frowned even more. And I started to cry.

"Dad? Are you my dad?"

"Paisley? No! Baby . . . is that you?"

He was smaller than I remembered, and not just 'cause I'd gotten taller. He'd lost a lost of weight, too. His face was hairy. He'd grown a thick beard and mustache, but underneath it all it was my dad, all right. His face lit up like there was a candle under his skin when he said my name. Just like when I used to run into his arms when he came home after work.

He was shaking. "Oh my God. Paisley . . ." He went to hug me, but stopped and put his hand over his mouth, like I'd told him not to.

"I can't handle this," he said and started to cry. He had bits of trash stuck to his clothes, and he smelled like he'd fallen down in a public toilet. But it was my dad and I didn't care, so I touched one of his hands and he grabbed on to it. I leaned over and hugged him. And he hugged me back. His cheek was cold and quivery against my face. And he held me like we were going to jump off a building. Normal hugs don't last long. A quick hug, a pat on the back, and then you pull away. Not this one. He was there, like all my sunrises at once. My dad.

"Please tell me this isn't a dream."

"It's not a dream, honey," he said, leaning back to look at me. "God. I can't believe you're here!" He kissed my hair and breathed it in, his tears forming a little damp patch on the top of my head. He held my face in his hands.

"I knew it," I told him. "I knew if we got on that screen, you'd see us. I knew we'd get to you somehow," I said, holding on to him again so tight. I didn't ever want to let go. I didn't even care how dirty he was. I buried my face into his filthy red shirt and breathed him in like he was lavender. The last time I'd hugged him, I'd only come up to his waist. Now my head was on his shoulder. We stood there for the longest time. I had my dad and he loved me. And that was all that mattered. . . .

I pulled back. "Dad . . ."

"We've got so much to talk about, Paisley," he said, wiping his eyes on his shirt sleeve. "God, look at you. You're so beautiful. My little girl. I've been watching the news. I saw you." He rubbed his eyes. His fingers were blackened with dirt. He saw the bottle of

Scotch in my hands and took it from me. "What are you doing with this? You don't need this." He aimed it at the trash can he'd been searching through days before.

"Dad, everything's gone wrong. We've done some pretty bad things. Well, I have."

"Yeah, I saw. . . ."

"No, before the robberies. Beau and the fire and I . . . shit, sorry, I don't know where to start . . . I got expelled . . . like, five times."

"Well that's—"

"And I punched a girl."

"Okay."

"And I burned down Virginia's house."

"Whoa."

"And I drugged a guy and robbed him."

He held his hands up. "All in good time. But I saw you guys on the news. You did all that for me?"

"Beau said it was a stupid plan." Beau, oh my God, where was he?

"It was a stupid plan," said Dad. "But it worked. We're here, together. That makes it a perfect plan." He hugged me again, but I just stood there like some stupid pillar. Everything was so fast in my head, it had made my body completely still. Dad was still talking, brushing the hair from my face.

"My baby's gone all Bonnie Parker just for her old dad?" He laughed. "I can't wait to see Beau. Is he all right? Paisley? Paisley?"

I snapped out of it when he said my name twice, like he used to when he caught me doing something I shouldn't, like coloring on the wall or clogging the toilet with Legos. "I . . . I lost him in the crowds. We were headed back to our motel, but . . . Oh God, the fire, Dad, our room was on fire. Our stuff . . . It's Virginia, she's got him."

"Whoa, what do you mean, 'got him'? Where is he?"

"She took him, her and her gardener boy toy. . . . They've got him; I know it. They've probably been trailing us for days. They trashed our motel room, set the letters on fire. . . ."

"Set *fire* . . . were either of you hurt?"

"No. She just burned the letters you sent."

He looked at me. "You got them? You kept them?"

I nodded. "She hid them from us. We got the last one you sent from Paradise. That's why we came. We found Eddie, he told us to look for you on the Strip, so . . ."

"Where did they go?"

"I don't know. Dad, I don't know!"

"It's all right, it's all right . . ."

"No, it's not, Dad. I have to know! What's she going to do to him? I'll kill her if she hurts him, I'll fucking . . ."

"Paisley, watch your mouth."

"I'm sorry, but Dad . . ." A thought hit me like a wrecking ball. I could hear Beau's voice in my head.

"The lake house. In Utah. I saw a picture of it in her desk drawer. Mirror Lake. She bought it a while back. It's pretty remote. . . . For vacations, I guess. A retreat."

I almost spat it back out at Dad. "The lake house. She must have gone there!"

He held my hands, just like he used to when I had one of my tantrums.

"All right, calm down, talk slowly."

"I can't! We have to go there now. We have to get Beau!"

"You think that's where they've gone?"

"I can't think of anywhere else. Beau said it's remote. She probably wants to lock him up again, keep him until he's eighteen. She might kill him, Dad. She might wanna come after me and kill me. Just so she can claim all the money . . ."

"*What?* What money?"

And just then he looked down. Mom's necklace. I didn't think he could cry anymore. He kind of cry-laughed.

"You got it back for me. You got it back," he spluttered.

We hugged again.

"Oh Dad, I've got so much to tell you."

BEAU
TWENTY-TWO

I woke up, my brain feeling like it had been kicked around on cobblestones. All I could see was blue. My body was being bumped and jerked around, and as I fully opened my eyes to see the scratchy blue tarp lying over me, I remembered where I was. My heart started pounding. I was in the truck. I was tied up. My mouth was stuck closed behind a strip of duct tape. It was daylight outside the blue sheet. I could feel the sun. The truck clattered on, metal clinked, loose tools rattled. Lying beside me was the lawn mower, and as I turned onto my side I stared straight into the blades. Bits of lawn cuttings were stuck to them. I could hear some country-western song coming from the cab. Hear voices over the top of it.

Virginia's voice. "You're very quiet."

Matt's voice. "What?"

The music went off.

"I said you're very quiet. Something the matter?"

"I was just thinking over something you said."

"What?"

"About keeping him chained to a water pipe for two years."

"It's not two years. It's barely eighteen months."

"You'd really lock him up?"

"He's always had a strict curfew. . . ."

"Yeah, but that didn't involve tying his hands together."

"We'll have to see how he behaves. If he promises to comply, we won't have to tie him up."

Matt's voice. "What if he gets out again? He'll go straight to the cops."

"No, he won't. The police are already after them for everything else. Arson. Car theft. Armed robbery. I don't think they're going to care too much about a tiny case of kidnapping between family members amid all that, do you?"

"What if he won't play ball? Goes on a hunger strike or something?"

"It won't get that far. I told you, Beau's a pussycat; he won't cause us any trouble."

"Yeah but—"

"Matthew, darling, I'm getting a little tired of all these arbitrary questions. Don't you trust me?"

"Yeah . . ."

"That almost sounded convincing. I'm starting to think your heart isn't in this."

"I just gotta think about the pitfalls, Ginny. I don't wanna go back to jail. I wanna go straight now."

"Yes, and won't it be nice when all this is over to go straight with millions of dollars in the bank? Your own business?"

Silence. The radio went loud again. Then down again.

Matt's voice. "What if she comes back to get him?"

"She won't. Darling, she's been away at boarding school for months. She doesn't even know we bought the house. She won't have a clue where we are. And he won't step a toe out of line."

"But if she does find him . . ."

"Matthew, if I ever see that girl's face again, I'll make sure I never have to see that girl's face again."

"What does that mean?"

No answer. I didn't need to hear anymore. If it came down to it, our grandmother would kill us both, of that I had no doubt. She had nothing to lose and everything to gain.

I had to get off that truck. I twisted my head around to see a wooden board propped up against the cab. They couldn't see me. I wrenched my hands, but they wouldn't budge. The rope must have been coiled around them at least six times. I wrenched my feet, but the rope was too tight and I was too weak. I couldn't even open my mouth with the tape there. I lay back and closed my eyes and felt the tears coming. There was a clattering from the other side of the truck. The blade from Matt's hedge trimmer, a large jagged blade, was jutting out of the side of his toolbox. I writhed over to it and held my hands up to the blade and started to rub against it, trying to get some friction going.

Rubrubrubrubrubrubrubrubrubrubrubrubrubrubrubrubrubrubrubrubrub rubrubrubrub . . .

Every breath I took into my nose was laced with the stench of hot, rotten grass and gasoline. Sweat beads trickled down my forehead and into my eyes, but I didn't stop rubbing that rope until I felt it fray.

I lay back down to catch my breath for a second, rubbing my forehead against a wooden board to wipe away the sweat. Then I started again.

Rubrubrubrubrubrubrubrubrubrubrubrubrubrubrubrubrubrubrubrub rubrubrubrub . . .

A strand from one coil of the rope came free, making it easier to cut through the rest of the pieces. *Swip swip swip* went the rope as it loosened and fell off my wrists. The relief was amazing. I had my hands back. I arched them back and forth and stretched my fingers out. Lying back, I brought my ankles to the blade and worked on the ties until my legs were unburdened by rope, too, then stopped and caught my breath again, my chest rising and jumping with the heaving from my lungs. My shirt was soaked through with sweat, and I pulled the neck up over my face to wipe it. Must have been a hundred and five degrees under that tarp. Another hour and I bet I would've cooked under that scratchy sheet.

"I love this song!" I heard Matt shout.

The music got loud again inside the cab.

It was the song from the dance machine. I was sure of it.

I snaked under the tarp and crawled my way along the truck, poking my head up at the other end. The sunlight was blinding outside. I craned my neck over and looked ahead at the cab. With that board blocking the back window, I couldn't see Virginia or Matt, so hopefully they couldn't see me, either. Then I looked over the tailgate of the truck bed to see the desert road stretching out behind us. It was like the road we'd taken from LA to Vegas, but it definitely wasn't the same one. The mountains were closer and the blacktop was darker. The truck was moving pretty fast, but there wasn't another car for miles. Not in the rearview.

I closed my eyes. "Come on. Come on," I muttered. I could feel the tears coming again. It was all my *carpe diem* moments rolled into one. Every time I'd had to take the plunge into a cold swimming pool. Every time I'd had to walk into class after summer vacation and look into O'Donnell's eyes. Every time Paisley had pulled the gun out. It was being back on the Stratosphere, about to go on Big Shot.

And I wonder . . .

I heaved my upper body over the tailgate of the truck. It wobbled. Any moment, the chain could have snapped and I could have fallen out onto the road. The tears came. I jabbed myself in my stomach with my fist. "Come on!" I muttered louder. I punched myself again.

If anything could ever feel this real forever . . .

I had to get on that road. I had to stop going where I was going. I had to be free of our grandmother.

Gotta promise not to stop when I say when.

I had to jump off the truck.

PAISLEY
TWENTY-THREE

"Oh my God! Paisley? Is it really you, Paisley? Guys, it's Paisley!"

"I'm sorry, what?" I said as this fat, straggly black-haired woman darted toward me, her sandals slapping on the sidewalk as she ran. She had a lip ring, and emblazoned across her chest was the black-and-white screen shot of mine and Beau's faces from the security camera at Doh-Nutty's. A big girl about the same age as me and wearing a black AC/DC T-shirt just like mine was sitting on a bench eating a burrito but dropped it and ran over. Then another kid, a skinny blond boy in a marching band jacket with big gold buttons, trotted up behind her.

"Oh my God, this is a total honor," said AC/DC. "You and your brother, you're like . . . our heroes. You're legends!"

"We've been following your story, and we've set up this website for the Argent Army, which is, like, this group of kids who just adore you," said Lip Ring. She had gray strands in her hair and a huge boil next to one of her nostrils. "We got, like, seven thousand members on the site. The hits go up every day."

"Seven thousand members?" I said.

"Yeah, and there's other sites, too. There's TotallyArgent.net and Wonder Twins Inc, too. You two are idols. Everybody loves you. Well, kids love you. We came here from Ohio. I'm Vicky, Vic for short, this is my daughter, Eliza, and this is Eliza's boyfriend, Robbie. I remember you guys from the first time around, when you went missing. We sent teddy bears to the hospital in Jersey. Oh my God, is this your dad?"

"Uh, yeah," I said.

"Where's Beau?" said Marching Band.

"He's . . ." I didn't know what to say. I couldn't think of a lie, either, so I just came out with it. "Our grandmother kidnapped him."

All three of them laughed hysterically, then stopped when they saw my face. I thought Marching Band was gonna start bawling.

"We thought you were joking," said AC/DC. "Oh my God, we're so sorry. When?"

"'Bout three hours ago," I said, reaching for my dad's hand.

Lip Ring snorted through her nose like a dragon. "We knew it. We said when we saw her on the news, that woman won't let this lie. She'll go after them. Didn't I say that, Eliza?"

"Yeah," said AC/DC. She opened her bag and got out a rolled-up copy of *Teen Times*. "Could you sign this, please?"

She handed it to me with a small Sharpie. Me and my brother's grainy black-and-white faces were on the front, and the headline read, BONNIE AND CLYDE FOR THE NEW MILLENIUM. I scrawled my signature across my own face. Marching Band offered me a small thick notebook plastered with pictures of me and Beau cut neatly from newspapers. I looked through it and found my own page to sign. He had written a short poem titled "Paisley's Ode." I can't remember much about it, but he likened me to a starfish and I liked that. I scribbled underneath, *So not worth it. Lots of love, Paisley xo*.

He smiled like a dolphin and eagerly showed the other two. "Look what I got. Look what she wrote. Oh wow. Oh wow."

When I'd finished my signing and photos, the three of

them stood there looking at me. I didn't know what they were expecting.

"What? You want me to open a vein or something?" I said. They all laughed again. Then Lip Ring looked at Dad, who had just been standing there by my side the whole time.

"Is this really your dad? Is this Buddy?" she asked. I nodded. She pulled him toward her and hugged him like they were good old friends. "I've been following these kids since they were little and they were on *Oprah*, and when we heard what they were doing now, we had to come here and show our support. They've done all this for you. Oh my God! It's an honor to meet you, sir."

"A real honor," AC/DC echoed.

Lip Ring ranted on. "Your kids are amazing, always have been. My sister lives in Jersey and she went out with one of the search parties when they went missing. Never thought they'd find them. But they did! And here you are."

Marching Band turned to my dad. "Can I shake your hand?"

Three hours ago, he was rooting through trash cans and bathing in public fountains. Now he was getting called "sir" and having his hand shaken? And *I* was amazing? I didn't know what was happening. I thought it might be some prank. I turned and walked away, pulling Dad along with me.

"Wait! Where are you going?" called Lip Ring, and the three of them caught up with us. I kept walking. So did they.

"I'm sorry, but I'm not this big hero, all right? All me and Beau did was hold up some candy stores, and we only did that to get on the news. So we could tell our dad we love him. So we could find him. Okay? I've found my dad now. That's all I wanted. You can get on with your lives now. Stop stalking me."

I kept on walking. Pretty soon, I noticed they'd stopped following. So had Dad. I turned around. They were all standing in the same spot a couple of yards away, staring at me.

"Dad?" I said.

"Paisley, apologize. These people have come a long way to see you."

"What? I didn't ask them to, Dad. . . ."

"Paisley . . ."

"Okay, I'm sorry. But, I didn't ask for any of this, okay?"

"But you got it," said Dad, walking toward me. "So what are you gonna do with it?"

I shrugged.

"We've got a car," said Lip Ring. "If we can drive you guys anywhere, it'd be a total honor. Do you know where your grandmother might have taken Beau?"

"No. Well, I have a hunch, but it's risky. . . ."

"We know the risks," said AC/DC. "If your grandmother wants to kill us, it'd be a total honor."

"Yeah," said Marching Band. "We don't mind getting shot. I'll get shot for you." He bowed his head like he was totally embarrassed.

"You're so cool," said Lip Ring. "Everybody loves you guys. Well, everybody under fifty, at least."

I shook my head. "But I don't get it. Why so stalky? Just 'cause we got a gun and there's some montage of us on YouTube with a Bon Jovi soundtrack?"

"It's The Who, actually," said AC/DC.

"'Baba O'Riley'?" said Dad.

"Yeah." AC/DC smiled.

"Cool," he said. "Classic."

Look at my dad, I thought, *down with the kids.*

"We just want to help you, like you helped us," said Marching Band. "We want to show you our gratitude. Please. We could help you find Beau."

"How have we helped you? Me and Beau are thieves, guys. We're not rock stars, we're not heart surgeons. We stole from people to get on TV. That's all. We're not exactly role models." ·

"We don't want role models," said Lip Ring. "We're sick of role models. You're the coolest thing since Bonnie and Clyde. It gives us all hope."

"Yeah. And I know what it's like to lose your dad. I'd do anything to get mine back." AC/DC shot Lip Ring a knowing glance and the woman reached for her hand and gave it a squeeze.

"And the governor here hates you," added Marching Band. "He says you're an example of everything that's wrong with America."

"Praise indeed," said Dad.

"I think you need us," said Lip Ring. "We could really help you out."

I looked at Dad. He raised his eyebrows, like he always used to when he was waiting for me to make up my mind which cereal I wanted for breakfast. It was always the chocolate one.

"Okay, guys," I said. I remembered what Beau had told me about one of the Hansel and Gretel stories. How they got out of the woods on a white duck. This was our white duck. "We're in your hands, I guess."

As the three of them leaped up and down in utter joy, they didn't look much like white ducks, though. More like baby black rabbits.

So we went to find Lip Ring's car. It was beyond cool. A black Trans Am with scratches and dents and zebra-print seat covers. When we were on the road, Marching Band told me they were turning it into the Wonder Mobile, black-and-white themed throughout, and they were gonna follow us in it everywhere, wherever we went. Keeping their distance, of course. They didn't want us to get caught. They just wanted to be near us. Batshit, I tell you. Totally batshit.

Somewhere on the I-15 to Salt Lake City, Lip Ring said she needed gas, so we pulled over at a little rest stop called Moriarty's Diner. Dad was starving, so Lip Ring fronted us some cash and me and him went inside to get some pie to go. The TV was on in the corner.

CNN BREAKING NEWS:
WONDER TWINS BANDIT FOUND IN UTAH DESERT

"Welcome back to Headline News. I'm Kim Slaughter, and we take you live now to the Dixie Regional Medical Center in Utah, where Jake Williamson is on the scene. What's the latest, Jake?"

"Thanks, Kim. Yes, I'm standing outside the hospital where Beau Argent, one of the Argent twins who have been causing mayhem in the city of Las Vegas over the last couple of weeks by holding up candy stores, has been admitted. Early reports say he has suffered head trauma after having jumped or been pushed out of a moving vehicle. He was found on the roadside off I-15 near Highway 9 around five thirty this morning by a fisherman heading to the reservoir there, and was brought here to the Dixie Regional Medical Center in Saint George."

"For anyone watching who may be unaware of the

Argent twins, Jake, can you tell us a little more about them?"

"Well, Kim, in recent weeks these kids have become kind of Bonnie and Clyde figures for a whole new generation, and as you can see behind me there are literally hundreds of young people who have gathered to show their support for Beau Argent and to light candles, wave banners, and wait for news of his condition. They're also waiting to see if his sister, Paisley, shows up. She has, perhaps, been the more vocal of the pair, and in every robbery it has been Paisley calling the shots, so to speak. Last night it is believed the twins pulled off their last robbery at Cornucopia in Las Vegas, before firing shots at a popcorn machine and causing thousands of dollars' worth of damage. There are a lot of very worried fans of the Argent twins, but you can bet store clerks all over Vegas won't be saying any prayers for these two right now, Kim. . . ."

"Thanks, Jake. More details on that story as it develops. In other news . . ."

"They said head trauma, Dad. He could be brain-dead. It's all my fault. I did this to him. He was better off without me. . . ."

Dad looked me straight in the eyes. "You just did what you thought was best," he said. "It was her. It was your grandmother who did this to him, not you. I mean, we don't know for sure whether she pushed him out. . . ."

"She did, I know she did. She left him for dead. If he hadn't been found and taken to the hospital . . ."

"Yeah, but he was. And now doctors will be doing everything

they can to make him better. You gotta hold on to that, Paisley. And we're gonna go get him. Okay? Are you with me?"

I nodded. We walked back out to the parking lot with our pies.

"It's okay to be scared sometimes, Paisley."

"No, it's not. I need to be angry."

"Why?"

"Because then I can kill her. If I see her again, I'll kill her. I need to be angry."

He put the box of pies on the hood of a car and took my hands. Somewhere inside me, a plug was being pulled and, like water in a bathtub, all the pressure was draining out of me.

"You still got the gun you did the robberies with?" he asked.

I nodded.

"Let me have it."

I tucked my hand into the back of my jeans and grabbed the Eclipse. I handed it to Dad.

He shook his head. "This can only lead to no good, baby. Okay? I don't want you getting into no more trouble." He tucked it into his own belt. I hadn't realized it until then, but he was still wearing his wedding ring.

"Come on," he said, picking up the box again, and we ran to the Wonder Mobile and told the White Ducks about the news report.

"How many fans are out front at the hospital?" asked Marching Band, biting his bottom lip.

"They didn't say, but from the pictures it looked like a lot, maybe a hundred," Dad answered.

"Were they all wearing black and white?"

"Most of 'em, yeah. Why?"

"That'll be Totally Argent," said Lip Ring. "One of our sister sites. If it was Wonder Twins Inc, they'd be wearing candy colors, and the

Argent Army wear whatever they want. They're not dictated to by anyone, not even you guys."

"God," I said, "I've created a monster."

Lip Ring started the engine as I squeezed into the back with Marching Band and AC/DC, and my dad fiddled with the radio from the passenger seat.

"There were police there, too. And doctors and press. How the hell are we gonna get past all of them and find Beau?" said Dad.

"You need a diversion," said AC/DC, "and we can give you a diversion."

BEAU

TWENTY-FOUR

DIXIE REGIONAL MEDICAL CENTER,

ST. GEORGE, UTAH

Not for the first time in the last few weeks, I woke up wondering where the hell I was. I felt like I was juiced, like my head was being put through a pencil sharpener and my whole body was turning in circles. As my eyes focused, I saw white bedsheets. A TV on a shelf in the corner. Sunshine blazing in through a window between walls the color of a rainy day. It wasn't the motel room. There was no other bed. It was just me and a TV and white bedsheets. A little red light blinked on the bottom of the screen. A remote sat on top of a nightstand to one side of me. I reached for it, but found I couldn't move. My left arm was in a sling, plastered up. I tried to wrench my body over slowly so my other arm could grab it, but everything hurt. I couldn't move. The door opened. A nurse came in.

"Where am I?"

"Oh, you're awake. You're in Saint George, in the hospital, sweetie."

"Where the hell's Saint George? I was in Las Vegas."

"Well you're not in Vegas anymore; you're in Utah. Boy, you must have banged up your head pretty good."

"Utah?"

"Mm-hmm. How are you feeling?"

"I'm in Utah? I can't be. Where's Paisley? What happened?"

"You've got a badly broken left arm, a sprained right ankle, multiple bruises, and a nasty head wound. From what I hear, you are darn lucky that's all you've got. We're keeping you overnight for observation, and then I'm afraid you've got some explaining to do."

"Are the cops here?" I asked her.

"Here, there, and everywhere. One right outside the door just in case you try to pull a fast one, and a dozen trying to keep the crowds at bay out front." She sighed, and went around my bed to the window to open it a crack. "Can I get you anything, a drink?"

"I'm not allowed. I'm sixteen."

The nurse chuckled, pointing to the pitcher of water by my bed.

"No, I wanna watch TV. Are we still on TV?"

"Yep," she said, reaching for the remote and stirring the TV into life. They were broadcasting live from outside the hospital, where there was some kind of riot going on.

"What's happening?"

"I don't know. Looks like your fans are going crazy out there. Fighting over who loves you the most."

There were all these kids on screen outside the front entrance, waving makeshift cardboard signs spelling out WE LOVE YOU BEAU AND PAISLEY in glued-on candy. Some kids had linked arms and were chanting. Others were throwing donuts at cameramen, others being restrained by cops.

All for us.

All 'cause we robbed some people.

All 'cause of Dad.

"Is my sister here? Is Paisley here?"

The nurse shook her head. "No. Though I wouldn't be surprised if she turned up. She'd better give *them* a wide berth, if she's got any sense . . . but coming from the same family as you, I'm thinking maybe she ain't got a lick of sense, neither. Jumping out of cars . . ."

"I jumped out?"

"You tell me. Some fisherman passing along I-15 found you lying by the side of the road. Like a bloody carcass waiting for the buzzards."

"Shit. Why don't I remember?"

"When are you kids ever gonna learn that roughhousing always leads to no good?"

I smiled. "I did it. I jumped out."

"You need anything else, just give that cord a little pull, okay? When you're feeling up to it, someone will be in to show you how to use those," she said, and nodded to a pair of crutches leaning up against the corner by the door.

"Okay," I said as she wobbled out of my room.

I really jumped. It was all coming back to me. I'd heard Virginia talking about us and how she'd do whatever it took to get the money. Locking me up for another two years. Killing Paisley if she had to. And I jumped. And between jumping and landing here in whatever middle-of-nowhere hospital I was in, I remembered nothing.

The TV flickered in the corner. Girls were taking their tops off and parading around half-naked, cops trying to cover them up with their jackets. Girls were painting *We Love You Buddy* in melted chocolate on the hospital windows.

How come they loved Buddy? I didn't even know if I did, and I was his son.

Was I thinking straight? Didn't I love him? Didn't I want to see him? Not as much as Paisley, I knew that. Not enough to get us both killed. Not enough for all this.

Not enough.

Amanda Peace was being accosted by a kid in a military-style coat and a big girl wearing an AC/DC shirt just like Paisley's.

And then I heard a little voice in the room.

"Beau?"

And Paisley was standing there in a candy striper's uniform.

"Oh my God!" I said, and she shushed me and came over, throwing her upper body on top of me in a hug. I groaned.

"Oh shit. I'm sorry," she said, drawing back.

"It's okay," I said. "I'm just a little bruised. How did you find me?"

She nodded at the TV. "The news. God, I'm so glad to see you, Beau. I'm sorry, I don't care if it hurts." And she hugged me again.

I laughed in my pain. "By the way, what are you wearing?"

"Don't ask," she said. "We haven't got long. The cop outside your room went to get coffee from the top floor. Coffee machine on this floor's broken. Somehow. You hooked up to monitors or anything? One of those bags you piss into?"

"Uh, no," I said.

"Good, 'cause we gotta get you outta here."

"Who's we?"

"Oh, I met some people. Made some friends."

"YOU made some friends?" I laughed. "You gotta be kidding me."

She eased me up to a sitting position on the bed and then gently swiveled me around. "Can you walk?" she asked me.

"I think so," I said, standing up. I stepped forward. My whole body was screaming with pain, throbbing in too many places, but I could walk.

"Come on, we gotta get out of here before that cop comes back.

I got a car waiting at a back entrance, but we got, like, a five-minute diversion before they start getting suspicious."

"Where did you get a car from?"

"The fans out front," she said. "They're giving it to us. Like a gift. They said they'd be honored."

"They're rioting for us? You did that?"

"Of course. So we can get you outta here."

I was shuffling a little from all the pain, and she was urging me to hurry up. "We're not gonna get very far like this. I'll go get a wheelchair. I saw some old lady using one a couple of doors down. I'll go and scam her."

As she opened the door, a man stood there in a red shirt with a white doctor's coat over the top. A scruffy man with a thick brown beard.

I felt my heart sink.

"What's the problem, Pais?" the man said. "Is he awake?"

"Yeah," she said. "But it's slow going. I'm gonna grab him a wheelchair."

"I'll carry him if I have to," the man said, coming into the room. He stopped when he saw me, as though waiting for me to say something.

She'd found him. I knew she would.

"Dad," I said without thinking. He was a little grayer and he'd lost some serious pounds, but it was still him.

He walked over, smiling, though there were tears in his eyes. "Hey, son. You need some help there?"

"No, I'm okay," I said, making a lame attempt to cross my arms and just sticking out the cast instead. But I didn't want him to hug me. Paisley must have hugged him half to death. My whole body was screaming in varying degrees of pain, but no way was I gonna show him that I couldn't manage. I didn't want anything from him. I didn't need anything from him.

I took another step, carefully and purposefully, holding on to the nightstand with my good hand until I was sure I wouldn't stumble.

"You all right, Beau?" asked Paisley.

"Yeah, I can manage," I told her.

PAISLEY
TWENTY-FIVE

DIXIE REGIONAL MEDICAL CENTER,
ST. GEORGE, UTAH

So here's where you want us all driving off into the sunset, Dad throwing candy back at us like he used to, and me and Beau bundled up in blankets on the backseat. That's what I wanted, too. But life's not that kind.

"Which car is it?" said Beau. Dad's hand had been clasped around his good shoulder all the way out to the car.

"Over here," I said, opening the door of the Wonder Mobile. The sunlight was streaming across the pavement. Beau got inside.

"Won't they want it back?" he asked, squinting up at me.

"Nope," I said, holding the top of the open door. "And they're gonna keep the cops away from this side of the building for us so we can get away. Pretty sweet, our fans!"

"Yeah, pretty sweet." He winced, his head obviously in agony as he leaned against the backseat. Dad took his doctor's coat off and bundled it up for Beau to rest his head on. Beau lay down and closed his eyes.

We could hear the fans chanting from around the front of the hospital, so we knew the cops would be busy for a while, but we still had to hurry. The only thing I could see for miles around was dust. Dust and desert and rocks, and beyond the rocks, mountains. Where the hell would we go now? Dad would know what to do. He always knew.

But before either one of us could get in the car, there she was. The Skankmother. With her own private garden gnome, standing beside his pickup. She had a gun. It was pointing right at me. The gun looked exactly like the Eclipse.

"Shit."

"Didn't know I had another one, did you? They came as a pair. Two for one. Twins! If only you'd bothered to look harder, Jane, you might have found it."

"Maybe if you'd bothered to look beyond Beau, you might have seen me coming," I said.

She laughed and swept the gun across to Dad, her long red nails clutching the handle. Then I got kinda nervous. She hated me, but she truly detested my dad. Suddenly my heart was a madman slamming his head against a stone wall. I felt myself move over to Dad. I wasn't going to lose him again.

"Where's the other gun?" she said.

Dad looked at me and took the Eclipse out of his pocket.

Virginia held hers with both hands. "No funny business. Empty it and put it on the ground. I'm warning you, Michael."

Dad did as he was told and emptied the chamber. *Plink plink plink.* The shells fell to the ground. He didn't take his eyes off her. Then, keeping one hand raised, he placed the Eclipse down by his feet with the other and kicked the gun over to her.

"Now you, Virginia," he said, straightening up again. "We can settle this without violence. We don't want trouble. We'll just go, okay?"

"Michael, you're quite the unexpected irritation. They didn't mention *you* on the news."

I'd never heard anyone call my dad by his real name before. He was always Buddy to everyone who knew him. But not to the Skank. Just like the way she insisted on calling me Jane. I hated that.

Dad didn't take his eyes from her gun. "Yeah, well, I fly under the radar these days."

"My lawyer tells me that in the sad event of your deaths, I am legally entitled to your estate as your next of kin."

"What are you gonna do, kill all of us?" he asked her, still staring down the barrel. "That's what you want, isn't it? To get us out of the way so you can lay claim to their money."

She shrugged. "I've got my future to think about."

I scoffed, starting forward, ready to wring her scrawny chicken neck. "Stop pointing that gun at my dad!"

Dad held me back. "What if we signed it all over to you? Legally," he said.

I looked at him. "Dad?"

"It's okay. Let her have it, if that's what it takes for her to leave us alone. What do you say, Virginia?"

She shook her head. The gun moved over to me, and it didn't waver. "No. We have to do things the hard way, I'm afraid. I was quite willing to take your children as a down payment until the time came. And I was more than happy to settle just for Beau, but then he listened to his pathetic excuse for a sister. . . ."

It was my turn to look down the barrel. "Aw, if it weren't for us pesky kids," I said.

"Shut up!" Skank snapped. "Shut your dirty mouth, you pathetic little whore."

"Don't call my daughter that," said Dad, his hands still raised.

I didn't think I could love my dad any more than I did at that moment.

Virginia was still spluttering her fumes. "Your brother could have died, and it's all *your* fault. Anything bad that has ever happened to you two has been *your* fault. Beau was happy with me. You are the root cause of everything, do you understand me?"

"You mumble a little bit, but I get the general idea," I replied.

"Vile girl!" she spat, the Eclipse gripped in her rock-hard grasp, still aimed straight at yours truly. I wasn't worried. It kinda worried me that I wasn't worried.

"Don't you dare talk to her like that," said Dad.

Yay Dad.

"She's said far worse to me," said the Skank, holding the gun out farther in front of her, making the bullet's flight an inch shorter. I watched her trigger finger. Dad moved across me.

"So there really is no other option. I have to get rid of all three of you right now. Which one of your twins do you want to see executed first? The boy or the girl?" She moved the gun so it was locked on the rear window of the car, where Beau was, then back to me. Then back to Beau. Then back to me.

"Eeny, meeny, Paisley, Beau. Ooh, it's like *Sophie's Choice*, isn't it?"

"There are hundreds of fans out front," said Dad. "They hear a gun going off, they'll be around here faster than you can scream. They'll find you. You'll be seen. How the hell do you expect to get away with it?"

"Who's going to miss you three?" said Skank. "A vagrant and two thieves?"

"I take it you haven't been watching the news, then," he said.

She cocked the gun.

"You hate that, don't you, Virginia?" Dad smiled. "You hate the fact that they've gotten more famous in a couple of weeks than you ever were in your entire career."

She squinted a little, pointing the gun at Dad's head now.

And with that, Matt turned and headed to his truck.

She looked around at him. "Matthew . . . ?"

"I can't handle this, Ginny. I'm sorry. I have to go."

"You stay there. You damn well stay there!" She aimed the gun at him.

His hands flew up, his face twisted in sheer terror. "What, you gonna shoot *me* now?"

"You're in this up to your neck anyway, sweetheart. Even if you go and I do get caught, I'll name you. Don't think I won't."

"You bitch!"

"Bitch with brains. I want that money. And you are going to help me get it."

She turned back to Dad and cocked the gun again. "First things first. Let's deal with the irritation."

There was no time. No time for anything else. My legs started moving, and I went with them. I can't remember what I screamed. I ran toward her, and I got hold of the gun. I shook it. I pulled it away from her. I had it. A shot rang out. Dust flew up.

And Dad went down.

It was just like in the movies. Everything went all slow. My legs wouldn't move.

"DAD!"

I dropped the gun. Dad was slumped against the back wheel of the car, blood pouring out of his shoulder. I went to him. He was crying in pain.

"Oh my God, Dad. I didn't mean . . . Dad, I'm sorry. . . . Shit . . . SHIT . . . You need a doctor. Beau?! BEAU! Go get a doctor!"

The sun disappeared behind me as the shadow of Virginia loomed larger than ever. Laughing.

"You shot him! You shot your precious daddy! How awful. That's so awful, I don't think I'll ever stop laughing."

Her words burned me slowly, but she was right. I had done it. I had pulled the trigger, whether I had been aiming at him or not. It was me. And she had the Eclipse again. It was poised to take my head off. I stood up. I stood up and looked at the face I'd only ever back-talked, bitch-slapped, or shouted at. And I begged her.

"Please." Suddenly I didn't care anymore about our pathetic little war. I just wanted my dad to be okay. For Beau to be okay. I didn't give a shit about anything else.

"What?" she said.

I held my hands out. They were shaking. Tears poured down my face like rain. "I'll go with you. You can tie me up, whatever, I don't care."

"Paisley, no, stop it. Get in the car," Dad mumbled. I thought blood was gonna come out of his mouth, but it didn't.

Beau was getting out of the car.

I turned to Dad, my hands still in front of me, waiting to be tied. "It's okay. You go on back inside the hospital with Beau, and they'll fix you up."

My chest thumped like a thousand marching soldiers. There was a horrible silence. I turned back to Virginia.

She was still laughing. "You think I'd trust YOU, after all you've done? I wouldn't trust you as far as I could throw your miserable body, Jane Argent."

"Tie me up, then!" I shouted. "I'm giving you myself on a plate. Gag me if you want. I don't care. Just let them go. Dad needs a doctor."

She looked over at Matt. He still had his hands in the air. "Matthew?"

"I'll get the rope," he said, and walked backward to the cab of the truck.

She glared back at me. "If you try anything, anything at all, you know what will happen, don't you?"

I nodded. "You'll let them go, then? Let them go."

The gun was still fixed on me. "Who shot your father?"

I looked at her. I hung my head. "I did."

"I didn't quite catch . . ."

"I DID. I SHOT HIM!" I shouted, and thrust my hands out farther.

She smiled. "They can go."

Beau was helping Dad to his feet. Dad had one hand pressed against his shoulder, and blood was seeping out between his fingers.

"No, Paisley."

"There's no other way, Dad."

Beau appeared by my side, his good hand clasping my arm. "Paisley?"

"She'll kill Dad if I don't, Beau. You know she will. I can handle it. It's my turn. I always said I needed locking up anyway."

"No, no way," he said. "No way, Paisley. I can't leave you with her."

"You'll be better off," I sniffed through my tears. "Look what I did." We both looked at Dad. "I have to go. You go get a doctor." My voice dropped to a whisper. "Tell 'em it was me. They'll come looking for me."

An engine started, a door slammed, tires screeched. Matt was getting out of there, ducking behind the steering wheel.

KA-BLAM! BLAM! BLAM! Skank fired at the truck, cracking the windshield, smashing a taillight, running after him, but Matt drove on, drove away. Left her.

"You bastard! You lying bastard!" she screamed after him.

Everything changed in a heartbeat.

"Quick!" said Beau. I helped him put Dad into the backseat of the car and propped him up. I climbed in beside Dad and scraped away my tears with the back of my hand. I looked at him. His head was back and he was sweating. I looked at his chest. I felt over it. His shirt was soaked in blood. My hand got to his shoulder and he winced in complete agony. I snapped my hand away.

"I'm sorry, I'm sorry!"

Beau struggled into the driver's seat, straining with his right arm to shut the door. Once inside, he jammed down the lock, and I reached over to do the same on the passenger side.

"Does he have an exit wound?" Beau asked, turning to me but keeping an eye on the Skank through the windshield.

"What?"

"An exit wound, does he have an exit wound?" he asked again. I couldn't fuse the two words together in my brain, and before I understood what he meant, he reached awkwardly through the seats to check it himself, pulling Dad forward with his good arm and looking at his back. Dad howled.

"Yeah, it came out," said Beau. "That's good." He twisted back around in the driver's seat, *ouch*ing and *aargh*ing as his cast knocked against the steering wheel.

"How is that good?" I asked him.

"The bullet came out. Means we can patch him up ourselves."

"But he needs a doctor, Beau. Look at him."

"She's coming back!" Beau yelled.

From the backseat, I looked past my brother to see a totally unhinged Skank tottering toward the hood of the Trans Am.

"Keep applying pressure to his shoulder, Pais. Use one of your socks or something, turn it inside out."

"Okay," I said, taking off my boot. The stack of Wonder Twins stickers dropped into the foot well.

BLAM! BLAM! BLAM!

I leaped on Dad and pushed him down. He cried out in pain. Beau was huddled down in front, his head between the seats. He was okay. Dad was okay.

BANG. A bullet plinked off the metalwork. Glass tinkled at the window. Shattered pieces fell on my legs. I didn't dare move.

"How many more does she have left?" Dad whispered.

"I don't know," I said, my head hard against his.

The driver's door slammed.

Me and Dad both jolted. I looked up. Beau was making his way slowly, slightly limping, around to the front of the car where our grandmother was now standing, pointing the gun at us. We watched as he walked right up to her, took her gun with his good hand, and threw it to one side. He then grabbed her by the throat with the same hand. Beau had one arm in a sling, but he grabbed our grandmother by the throat. I couldn't believe what I was seeing.

He talked the talk, too. "What you got now, Grandma, huh? What you got for me now?!" He looked her hard in the eye. She was shaking, pawing away at him, but he held on, and he pushed her down. She pleaded. She *begged*. Beau had her begging. He had her on her knees. He was a fucking superhero!

The Skank stumbled and twisted in his grasp, wide-eyed and helpless. He seemed taller. She seemed older.

"Beau, there's no need for this, please." She writhed, scratching at his grip with her fake nails. "Oh God, let . . . please, you're hurting me!"

"You come near my family again, I won't need a gun. I will kill you with one hand."

And he shoved her onto the rough pavement of the parking lot and limped back around to the driver's door. He stopped. He opened it and got in.

He started the engine and rolled down the window.

"If you don't move, I'm gonna fucking run you over!"

Our grandmother scurried away like a frightened mouse looking for a hole in the sand. My brother, my little wuss of a brother, shifted into drive with his good hand, his broken one propped in its cast on the open window. We drove out of the parking lot and back onto the road.

Nothing else happened for several minutes, nothing but the sounds of my breathing, Dad's breathing. The lull of the engine. Glass tinkling at the window. Beau said nothing, and he didn't look back at us. I couldn't find the right words, either, so I just stayed quiet and held my bleeding dad in my arms. Aside from pressing my soaked-red sock against his shoulder, I didn't have a clue what to do.

"You knew she didn't have any bullets left, didn't you?" I said eventually.

My brother looked back at me through the rearview mirror. He smiled. I smiled. We started laughing, but it was a weird laughing. Beau couldn't stop himself. He laughed until he had wet eyes; I could see them in the mirror. Nothing was funny. I guess it was just relief. But it didn't last long.

"We need to get Dad to a hospital," I said. "I can't stop the bleeding."

"We just came from a hospital."

"Another hospital, then."

"No, we don't, I'm okay," Dad piped up, trying to act the martyr, but all the while I could see in his eyes that he was scared. And in so much pain. "The blood would be darker if we had anything to worry about."

Beau looked at him in the rearview. "You been shot before, Dad?"

"No, just watched a lotta movies."

"Sure?"

"Yeah. We'll go to a rest stop or something. Buy some gauze bandages, rubbing alcohol. Patch me up."

"No," I said, "you have to see a doctor, it might get infect—"

Beau looked back at me, his right hand steady on the wheel. "You can't just go into a hospital with a gunshot wound and get treatment, Paisley. The doctors have to report it. The cops'll be onto us in a heartbeat. We gotta keep on driving."

"Keep on driving where?" I said, folding the sock over and pressing it down again on Dad's shoulder. I looked at Beau in the mirror.

He shrugged. "I didn't plan on being alive for this part, so your guess is as good as mine."

"Don't say that, Beau." I couldn't believe what he was saying. Me and him had totally switched places.

"It's true. I could have taken my chances with Matt and Virginia, but I chose to jump off that truck. I never thought I'd make it."

"But you did make it. And so did Dad. And so did I. We can go anywhere we want now. We're a family."

"No, we can't," said Dad.

"Why not?"

"Because we're outlaws now, Paisley," said Beau. "And outlaws gotta watch themselves. We make ourselves known, they'll send you and me to juvie, they'll send Dad back to jail, and that will be that for another ten years. At least. Face it, Paisley. We gotta keep running."

I nodded. He was right, and I hated it.

I looked at Dad next to me. His eyes were scrunched up like he was trying to think really hard, trying to concentrate on something other than the pain. The pain I'd caused him.

"I'm sorry, Dad," I said. "I just wanted to find you. Beau was right, I shouldn't have taken her gun in the first place. I shouldn't have done a lot of things; then maybe this wouldn't be happening to you. It's all my fault. I'm sorry."

He opened his eyes and looked up at me. He smiled and the pain disappeared from his face. "It's all right, Paisley. I'm gonna be all right. I got my Wonder Twins back." He raised his other arm to my face and brushed back my hair with his fingers.

I would never, ever touch a gun again.

It was then that I caught sight of the stickers in the foot well. I reached down, grabbed them, and threw them out the shattered window. They fluttered behind us onto the empty road.

I looked in the mirror at Beau again. He caught my eye. If he could sense my anxiety, he didn't show it. His face was unmoved.

"So what do we do now, Beau?" I asked him.

"Try to get some sleep, okay?" he said as we rolled along through the rocky desert. "We got a long drive."

THE END . . . ?

ACKNOWLEDGMENTS

Barry Cunningham and everyone at Chicken House.

My mum for always believing in me even when I don't. My big sister Penny Skuse for showing me *Platoon* when I was eight and for teaching me to always swim against the tide. Nan. Auntie Maggie and Uncle Roy. My big brother Jamie, Angie, Alex, Josie, Joshua. Matthew and Emily Snead, for all the years I spent at your mansion while mine was being decorated. Karen and Danny for letting me burn their house down.

Wendy Griffin at Yew Trees Nursery for keeping my job open throughout my studies.

Julia Green and all the Creative Writing staff at Bath Spa University. Dawn, Diana, Titania, Lila, Eden, Roy, and my fellow witches Fliss Crentsil and Ali Killeen.

Gill and John McLay, Barry Timms, Owain Gillard, and Jo Baker, for their advice.

My Chemical Romance, Linkin Park, Blind Melon, The Killers, All Angels, Limp Bizkit, Slipknot, Feeder, Kings of Leon, Paramore, and Foo Fighters, for always unlocking the block when I needed it.

Gerard Way, Jeffrey Dean Morgan, Bonnie and Clyde, Brothers Grimm, Grant Morrison, Jack Nicholson, Anthony Perkins, Al Pacino, Quentin Tarantino. Whether you know it or not, you've all helped in some way to make my dustland fairytale come true. Thank you.